"**INTELLIGENCE AND CORROSIVE SATIRE**
distinguish all of Bernard Wolfe's writing. Both
qualities are displayed to brilliant advantage in his
latest novel, THE MAGIC OF THEIR SINGING.

Pages overflow with as brave a company of eccen-
trics as may be imagined: reefer peddlers and ad-
dicts, amateur prostitutes, rapists, voyeurs, switchblade artists, bongo devotees, juvenile delinquents
searching for a rumble . . .

The book is strong medicine . . . But for the knowing reader tolerant of youthful peccadillos and
sophomoric revolts, here is just what the doctor
ordered: a lively, uncompromising satire written
with intelligence, discernment, wry humor and a
pitiless scorn."

—Richmond News Leader

For
Al, Jean, Karen, Robert

THE MAGIC
OF THEIR SINGING

by

BERNARD WOLFE

MB

A MACFADDEN BOOK

THIS BOOK IS THE COMPLETE TEXT OF THE HARDCOVER BOOK

A MACFADDEN BOOK . . . 1962

Copyright, ©, 1961 by Bernard Wolfe
Library of Congress Catalogue Card Number 61-7211
All rights reserved
Published by arrangement with Charles Scribner's Sons

Chapter 9 was first published in THE DIAL,
Number 3 under the title "Miss Shoshana,"
© 1960 Bernard Wolfe

**MACFADDEN BOOKS are published by
MACFADDEN-BARTELL CORPORATION**
205 East 42nd Street, New York 17, New York

PRINTED IN U.S.A.

1

"ONE UNAPPETIZING thing about you, Worthington, one among many, y'always being y'self."

The bigger one holding the bottle of Johnny Walker Black Label, Hoyt Fairliss, said it, pressing harder against the steering wheel. The girl, a young girl with auburn hair and astonishing breasts, sipped again from the beer can and ran her tongue over her lips. She made an editorial sound like gler, gler.

Worthington Rivers, the tighter, trimmer one with the bottle of Jack Daniel's Sour Mash in his lap, adjusted his foulard tie and palm-pressed his stubbed wheatstraw hair and that was all.

"The ladies can't make a fool out of *you*, Worthington. They see the inalienable, incorruptible, insupportable foolishness already in you'n use it. Y'readymix fool, open along dotty line and use. *When* y'y'self. *Always*."

This was a brilliant day in May. The Goldthwaite Cup intercollegiate eight-oar races were being run off here in Derby, Connecticut. All three of these people were crowded into the two low seats of the scuffmarked T-bird, the girl in the middle. From the hill on which they were parked they had a view of the lazing wide Housatonic in both directions, which they were ignoring in both directions.

Worthington Rivers recrossed his long flanneled legs and tamped down his close barbering and that was all.

Hoyt Fairliss had a bad and worsening stomach ache. For this reason he was working hard to bait Rivers into a usable response. Something, something had to be hit. A transfusion of knuckles could more easily be made into the imperturbable one's face than into a looping stomach. The imperturbable one was not being coaxed into any usable moves. Fairliss forced his ribs harder against the tilted steering wheel to turn on another pain whose considerable merit was that it could be turned off.

He was a lesson in the ample, a space-taker. His arm and shoulder and neck muscles strained against his confining clothes when as now he was curled in on his ache. His long copperish

5

brown hair, his one collapsed feature, ran in unrelated driblets toward his eyes.

More was needed: "Couldn't you stop being foolish and made for stepping on on weekends anyhow? Busy man though you are, you have a tight schedule, yes, y'follow each systole with a diastole."

Worthington Rivers gave his undivided attention to the antiqued bronze buttons on his hopsacking sleeve.

"Well," he said with his trim, trued nasalities, "there's nothing else to follow a systole with. You think about it."

Hoyt Fairliss took a prolonged swallow of scotch. He wiped his upper lip. "I'll state my p'sition one more time. Either you take y'hands off'r and keep'm off—"

The girl made more partisan glottal sounds. She pulled up from her slump, unheld masses quick under her sweater. She thinned her green eyes to look along the river.

"There, there, they come, come," she said. "It's, yes, Hahvahd."

"You've made your position clear," Worthington Rivers said. "In my pinion it's untenable."

"Hahvd by three lengths easy. Rotten Hahvd'll go to any lengths." The girl tossed the empty beer can over her head toward the flaking silver birches and posed back. "I can rub m'stomach and m'head in differend directions at the same time." She demonstrated. "Shoot anbody else who tried to ruff m'stomach and head in differend rections, though." She took up the bottle of Jack Daniel's from Rivers' lap and drained it with one maximum intake. "I hate and *de*-spise to be handled."

"Except by Himself Rivers," Fairliss said.

"Bart," the girl said. "Gent." She looped the empty bourbon bottle high over her head, drew Rivers' hand down from her shoulder to her chest and began to play with the fingers. "He can put his hands any old place he wants and some not s'old."

"The thing you're assuming, unwarrantedly, I think," Worthington Rivers said, "is that the party is your girl."

"What I'm assuming, warrantedly," Hoyt Fairliss said, "is, the girl's my party. You're not invited."

"You have a lease or a bill of sale or something?" Worthington Rivers said. "Something that'll stand up in a courtalaw? Think right now *you* could stand up in a courtalaw?"

"The slave block?" the girl said. She began to hum *John Brown's Body*. "They abolixed the traffic in flesh."

"There's entirely too much traffic in *your* flesh," Hoyt Fairliss said, cradling his stomach. "There's a traffic jam whever your

6

flesh is. You give freely of yourself. To all comers. Some goners."

"We can do without that kind of talk," Worthington Rivers said. "Enough, ample, Hoyt."

."Get this straight." Fairliss pushed himself erect and shook his head with energy. "Girl comes down Bennington see me, comes see me, *me*."

"Suppose we leave it up to her?"

"We'll leave it up to me. Unless you want your bones taken apart and reassembled. You going to take your hands off'r?"

"You apparently don't know the sort of man you're dealing with'n W. Rivers," the girl said. She arched her back and collapsed again. "His middle name's Missouri."

"Last name's Okloma," Worthington Rivers said. For the first time, unexpectedly, he smiled, with a slow cranking back of the lips.

"Can't you even learn to smile right?" Hoyt Fairliss said. "You open your mouth as though you're going to spit or say ah and you call yourself the bluebird of happiness."

"Missouri, you dog," the girl said, "you absolute *dog*. Missouri loves company." She moved closer to Rivers and locked her long tennis-tanned fingers with his.

"Say you're all forty-eight states," Fairliss said. "I'll break one bone for each state. Well?"

"Bring me around to your way of thinking," Rivers said. "Give's a sample of your bess suasion."

Fairliss took the other man's hand from the girl and heaved it away. In the same motion he leaned over and butted River's chest full force with his palm. Immediately his stomach felt much, much better.

"That's not all of it," he said, "just a sample."

"In that case," Rivers said through his patrician thin nose, "in that case, the thirty-five pounds you have on me notwithsanding. Step out of the car and settle this?"

"Now you're talking, buddy."

Fairliss fumbled at the handle of the door. When it opened he fell out.

He said to the grass against his face that he could not distinguish from his hair: "They use you and use you until you're useless, remember that, Worthington."

"Makes a big thing about breaking people's bones," the girl said. "Talk, talk." She slid over to the driver's seat and switched on the dashboard starter. When Rivers made a wavering move to climb out on his side she gripped his hacking jacket near the

7

side vent and pulled him back. "Let him lie there and be *him*self. Hoyt Fairliss! The examiner! Bed his dominion! I never liked his hambone pimp clothes anyhow. Who d'you think you are!" She stepped on the accelerator. "Been a race to r'member, you lost, lost, lost."

She was singing in a stretched voice, something about "he's made his position clear, it's ho-ri-zon-tal," as the flatted bug of a car swung down the hill's spotty grass to the highway.

2

HOYT FAIRLISS was twenty-seven. Undeniable dampness on right wrist to elbow. Hoyt Fairliss had an M.A. for his very own. Thin querulous lament of T-bird on far-off highway shoulder. Hoyt Fairliss was best regarded doctoral candidate in the Department of Powiticow Thienthe. Stomach on a trapeze again. There was a cushy career spot in State arranged by his father Sam'l and waiting for him when he got his very own Ph.D. Science fiction ants nudging behemothly at these great green monoliths of grass and fat copper hawsers of hair before his nose. He was just now finishing up his dissertation on Miwwel Eatht Fowwin Powithy. T-bird gone from earshot. Said dissertation would eventually be brought out as a trade book by a good New York publishing house, thanks again to said Sam'l's good oak-paneled offices. Stomach on a trampoline. The first Sam'l of his tribe had signed the Declaration of Independence with his left hand. Definite wet on right forearm. He was in reasonably good physical health except for left leg's slight tendency to buckle. Pale buff worm the size of three amalgamated Loch Ness monsters glistering through these vaults of chlorophyl to one side of his nose. He was taller than most and shoulder big and with a certain not displeasing trend to hyperpotency and he of these big bones and these large boons lay in this heap on this hill overlooking this Housatonic and he did not know if the Hahvd shell had kept its lead over the Yale and Princeton shells or which way the Thunderbird had gone on the highway or where the withholder and chopper of a Penelope would be found again or what to do with all this unused hyperpotency on his hands, nor was there any easy explanation of the spreading wet along his right jacket sleeve. He raised his head. He spat out quantities of sand and grass. The ants diminished back to rampageless specks. He saw that the bottle was in his left hand, its open mouth emptying with modest gluggings over his right forearm.

He got to his feet and swayed, looking at the place where the car had been parked, and he lifted his head and shouted "Who did you say won the races, Penelope," swinging his arm in a pitcher's warm-up gesture. The bottle flew off and fropped on the strip of beach beyond the cliff. Stains from the scotch began to spread on his unpressed cashmere hound's-tooth jacket. "Hambone clothes?" Tell that to Giacomo. "Pimp clothes?" Let her tell that to Giacomo D'Amici of the Via Veneto.

He saw a stiff straw hat lying on the ground. Mr. Rivers' boater. Just-so belled crown with just-right Old Eli blue and white band. When he stooped to pick it up he lost his balance and fell again.

His head dropped down between his knees and he started to cry in a manner he thought copious. He heaved his shoulders in the just-so lamentation rhythms and when he judged that a minute of dedicated keening had passed he put both hands to his eyes to see if he had produced any just-right tears. His palms came away dry. "My position is thus clear." He took hold of his hurting stomach and began to laugh without control.

He climbed back to his feet. He put the straw over his ears and ran off, favoring his left leg a little, toward the highway, to the long line of jammed traffic moving a crawl at a time. He wove his way between the cars, peering into each one as he passed. "I'll use him, I'll use him down to his all-wool Saville Row ribbed socks and hand-stitched cordovans." Someone called out to him and he answered, "Bring'm out, fight like man not a mice, best laid plans, my girl." He climbed on the back of an old roadster, steadying himself on the spare tire. "Atta boy," somebody yelled. "Ride 'em, Bat Masterson!" The car began to move forward, came to a sudden stop. Fairlisss rolled off. "Hey, look out!" somebody shouted. "For Pete's sake!" Fairliss turned over a few times until he came to rest against the curb. "Leave Peter Masterbate out of this," he said with insistence to the slate curb. "And his brother Worthington." The line of cars inched on.

When he picked himself up he reached for the hat and found it had been bashed in on one side. He tried to punch it back into shape and his fist came through the crown. "What you get from talking through your hat all the time, Worthington. I'm as badminton, as broadminded as the next fellow. Worthington minds all the broads. Used up by the users. Don't

9

you talk through any hat or nostril of mine, Worthington."
Laughing, on the whole quite pleased with the unsequential
trending of his thoughts, he put the hat on again and zigzagged
down the road until he crossed the bridge into Derby proper.

He walked along hilly streets, aimlessly, the limp more pro-
nounced now, and at the center of town a five-and-ten caught
his eye and he went in. He leaned over the toy counter to tell
the salesgirl in a whisper, "Her name's Penelope and she's inclined to give it away, I've got to stop them. We can do without
that kind of talk. Listen, what've you got in the way of guns and
similar lethal pliances?"

"Whyn't you go home and sleep it off, Junior? You smell
like two leaky breweries. Some Junior."

"Give me water pistol, clam juice in's eye and drown him.
For her, traffic control."

He handed over a bill, wagged his finger as he said "Keep
a change," and went out. Shouldering through the street crowds,
he saw a sign for the New Haven bus stop halfway down the
block. He got to the curb and lowered himself next to several
young students, most of them in thin-lapeled tweed jackets and
back-belted tweed caps. He brandished his pistol, aiming at a
fly. "Five dollars for this shooting iron. Cost of killing's up,
up." A bottle of vodka was being passed along the line of
students. The last man, a husky one in a multi-colored Madras
jacket, staring now with rivetted interest at his own streaked
white bucks, handed the bottle on to Fairliss.

"Waiting for bus?" Fairliss said. "Somebody steal your car
too or didn't you drive out?"

"They took my license away from me and busted me to
pedestrian," the other man said to his smudged shoes. "Judge
said I was a menace to navigation and the all-time winner of
the son-of-a-bitch sweepstakes but I can name some that
beat me."

Fairliss inserted the barrel of his pistol into the mouth of the
bottle, carefully tilted the bottle, filled the gun's chamber. He
took an upending swallow, held the bottle bottomside up and
scowled at it.

"That judge knew what he's talking about." Fairliss deposited the bottle in the gutter. "Nobody beats you. I can tell
from the way they stuffed up your Worthington nose for good
at Groton. Don't I know you from somewhere?"

"You might have the decency not to slop up the last drop,"
the young man said through slowed lips without raising his
head. "I'll stuff your ugly ungratiating nose down to your tonsils

10

if you want. You make a habit of slopping up the last drop?"

"Some Junior." Sophie, Sophie of the runaway hams and tired size eights, said it. "Some Junior," Sophie said and made her pout-riped lips go thicker. She was maybe three years older than he, at the big dividing line of thirty, close to the halfway mark in the race without Goldthwaite Cups, race with no training periods, no coach, no summer vacations, her fingernails were cracking, her surging meat defied the latexes, the varicose veins from being on her feet all day were surfacing, and so her clear meaning was, who was he to play the game of the workfree? She had to sell the water pistols. He, her contemporary, had no right to buy them gaggingly. She knew the difference between exacted labor and fooling around. Student of those with the loose tourist air, the over-interested and under-involved, she tried him and found him wanton. Wonton? Always in the soup? She would not acknowledge *his* headaches. Then he said "Keep a change" and her tired smear of mouth came open. The five-dollar bill was in her hand and he was wagging bye-bye. Five dollars for a water pistol. These silked-up Yalies didn't know the meaning of a dollar. She had studied the Yalies staggering and hollering through town each year at boat-race time and she saw how they threw their unearned money around. She watched him go egg-walking out of the store and wondered how come the limp? Must be he was falling-down drunk. He had fallen on his lushie face somewheres and cracked his knee and served him right. Grown man acting every damn age but his own. Not a snotty kid like the others but clowning round like a kid. Looking him up and down from the back she could see another thing off about this one. Sophie had been studying these Yalies for some years now and she knew how the shoulders were supposed to be slopey and pinched and the coat snugged down the body and long. This overage joker had these squared-off hiking shoulders and the coat ending mid-ass and with a flare. He was an off one, all right. One of them and not one of them. She wished him no happy days as she checked around to make sure the floor manager wasn't looking and rang up a no-sale on the cash register. She wished him another healthy fall on his fleshing Park Avenue face as she slid the five-dollar bill down behind her stocking garter close to the bloom of varicose. Too bad her feet hurt. Damn shame her chunking Warsaw face would not stop broadening. But Sophie, but Sophie, is *Worthington Rivers* too big for the kid stuff? Seriously, Sophie, can't you spot a

11

Worthington Rivers All-American Junior when he hands over a five-dollar bill for a water pistol? That wasn't *me* buying the gun, I'm too old for such damfoolery, that was the Worthington hiding out in my skin, Worthington, the perpetual damfool college boy. Admittedly the stuffing in the shoulders instead of the nose can fool you. Granted the close shaping at the waist instead of on the pate can confuse the picture. Especially when on top, where the prescribed crewcut should be, there's a three-month pimpy hambone mop shagging the neckline. But Worthington is as Worthington does. Himself. Full of self hymn. Sophie, Sophie, you've got to train the eye to recognize behind the decoy splashes of makeup and wig these all-time winners in the son-of-a-bitch sweepstakes—

"Wish to report a stolen car," Fairliss said. "Bennington girl stole my hubcaps without taking them off."

"How's that again?" the young student said concernedly to his shoes.

"I wish to report that September of Fifty-Five was when I stopped apologizing for my shoulders. Rome. Via Veneto. Giacomo D'Amici. Granted I could do with a haircut, Sophie." He sighted at a fly along the barrel of his pistol and said very loudly and headmasterbately to the sagging young man in Madras, "I most emphatically do *not* drink the last drop, not unless some all-time swine has had the emphatic temerity to drink the *next* to last drop. If you want to start working on noses, buddy, I'll be only too happy to twist yours into a parody of a pretzel, you miserable hooked turd of a perennial sophomore." It worked. Nothing like some iced Grotonism to make them snap to. Madras Boy's eyes widened as by signal to respect. Deferential phrases automatically forming like loud saliva on his lips. At this point the bus drew up and its door folded open. "Know where we stand now?" Fairliss said genially, dropping the headmaster's sinoid tone. "See *if* we can stand, right, Junior? Know you from somewhere, Beta house? You a friend of Worthington Rivers, Some Junior? You and he seem to have the same breathing problem."

3

FOLLOWING THE line into the bus the student said, "Sure, I know Worthington, that any reason to make a person's nose into a pretzel?"

Fairliss secured the pistol in his belt and said, "What's your name? You always address yourself to people's clothes?"

The student said, "Endicott, do I always what?"

"For your own good, Endicott, I point out that you have this habit of addressing yourself to people's clothes. Minute ago there you were talking to my jacket. My haircut too, rather, my lack of haircut, but essentially to my jacket. You were lucky, this is an Italian jacket and very hotblooded, it could have slugged you for the snide tone, Endicott. Can't you stop talking with Worthington's Tuxedo Park diminished nostrillings, for Christ's sake?"

"I don't—"

"Addressing the world like hired help. Get yourself very slugged that way, Endicott. It happens one of my ancestors in direct line signed the Declaration of Independence, wrote his name Sam'l, abbreviated form, didn't know how to spell much and probably saving face along with ink. From here on in, Endicott, little respect for the other fellow's wardrobe, right?"

"I really can't—"

"On with it, Endicott. Pay the man."

Endicott dropped his coins in the meter and shot through the turnstile, propelled by Fairliss. The aisle was filled with passengers, mostly students. When the bus growled off with a jolt, Fairliss collapsed, pulling the younger man down with him. He put his hand out tentatively. It came in contact with a leg, which he explored with his fingers to the knee. "Now what have we here," he said with scholarly interest. "Proverbial fatted calf in its lean years. It's a small and drunk world and bus."

The thin young man whose leg Fairliss was holding sat stiffly in his seat, with a paste-up smile. He was toy-chested, with the miniature craters of acne on his face, and he was wearing a yellowed straw. His off-the-rack jacket of nubby

13

tweed, lined vertically with slashes of grey, brown and black, was pinched in the waist and wide in the lapel and long in the peak.

When Fairliss saw this man's kindled eyes he pulled his hand away hurriedly. "Sorry, very, being Worthington again."

Endicott looked up curiously and said, "They steal your car'r take away your license?"

"What?" the thin man said. "No, came *up* on the bus, don't drive." The stout-armed girl next to him, in a heavily flowered print dress and an elaborate hat with a runaway icing of purple veil, said, "Who's your friend?" Her tone was merry.

"My girl's up in Poughkeepsie," Endicott said to the world in general. "She won't take busses and I'm not allowed to ride in any private vehic, hic, hicular conveyances during my probation, not even as a passsenger. The judge was very pussed off because I was driving on the sidewalk up Prospect Street but where the Harry-hell else you going to drive with these traffic conditions? I was late for thermodynamics lab and this country needs thermodynamicists. Judge had a nose like a pretzel stick."

"Poughkeepsie," the girl in the veil said, "that's where Vassar is, isn't it?"

"Smith," Endicott said.

"Endicott," Fairliss said, "you're talking to people's clothes again."

"You go to Smith?" Endicott said.

"No," the girl laughed, "I'm up at Storrs. That's where Connecticut U. is. Of course, it's not a very old school."

"I've heard of it many times," Endicott said. "Where they have the agricultural station, cows." Across the aisle he noticed a squat, Slavic-looking man in a leather jacket. "Friend, sir," he said, "who won the races?"

"I couldn't tell you," the man said, smiling as he dug at the grime linings of his fingernails. "I was going to go, then the way it turned out I had to work."

"Need a union's what I always say," Endicott said. "A man can't get to see the races without union. Fellow workers."

"Endicott," Fairliss said.

"No way to get off," the Slavic-looking man said, picking at the mourning borders of his nails. "They got these rush orders up to the plant. We make hand grenade fuses, see, for the Picatinny arsenal."

14

Endicott said "I see and that's nice" and turned back to the thin young man. "You in my class?"

"Fifty-eight," the thin man said. "Fifty-eight's my class."

"Oh, no, it isn't," Endicott said. "Fifty-eight's *my* class. You get yourself your own class and take your hands *off* my class."

When the thin man opened his mouth to say something the girl put her hand on his arm and shook her head. "Ritch," she said. "Ritchie." She leaned toward Fairliss and said, *"You* look more like you're in grad school or an instructor."

"My years are as advanced as my opinions," Fairliss said. "I *am* in graduate school and I *am* an instructor, I instruct Endicott here on how to keep his Tuxedo Park nose clean. I must apologize for my friend, he looks more like he's in reform school, should be. Now, Endicott."

Endicott looked at the thin young man and said, "You in Pierson?"

The thin man shifted in his seat. "No, don't room in a college, live home, come from New Haven."

"I know people come from New Haven," Endicott said. "Where they go is the question. Far, we can hope." The other students to the rear, the ones in tweed caps, started to sing "The Whiffenpoof Song" and he joined in for a few bars, then stopped and said to the thin man, "That's a nice hat you have there. Mind if I look at it?" When no answer came he repeated loudly, "Let's see the hat, will you?" and the girl said, "Oh, go ahead, if he wants to see it. Ritch." The thin man took off the hat and handed it down. Endicott examined the label. "Adam, fine house." He laid the hat down on the floor beside him.

The girl leaned closer to Fairliss. "What did you say your field was?" she said good-naturedly.

"He's in weight-lifting and wop haberdashery," Endicott said.

"Endicott's majoring in fife-and-drum corps and snidery," Fairliss said. "I'm in chronic alcoholism and political science, in that order."

"I'm taking Pol Sci this year," the girl said.

"Marcia," the thin man said.

"I've got to write a term paper on Quemoy and Matsu, on whether we should give them up."

"No question about it," Endicott said. "Gave them up years ago myself."

"Endicott, get hold of yourself," Fairliss said. "I don't want to speak to you about it again."

The thin man, looking out the window, said softly, "That

15

will make Nikita and Mao very happy. Marcia." He put his hand on the girl's shoulder and tried gently to push her back in her seat.

"Oh, you're kidding," she said. "I was hoping you'd know something about it. I guess I'll have to look it up in Bemis."

Endicott said, shaking his head, "Didn't you know about Bemis?"

"What about him?" the girl said uncertainly.

"Trouble with Bemis," Endicott said, "he gets all these ideas in his head before he sits down to put them on paper, and then he sits down and puts them on paper and people go ahead and read him and don't suspect anything."

"Oh." The girl looked disturbed.

"Warned repeatedly," Fairliss said. "Stand up, Endicott." After several unsuccessful tries he made it to his feet. "Up, Endicott."

"Up yours, you perennial bloated bastard." Endicott did not move.

"Respect for your betters, Endicott. Up, immediately." He was speaking with his full nose resonances again and Endicott stared up at him. Fairliss bent to get a grip on the young man's Madras lapels. "Hoyt Fairliss majors in advanced horseshit," Endicott said. In an abrupt gathering of purpose Fairliss heaved him to his feet. The other passengers watched without understanding but spectacle-bound. "Roman jacket's very hot under the collar now, Endicott, going to rearrange your teeth some. If your J. Press thin-blooded garment wants to put up a fight that's all right."

"You're a drunken bastard and you're ugly," Endicott said. "If you think for one minute—"

Fairliss raised his fist and let it go into Endicott's jaw. His stomach began to sing with happiness. It was the next best thing to slugging Hymnself Rivers himself. Endicott fell over backwards. He lay on the floor rubbing his cheek and considering Fairliss with clouded, clamorous eyes. Fairliss' stomach chirped.

"Little gentlemen's disagreement between Giacomo D'Amici and J. Press," Fairliss said to the startled standees. "Giacomo wins hands down. Naturally. His shoulders are twice as big."

Tears were sprouting in Endicott's eyes. "I know about you, you escaped convict. I heard stuff from Worthington. You're his roommate and you read crazy stuff in Russian and Arabic. You could be plotting something. You buy secondhand T-birds and put more scratches on them because you're against con-

16

spicuous consumption and what do you get but a halfass conspicuous unconsumption? What the thin-blooded hell you have to go hit me for, what did I—"

"That, Endicott, was for seeing the world as a counter of dry goods, like a Worthington."

"He's a particularly ugly bastard and he's not right in the head," Endicott said to the passengers. "Man who spends five dollars on a water pistol."

Fairliss didn't understand at first. Then he remembered. He took the pistol from his belt. "You miss the point, was going fill it with clam juice, vodka's no substitute, they stole my car."

Endicott had raised himself to a sitting position. He was trying now to get to his knees. "What the?" he said. He reached under him and pulled something into view, the thin man's straw, its crown crushed irretrievably flat. "Oh, sorry," he said. "Inexcusable. Make it up to you." He searched through his pockets, took out a bill and unfolded it. It was a twenty.

"Oh, that's all right," the girl with the veil said. "He won't need the hat after June anyway. He's reporting at the New London base right after graduation for active duty."

"My uncle isn't reporting at New London for active duty," the thin man said. "It's his hat."

"I guess you wouldn't have much use for a straw hat on a submarine," the girl said. "Ritch."

"The only submarine my uncle'll be anywhere near is a submarine sandwich," the thin man said. *"He'd have plenty* of use for that hat."

"I insist," Endicott said, holding out the bill. "Small tribute to men of our fighting forces. I myself expect to be soldiering among the cyclotrons." The thin man made a slight movement forward, only an inch or so, not with his hands but with his whole body as a unit. He stopped and held himself. He looked into the girl's eyes and his shoulders went back against the seat.

"Five dollars for a water pistol and twenty for a hat," he said to the window. "They've got money to burn."

"It's what conspicuous consumption will have to come to before it can be a pure art form," Hoyt Fairliss said. "Eliminate the intermediary steps and burn the money right off."

"They'll set fires to continents before they're through," the thin man said to the window. "Already have."

Endicott's face was thoughtful. "Money to burn." His face brightened. "Back home we have this money bonfire every Saturday. Nothing less than a ten-dollar bill." He groped in

17

his pocket until he found a book of matches, lit a match and held it to a corner of the bill. "What's the good of the filthy looker?" he said enthusiastically. "Makes them all want to hit you." The bill began to burn feebly. At that moment the students farther down the aisle began on "The Whiffenpoof Song" again.

Endicott spread his hands in front of his face. Fairliss was reaching down for him once more.

"Down to the musicale, Endicott. Raise the boarding-school whine without women in song."

Endicott kicked energetically at Fairliss with both white bucks. Fairliss bent lower, there was a scuffle, the sound of a hard slap. Endicott stopped struggling. He let himself be lifted and maneuvered down the aisle to the vocalizers. Fairliss held him by the collar, nodding encouragement until the younger man began with a cracked voice on the words:

> Sing the Whiffenpoofs assembled, with their
> glasses raised on high,
> And the magic of their singing casts its spell.

Fairliss twisted the Madras collar. "Louder, Endicott. Since you can't get funnier."

Endicott's voice cracked:

> We're poor little lambs who have lost our way,
> Baa, baa, baa,
> Little black sheep who have gone astray. . . .

"Louder, Worthington."

From time to time Fairliss reached down with his free hand to rub his left leg.

The bus was stopped down the block from the Hotel Taft, at the corner of Crown and College.

"What's the matter with your leg?" the Slavic-looking man said. "Fall asleep?"

"It does this sometimes," Fairliss said. "Can you just help me over to the steps? Once I start walking it'll be all right."

Leaning on the man, he made his way along the aisle. The two ruined straw hats were lying in a vacant seat. He picked them up, turned back to Endicott, and crammed them both on the younger man's head, one on top of the other.

"By rights I should make you eat them. I'm not sorry I

18

socked you but understand the circumstances. You were a stand-in, Endicott. For Himself the Rivers. Of course, you volunteered for the job. Don't go through life typecasting yourself, Endicott. Other things to be than a replica. Nothing inherently wrong with padded shoulders, right?"

"Hold on, feller," the Slavic-looking man said. He supported Fairliss in his careful maneuvering down the steps. As they proceeded along College Street the man, still gripping Fairliss' arm, said, "Funny, you ain't sloppy drunk or like that, you're pretty steady."

"As a grenade maker," Fairliss said, "you'll understand this. They all want their Goldthwaite Cups. Kept coming over the hill, through the snow where the 'copter was crashed, and we kept dropping the mortars in, then with the machine guns. Afterwards, in the hospital plane going to Seoul, the talk was our crew got sixty-seven but of course that wasn't official. *They* have good grenade makers too, that's what I want you to see. One of their grenades came over and a piece of it took four inches of bone out of my leg. See? Left leg's aluminum for four inches, it took two years to put together. Why I can't run fast enough after the chopping ones who steal my car but of course that isn't the reason at all," then they turned the corner into Chapel Street, Fairliss limping badly.

Ritchie and Marcia stood at the bus stop, they watched until he was out of sight. "What do you mean, nuts to my uncle?" Ritchie said. "Did you listen to those two clucks in the bus? That big son-of-a-bitch now, he'd fall down if there wasn't somebody holding him." "I saw you," Marcia said slowly. She was still looking down the street. "Do we quarrel about it? Marcia? With me going away so soon?" "It's not like that, I'm not quarreling." "It was just, I was just watching, then when it started to burn," Ritchie said haltingly. His voice was puzzled. He opened his hand and looked wonderingly at the bill, blackened at one end. He added, "But I didn't. I was going to, but. They were rolling around on the floor, hitting each other and rolling around, then it was in the cuff and not burning. You saw. It was there in the cuff. They've all of them got so goddamned much of everything." "What makes you think you have to explain?" Marcia said. "To me? But if he's so much like them why doesn't he dress and look like them?"

The exact words didn't matter. Something along those lines and with that tone. The lines wrong, the tone wronger. You miss the point, Ritchie. Assume they've got the same big

19

money and number of blooded generations behind them and the same consciousness of coat cuts and the same nasalities and still there's no lumpable they. Not all of them flare their nostrils at too much nub in the tweed and too much Saturday racetime veil. One can even come along with continental curves in his custom and hair that needs orthodoxing. Where he's going is another matter. Don't ask him. This comer may be a goner. But he may come. What Marcia was trying to tell you is, I make the effort to be inconspicuous but it's not one of my talents. My shoulders in lieu of my vistas are too big. I tried to put the spark out and slip it into your cuff discreetly but she's got scorekeeper eyes. Sorry I can't be inconspicuous where it counts. Sorry you need the twenty and we don't. In this sense there *is* a they, we *are* a we. We have this supply of twenties, thanks to our predecessors' good oak-paneled offices, and in this sense you are right to think of us disparate ones as one. In this sense only. There are all kinds of class wars. Remember, all those without acne scars are in a sense a one too, a dermatologically closed society, this is what is called the pity of it all. No one can expect you to see that there is a class war too between Giacomo D'Amici and J. Press, or between the Endicotts and me, imperfectly and inconclusively resigned, defected but not far enough, Endicott. Sorry you have to have an uncle who wears an Adam bargain straw if you think the trademarks and price tags are important, you too. Marcia, missy, you in the heartbreaking veil that only exposes, dressing like who knows what long-hungry them, I don't dress like *my* them because it's hard to resign from yourself and you've got to start somewhere, no?

"I'm sorry for people with Adam labels and I'm sorry for those with J. Press labels," Fairliss said. "I'd like to feel sorry for myself but where do you start, with the D'Amici label? I'm tired. Too bad she had to see me do that with the twenty. I didn't want anybody to see."

·The Slavic-looking man patted him on the shoulder. "Sure, you're all right, Johnny. I don't see why you fellows fight with each other, though. You didn't have to punch that kid, after all, you're the same kind."

Isn't that why people anywhere fight. Because they're the same kind? And how do you tell the sameness anyhow? Is there a total overlap of me's when two people have black machine grit under their nails? Wear the same leather jackets from the same Sears, Roebuck? If plain union makes the identity then how come the guy who collects your dues in the International Machinists' local beats his wife and you don't, *your* wife, I mean? Or is the one proof of sameness the fact that the two begin throwing punches at each other? Is that the way you recognize blood brothers? When they go for each other's jugular vein? Then Walt Reuther's wasting his time and there's no togetherness but in the gas chamber. Is it that the pitchest battles take place between mirror images? The bad blood between Russkies and Yanks is brothers' blood? But there's no big mirroring between an Endicott and a me. He's a much of Madras, I'm a huddle of hound's-tooth. Want to say this, though, and I'm soberer. Grenade maker, you do need a union and maybe we all need unions. Not to prove we're absolutely alike but only to suggest we're not entirely alone. For when the choppers and withholders dump you on the Housatonic hill. They will steal you blind and T-birdless. I'd join a union myself if they had one for unapologetic shoulders. Rest assured there are *some* samenesses. Otherwise there'd be no call for your grenades, maker. Wish I knew a way to get the giveaway grits from under the nails if managerial nails are so important to you. People with gritted nails sometimes itch to throw grenades too. When other targets lack, at others with gritted nails. I am going to find that footloose and other parts loose girl and give her the prime what-for. Oh, some togethernessing she won't forget.

4

IT WAS past five when Prosper beat the obstinate glue on his eyes and forced his grainy lids half open. This was on the top of an old commercial building southeast of Washington Square, on West Broadway, a floor-through loft whose partitions had been cut down to make one great and vacant room. The bare brick walls were white, so were the ceiling and the rough-planked floor. Most things here that could be painted were unemotional white, door knobs, faucets, skylight chains, refrigerator handle, the clothes hooks screwed into the moulding strips here and there.

The place was like the insides of a very large and meagerly

21

stocked refrigerator. Here you would want to wear an overcoat in the dog days.

The bed Prosper was stretched on, his own body a sample of mortuary white, was an oversize slab of foam rubber resting on the floor and covered with an unmoored length of black corduroy.

He considered the one piece of art work in the barn-dimensioned room, a print scotch-taped to the ceiling near the bathroom door, a Mondrian of abutting rectangles in the primary colors. The uncased tuner of a hi-fi, a conclave of tinted tubes and colored wires with a smokey blue glass plate to hold the adjusting knobs, lay in an elbowy all-black Hardoy chair close by his head. He reached over to turn some of the knobs and in seconds, from the black plywood boxes in the far corners of the room, the tweeter and woofer, came the twitching sounds of History Jones puffing soft and susurringly on his tenor sax through "How Hee the Moo."

Prosper listened as History began his flatted vocal:

Some air their mews thick,
How feign the tomb,
Some wear their muse sick,
How hee the moo.

There was a thirty-inch tumbadora drum standing on the floor close by the Hardoy chair, surrounded by lesser bongos. Prosper's hands went to its tight skin head and his fingers began to stroke polyrhythms. His eyes, neutral in their program as in their gray, shifted to the looking glass bolted to the ceiling just over the bed, a very large mirror of the type found in pre-Prohibition Hell's Kitchen bars, its blooming scrollwork frame lacquered black. He considered his floating image positioned back-up against the ceiling, an undernourished cherubim with tired blond hair and dented face and pulled-thin pale body, within those black wooden blossoms a 120-pound angel of deprivation with flapping black wooden wings from some old beer parlor, and he said through the trough of his extended tongue,

"My long lam. Down to me your domicile. Trend down and I will trend up for the togethering, you hear, Proper?"

It was his device on slow awakening to give the name Proper to the missing half of the down and outed Prosper. Minus Proper the Aeronaut what was there but Prosper the Airy Naught. The thing was to get the two parts together to make some kind of move possible. He faced this problem of a working unification each coming to.

"Us two to get to one agreed place and pacting for some one thing. You drag it a way down and I'll get lofting to it."

What bugged at him was the *second* body on the ceiling next to Proper's lank-shanked hovering body, the dim-dark one. He had enough work each day-facing hour to get back with the one lammer half. To talk down *two* necessary others was too much. Who wants to throw *two* shadows?

He began to get scared.

Just then the second up presence on the ceiling, the thicker and curvier of the hoverers, the shaded one, moved and said down to him,

"You say something?"

It was talking from the ceiling but he heard the words close to his left ear. He turned. Marga was propped up looking at him.

"Talking to the traveler me. To hip him on homecomings." She knew about Proper. When she was on the rise and focused toward the ups she sometimes spoke to him too. He blinked. "You been here long?"

"Since I don't know. From about sometime." She licked her lips and made a face. "Prosp, dads, that was wild and hangup pot. You should make them sift out the seeds and stems or maybe get with another contact besides Lewellyn. I got like burnt chocolate all *over* my mouth."

"Mine is all over kelp and kitchen rags. Did we make it before?"

She thought about it carefully. "You better ask somebody who was there. I was in I think the south of South America. Hug it and I'll check."

She urged herself to her feet and went across the bare white floor to the bathroom, dark hips narrow but hard back buns fisty, dark legs thonged along their lengths and bunched with power in the calves, the body of the dancer. After a time he heard the toilet flushing and the sound of water from the tap. When she came more stridefully back he said again, still finger-tapping the drum, "We made it?"

"You can't prove it by me. Though that proves nothing and a little less. You can't generally prove it by *you*. Man, what *is* your story, you are the story above the second story man, you sneak into the premises and gone without leaving trace one. You should sign your name in like some register so folks will know. Leave us some aftermath."

23

"You know my trend of thought on that. The thing is to lose the names and the trademarks. You author the good big state and it is bigger than the author and has everywhere dimensions and so why sign it? You can't get true lost keeping a map. Dissolve to all-state of non in this all-no and the need to autograph goes to melt too."

She did two quick bends, middle in heave with Martha Graham urgencies, then sank on the bed and began exercising her splatted prehensile toes. "Good. Congealed. Then why the quiz shows on did we make it? What's make got to do with dissolve and all the swim soft things? After the ecstatics the certified public accountants, that's a line from you."

He went on singlemindedly at the other, more attentive one in the mirror:

"Get to the un-me looser plane. It's beyond persons and projects. Being's better than fluxing and homing cuts coming. Immerse and rise above crossing the t's. The trip ranks higher than the destination. Hug it, that's a line."

For the first time he lifted himself up. He reached for a spiral notebook hung on a nail just behind his head, removed the ballpen clipped to the book's cover. He opened to a page and considered the words spelled out there in neat block capitals. He read them aloud:

"May 3, 1958, walking through Washington Too Square Park, directly across from N.Y.U. administrate building, I was touched by the finger of Hieronymus Bosch. On the groin, to the left, where I have the mole. All the strong itching powder in the universe. It pays not to wash regular."

He thought for a moment and said, "That is accurate in every detail."

He began to make another notation, speaking each word slowly as he printed the letters:

"Being vs. Coming. The trip is like better than the destin. The in is better than the thru. The with is better than the over. Done is the word to be (p) urged from the vocab of the seeker. Come and go the enemies of be and am. Seek and you do not hide. Seek is the end of it, find is for fools."

He replaced the notebook on the wall nail and said, "Do I care if we made it or about the measurements of finales? I'm not going for the credits. I want to know if I made a rich sideways something of my hours."

"Oh, oh," She was eyeing the alarm clock on the canvas seat of the Hardoy, holding to her cheeks with both palms. "Five? Five-*thirty?*"

"You can still go rounding. Some stores stay open."

She cringed. Immediately she was the little girl with track star's muscles, mummy's breasts tacked on for fun.

"Don't make me, Prosper. I don't want to go on the lift. Not today. Please."

"We need the loot, baby. We got to underwrite the nutriments for tonight and tomorrow anyhow. You holding?"

"One dollar and change. Yesterday I was rowing with Lewellyn on the lake in Central Park, those boats *cost*. It cleaned me."

"I told you what to do when you're going seagone. You take like the Staten Island ferry and hide in the toilets when it docks and that way you get your Atlantic crossings all afternoon for a nickel."

"Lewellyn had big eyes for Central Park. What could I do? I had to widen from *your* pad because you were giving the mamb lessons all day, Prosp, and I couldn't go to *my* pad because Lewellyn had his people there rolling the reefers you and others put in for. We took separate rowboats because when Lewellyn gets treetoppy, sequoia sent, and yesterday he was with the floats, he doesn't want company close, just somewhere around about to call when he feels he's falling. I had to pay for both boats because he says it's conformist slavery to carry money, so I'm next to empty."

"You could have done some rounds yesterday."

"I *can't* go back to the stores, Prosp. Not right now, togged down and way out as I am. It needs wardrobe, Prosp. This is no hype." She was on her feet again, doing high leg lifts. "I'm down to this one pair of black wool cablestitch stockings and my sailcloth toreadors and the Fire Island sweatshirt with the side pockets and the peaked hood. What could I lift in even a Third Avenue swap shop in that get-up but some eyebrows? Listen, Prosper, listen to me good, the eyes in those smooth stores have the hone for uncool threads. They'd have the handcuffs all over me before I could rabbit a nail file or a nickel Hershey bar into my pocket. I *know*. Last week I almost got bagged in Bergdorf Goodman's and then I was wearing a past-gone sharp suit *from* Bergdorf Goodman's, the one we sold on Wednesday to pay Lewellyn for the pot before the last, the one that Bennington swinger, that Penelope, gave me. Oh." She slapped her forehead. "Bring-down plus."

"What's it?"

"Penelope."

"Penelope? Saturday?"

"Listen." She held a cupped hand to her ear. "No trucks on West Broadway today. If not Saturday wouldn't there be trucks?" She listened some more. "Unless it's Sunday. But Sunday's bells."

"This is no Saturday because she was showing for her lesson two-thirty the latest on Saturday."

"It's Saturday, it's Saturday, I got the feeling. She must of got hung up, she only said she'd make the scene if she could get unhung. She's not coming and without her loot we are in the weekend with a long supply of the shorts. Prosp, listen, where's the gold from yesterday's lessons?"

"You know I gave it to Lewellyn for that new good weed we put in for. That was the much he was having them roll up yesterday." Prosper sat up straighter. "It can't be Saturday. She can't wash away. A whole weekend scoffing on air? Man, if there is no Penelope lesson we are looking into the black wall with no doors."

History Jones' record was playing through again. Prosper's fingers went back to the tumbadora and began to pick out the beat. Doing her broad leg lifts again, scrupulously in tempo, the beautiful dark Marga placed one hand on the drumhead and took to stroking the offbeat with the butt of her palm. They were looking at each other with eyes of deep trouble, she looping her bulge-thighed leg, he finger-snapping the riding accents of the beat, two tensioned drummers, when the vocal came.

Both of them began to sing along in tuneless, minored, spasmed vowels:

> Some wear their muse sick,
> How hee the moo . . . .

Their bodies came together, massy swells to skimped perpendiculars, dusted to bleached. Their hips, pared against rear-swollen, began to piston in an easy mambo. They moved well together, she was a member of an up-to-date dance group and schooled in today's chopper rhythms and he was a professional teacher of the jumpier mambos.

In this unstocked refrigerator, without overcoats, without underclothes, they danced as if in the hippest, highest ballroom.

She said, "Baby, you dance back."

He said, "All you do is lose the map and go with it. Go like there's no way home and no later."

26

5

His first thought was to check at Beta. There on York Street outside the fraternity house he found his patchy T-bird. There were beer cans on the floor with lipstick half-moons around the punctures. On the windshield, a message lettered in lipstick. HOYT FAIRLISS THE EXAMINER WHO FLUNKED OUT. A dime had been put in the parking meter, the hour indicator still had fifteen minutes to go. So they had a 45-minute head start on him. Nice touch. Puts a dime in the parking meter when he abandons stolen car minus stolen girl. What is known as not shirking responsibilities. Playing the game. Except that *Penelope*, who shirks all responsibilities and plays no game but chopchop, had stolen the car and incidental luggage, which happened to be Worthington, and Worthington was again the passenger in other people's souped-up projects. Wontoned projects. Fairliss went into the Edwardian-squiry stone house to ask around. Yes, Worthington had been by. Said he was called away on business. Left a letter with the steward to be delivered fastest. The steward remembered Fairliss as Worthington Rivers' roommate. He was happy to let Fairliss take care of the letter. Fairliss studied the address. Miss Shoshana Gasharid, Hotel Taft. Shoshana Gasharid, no less. He put the letter in his pocket next to the water pistol.

It took him only minutes to drive to his apartment on College Place just off Edgewood Avenue. Driving was hard with his head this clouded and it troubled him that his arms and legs were so sullen about doing their assigned work together. He closed his eyes as the elevator went up. He had the impression that as the rest of him rose his stomach was going sideways, a pendulum, and on the pendulum Penelope was sitting naked, remarkable breasts going sideways, and on the two pendular breasts two Penelopes were sitting, naked, singing out to him in hooting close harmony, "Hoyt the examiner! Hoyt the horizontal! Bed his daemonium! Bed his dim onion!" The tune was vaguely that of "The Whiffenpoof Song."

In the apartment he found precisely what he had expected, nothing. Penelope's matched Mark Cross dusty green bags,

27

both matches for her splendid eyes, were missing from the corner of the living room where he had left them this noon.

He went to Worthington's bedroom and examined the closet. Hoyt Fairliss the examiner. Worthington's stained saddle-leather Abercrombie two-suiter was gone. The hopsacking jacket with the slash pockets and antiqued buttons and turned-up cuffs, the one Worthington had been wearing, was hung up neatly, but another, a Huddersfield Prunelle worsted Glen check, was gone, along with a suit, a muted olive silk gabardine.

Fairliss went to the phone and dialed the garage. Yes, Mr. Rivers had stopped in for his Porsche. About a half hour ago. No word about where he was going. Thought he might be away till Monday, late Sunday anyhow. The attendant had not noticed if a young lady had been waiting outside.

No intelligence was needed about Penelope. As Fairliss put down the receiver he noticed something, some garment, that seemed to have been kicked under the night table. He reached for it. The Tailored Woman claret-red cashmere that had been inviting Worthington Rivers' cooperative fingers up and down the Housatonic. Fairliss placed his fists inside the sweater where the noteworthy breasts had nested. He made his knuckles plumply palpitate the wool. Ah, she made big fists out of the soft, soft things. So there was work to do.

He took all the clothes from Worthington's closet, suits and jackets and slacks in a heap, and carried them into the other room to dump in the fireplace. Even with crumpled pages from last Sunday's Times placed strategically in the sleeves and trouser legs the lovingly handmade stuffs would not burn right, too much smoke. He had finally to stamp out the sparks, as an hour ago he had done with the burning twenty, and carry the smelly mess through the hall to the incinerator.

When he came back he ran a bath and stripped, letting his clothes fall on his bedroom carpet. He felt dizzy. He dissolved two Alka-Seltzer wafers and drank the loud fizz, then repeated the dose.

He leaned close to examine himself in the bathroom mirror. Hoyt Fairliss was still, though patchily, patchily, the fair-haired boy. Though the fair hair was showing this tendency to ingest itself at the temples. For balance, the bile etch, the fleshslide called character, was showing signs of advancing on some fronts. Yet, and all in all, the contours of the mass-jawed and cheeky face were reasonably intact, despite certain Johnny Walker leavenings and pink traceries. Still detectible here the straight sure strokes of the chromosomic chisels of the many forerunner Sam'ls. He did need a haircurt badly. His tongue was fuzzed with stubborn white stuff. There was the continuing hydrochloric boil in his stomach. With trimming and retailoring he could yet be processed back into a reasonable facsimile of a Worthington or an Endicott. Only, scheiss, the shoulders *were* big. He just naturally had big shoulders. If her boobs were on her back wouldn't she be humpbacked? To get insulted by anatomy?

His stomach was plotting darkly. His infirm condition was nausea, definitely. He stretched out in the blessed zeroproof balm of the bath and, examiner that he was, began to examine the question of Sam'l.

His eyes closed. He gave himself over once more to the never finished job of composing The Letter.

Dear Sam'l. This is long overdue. So, incidentally, is my girl. Never mind the jokes. You must not conclude from my silence that I'm not grateful for the State Department arrangements. I'm not, but that's another matter. Obviously the desk of Miwwel Eatht Fowwin Powithy is where I can best put my talents to use or anyhow pasture. It's just that I want to hold off on the application forms for a few days until I work up some more singleminded enthusiasm for the brilliant career. The danger is in singling the mind prematurely. Sobering to think how this job might sober me up. You can see the drawbacks in an over-quick gelling when you look at Worthington Rivers. At twenty-five he's well on his way to being a fossil. What'll he be at fifty? A pterodactyl print on some sidetracked basalt? At three-score-and-ten? A petrified whale turd on the ocean floor? Well, I will work up a more monothink happiness for the aforementioned Miwwel Eatht desk in the next days and be monothunk about it from there on in and down, or, as you might put it, out and up. Listen, Sam'l, no matter what you've heard, I don't usually get this drunk. I get really loaded about once a year and always come out of it with this low opinion of myself. I never have a low opinion of myself *when* I'm drunk because then I'm not myself, I'm too busy being Worthington Rivers, who *never* has a low opinion of himself. For example, when I bought that water pistol, I wasn't myself. I was Worthington. You follow? I'll go into the matter with you sometime. I drink moderately, yes. I do most things in moderation except the things I'd like to do with Penelope, to Penelope, but Penelope's the moderator on those few occasions when she can't be altogether the chopper. I'm the examiner. She means, I like to put her to the test. How I like to put her to the test. I have this large urge to examine her straight through from abeam to abaft till her eyes bulge. But she's the product of progressive schools, she takes all positions but the horizontal, being too uppity, she doesn't believe in examinations. This is not progress no matter what they call those schools. I know how much you think of Worthington but the fact remains that he is a know-nothing shit for not stopping Penelope. He is always the object in these affairs of the heart or more particularly the spleen, very objectionable, subject to the ladies' objects. I should have known the day's course would turn out rocky when she stepped off the train in New Haven this morning at eleven. She bounced down from the Pullman with too much agenda in the eyes. Distinctly elbowy in manner. There was the smell of trouble about the upping set of her shoulders as she came toward me on those calvy clenchful legs carrying the matched Mark Cross bags. The first thing she saw, of course, was my jacket. She'd asked me please as a special favor to her, not to wear any of the Rudolph Valentino tango-master clothes I had made in Rome. I'd completely forgotten about this, at least I *think* I forgot. She ground her teeth at my hound's-teeth and with total warfare in her voice asked if I'd planned a weekend of pimp work. Certainly I saw the rumpus on her face and the too many fists on too many hips when she asked, what, please, *were* my plans for the weekend. She knew damn well what my plans were. It was all over my face, my mood for showdowns. She's been foxing me out of it entirely too much lately. Entirely, lately. *Her* mood, as I knew, as it always is, was for excursions. Hadn't she told me very precisely on the phone that she wanted this particular weekend to drive down to New York and lark around, make the scene at this big Waldorf Astoria party, catch some music here and there, gone and going musicians in town, the most of the most, far-out sounds, etc. Didn't I know she'd been avoiding these weekend hideaway examinations with me, and for good and ample reason. We could talk about New York, I said. At my place. First to my innerspring dominion. She didn't at all care for the novocaine in my eyes. What went wrong was that Worthington was still home when we got there. Penelope'd never met him. When I have overnight company I pry him loose from the apartment. This weekend he was supposed to go to the races in Derby, then shack up with some girl he claimed he had slobbering for him in the Taft. But he was still home and dusting off his crispy straw for Derby when I pulled Miss Holdout through the door. Worthington, you know, comes from a long line of Grosse Point Sunday skippers and was stroke on the crew as an undergraduate. You may remember that when he left Beirut in '56 he went halfway round the world to see the Yale crew cop the Olympic and world eight-oar championships in Australia. He loves all events watery because they go with his personality. I mean he has the aqueous style. A long drink of water redundantly watered down. As soon as she heard about the Goldthwaite Penelope was all ears and eyes. Suddenly she's the camp-follower, crew-follower, of all true blue oarsmen. Immediately she was saying let's go. Worthington was so perky, he broke out a bottle of Jack Daniel's. Her looks began inviting his hands. To get back at me, of course. For not taking her on to the out concerts and the big turn-on, that's weedhead talk, Sam'l, it means where there's jazz, her brand, there's pot, and she usually wants to turn it on to turn me and all examiners off. She was ready to go anywhere that was not bed, not bed with me. Worthington was the goner to her come-ons. I went to work on the Johnny Walker. This is why the line about my girl being overdue is a joke, Sam'l. There is no conceivable, and I use the word advisedly, way she could have been overdue, none due to me and my overtours anyhow. She's been outfoxing me like this for damn near two months now. After what we've been to each other. We've been everything to each other, I examinations to her, she progressive education to me. Sam'l, must dash now. Off to New York after the chopper and the choppee. She has a tendency to give it away when there's no spirit of examination in the air. What she hates is not so much sex as term papers. Did I ever tell you we were in bed twenty minutes after we were first introduced? You will therefore appreciate my reluctance to introduce her to others, especially non-examiners like Worthington. There's nothing to keep me in town this weekend. I think I've taken care of everything. Worthington's wardrobe is down the incinerator. Just have to make this one courtesy call and I'm off. Who do you suppose this Shoshana Gasharid is, for God's sake? How does Worthington get to know a Shoshana? More about Miwwel Eatht Affairth when I've disposed of the business at hand. You might like to know that your son and heir did not suffer a complete rout this afternoon, Sam'l. I won a major victory on the Derby battlefields. My position all along was that I did not want to see the races. I can report to you that I did not see the races. Well,

31

when I get to New York I'll pick up a paper and see who won the Goldthwaite Cup. I like to keep abreast of things. Abreast of something. I like to be of use but not used. I intend to use her until she gets used to it and usable. Before this itchy night is over. You'll be hearing from me. Your loving and mono-think son, etc.

He got the letter from his jacket, wrapped the bath towel around his dripping body, and went into the kitchen. Once the tea kettle began to steam, it took only seconds to get the envelope's flap curled loose. The text, in Worthington's narrow-shouldered script, was simple:

"Dear, dear Shoshana. Catastrophe. My father called. He flew into New York on business and he has some papers for me to sign. Dad only has one day in the East and can't get up here and he can't send these papers up by messenger because there are some technical matters he's got to talk over with me before I sign. The worst part is, I have to leave before your train gets in. I'll be back Sunday night or Monday morning at the latest. If you can stay I wish you would. Do, if possible. I've arranged some things that may help to pass the time. At the Shubert Theater there's a ticket in your name for tonight's performance of an interesting musical called Pajama Game. This is an incisive though not at all ponderous exposition of recent developments in labor-management relations in America and a visitor to our shores will find it instructive, I'm sure. Also, if you will go to the Hofbrau Restaurant on Crown Street I've arranged for you to have your meals there on my charge account. Aside from this, I think you may find the Peabody Museum and the Art Gallery of the School of Fine Arts both enjoyable and enlightening, in the first they have unusual prehistoric specimens and in the second the collection of French Impressionismists is especially good. I'm having this note rushed over to the Taft to save you the bother of calling my place or perhaps, out of concern, actually going there. It would be better if you did not try contacting my place at all. I don't know if I told you this but I have a roommate, Hoyt Fairliss, who drinks too much and can be a troublemaker, especially with women. I hope the hours pass quickly and profitably. We'll have a good long talk about water pumps on Monday. I mean to go into the pumps with my father in detail. Faithfully, Worthington."

6

"Miss Gasharid?"

"Yes, please?"

"Miss *Shoshana* Gasharid?"

"Please, New Haven is filled today with Gasharids? Yes, *Shoshana.*"

"I have to make sure, Miss Gasharid. I have a message for you."

"From Mr. Rivers?"

"Worthington, that's right."

"Well?"

"Miss Gasharid, you may not know this, but Worthington is easily carried away. Just two hours ago he was carried away. Not by anybody you'd know."

"This is your message?"

"No, I have this letter explaining things."

"Thank you."

"Hadn't I better wait while you read it? There may be an answer."

"All right. Come in, sit, please. Let me see. Ah, called to New York, his father, yes. Shubert, Pajama Game, Hofbrau, Hoyt. What? Troublemaker, with women, Hoyt Fairliss. I do not understand. Why do you stare?"

"Miss Gasharid, I'm not as easily carried away as Worthton, generally I object to being the passenger, but at this moment I feel myself lifted and transported and—"

"This says only that Worthington was called to New York. It does not specify the mode of travel."

"Feet first and with a lily in his buttonhole."

"It says he is called by his *father.*"

"I know Worthington's father, to the best of my knowledge he does not wear a size thirty-eight uplift. Of course, neither does Penelope. *If* she wore one it *would* be a thirty-eight."

"Worthington went to New York to meet a *woman?*"

"Not to *meet* her, Miss Gasharid. I said, he was *carried away* by her."

33

"How do you know this?"

"The party who did the carrying is, was my friend. You are an absolutely remarkable looking—"

"I begin to see. You are the troublemaking with women, let me see the name, Hoyt Fairliss."

"Worthington accuses others of making trouble with women because he makes women with trouble. He—"

"What? What does this mean, to make women? As in Copenhagen they make women?"

"It is an expression, not an operation. A self-expression, some say. I am not unpleasant to women, Miss Gasharid. I would welcome the opportunity to prove this to you. What I take a rather firm stand on is women who are unpleasant to me. Worthington says these things about me because he feels guilty over taking, being taken by, overtaken by, taken over by, my friend. How he could give up a weekend with you is beyond me, you have really remarkable looks—"

"He did *not* give up a weekend with me, Mr. Fairliss. I came to New Haven to discuss a business of water pumps with him, only that. You say you do not do unpleasant things with women? You opened this letter."

"How could I interfere with his plans unless I knew what they were? Be reasonable, Miss Gasharid."

"You offered to wait while I read the letter because there might be an answer. That was unpleasant, you were making an excuse to insinuate yourself in here. How could you deliver an answer to Mr. Rivers if he is in New York?"

"Try to quote me correctly, Miss Gasharid. I said there might be an answer, yes. I did *not* say I could or would deliver it. I made an analysis of the situation, not a promise of a service. I was genuinely interested in hearing your answer, that was why I wanted to stay. Where did Worthington get to know somebody like you? Your lips are *very* red."

"In Beirut. My lips are not *red* in Beirut, I met *Worthington* in Beirut. It would help if we could discuss one subject at a time."

"Certainly. Your lips are very red."

"Oh, this is most upsetting. He might have left a New York number. He knows I must discuss the pumps with his father. Of course, he says *he* will take up the matter, but, ah. Yes. If it is *not* his father he is meeting. This is annoying. What am I do do?"

"Worthington's paying for this suite?"

"He insisted. He also sent me my train ticket."

34

"In that case, Miss Gasharid, I have a suggestion. We can have some scotches and set-ups brought. Since they're being charge to Worthington we can make them doubles. Then we can sit down and discuss the situation in a relaxed atmosphere. Later we might go over to the Hofbrau and have some tournedos on Worthington. If we approach the problem in an unrushed spirit we'll think of something. Shall I call room service? I want you to know, Miss Gasharid, I've seldom seen such a remarkable looking—"

"I don't approve of this, Mr. Fairliss. Not one bit of it. Worthington should not have—"

"The situation has to be examined coolly, Miss Gasharid. I'm known as a not incompetent examiner. If we put our heads together—purely in the way of business—pool our impasses, as it were—we have each of us suffered a loss—the Hofbrau is right around the corner—"

7

"*Easy.* Penelope, if you'd like me to drive."

"I enjoy driving."

"I mean, if the European shift bothers you."

"I've driven most of the European makes, I'm used to it."

"But if you're tired and would like to nap for a while. *Look out.* It's better not to pass on the right, Penelope. They don't always see you."

"They pass on the right on the Hollywood freeway. Why doesn't the creep stay in the right lane if he's going to creep?"

"He's doing over sixty. You hit close to eighty passing him. *Careful.* It's a good idea to stay away from those shoulders. They're pretty soft along here."

"Don't worry, I've got good reflexes. I've studied with Martha Graham and once up in Kennebunkport I drove in a stock car race."

"Yes. Well, I haven't done much modern dancing but I've seen some of those stock cars after they've turned over four or five times. They often catch fire before the driver can get out. Are you sure you wouldn't like a nap? I wouldn't mind taking over, I'm wide awake now."

"Worthington, are you another Hoyt? You don't like being a passenger with a woman?"

"I think a lot of women are fine drivers, you're very, very good, you really are. I'm just saying if you're tired after all the excitement this afternoon and would like to close your eyes for a while."

"If you don't mind women drivers why do you keep pushing an imaginary brake and grabbing an imaginary wheel? That's what Hoyt does. I've been watching you."

"Better if you watched the road, Penelope, these curves are pretty tricky. Penelope, I've been thinking. I'm not sure we should do this."

"Don't think. We are."

"*Watch it,* it's best not to scrape the concrete dividers if you can avoid it, you can have a nasty spill. No, seriously, you did have a date with him, after all. No matter how he acted—"

"We had a date to drive to New York. He broke it, not me."

"All the same."

"Back's the nowhere route, back is where you find the done with and the done for, to quote my friend Prosper Merrymake, he's a very good poet, you may meet him tonight. Relax, Worthington. There are large wonders and lofting lifts up ahead. Bubbly balls, superior noises, supreme highs, the Waldorf, Prosper, History, all kinds of Varaderos—"

"All kinds of what?"

"Varaderos. That's the name of this beach in Cuba, I just use the word to mean everything good to the skin and the tongue."

"When were you in Varadero?"

"Oh, three years ago, about."

"Late summer? August?"

"I guess it was August, August of '55. Why?"

"Then *you're* the one."

"And aren't *you* the one. Why are you suddenly speaking in riddles?"

"You're the one went to Varadero with Hoyt when he got out of the hospital. Before he went to Rome."

"*That's* an insane idea. What makes you think I'd go anywhere with Hoyt?"

"He was there that August. With a girl."

"Damn him, he promised he'd never say a word! What did he tell you about me?"

"Nothing that would identify the girl, just abstract things, generalities, you know? I really think we ought to go back, Penelope."

"Because of what he said about me or because of *your* date?"

"I don't follow you."

"I've heard a couple of things about *you*. *You* had a date for this weekend. There was a girl checking in at the Taft and you were going to make it with her."

"You got that from Hoyt, of course. I recognize his lovely idiom. No, this girl was coming up because I had some, well, business to talk over with her."

"Some, *well,* business. The pregnant well."

"What?"

"The sterile what. If you want me to believe it was serious business why do you let your tone suggest it was monkey business? You're saying no with your words and yes with your eyes and tone, Worthington, you sly boots. You *were* planning to shack up with her, in Hoyt's lovely idiom. Hoyt said the deal was for you to stay away from the apartment until Monday. Where were you planning to sleep, on the grass on the Green?"

"There's no point in discussing it, Penelope. I really think we ought to head back."

"Why *not* discuss it? Because the less you say about it the more I'll believe the worst? You'd like me to believe the worst about you, wouldn't you, Worthington? That's a neat trick, you take gentlemanly reticence and turn it into a lewd and loudmouth confession. Bro-ther. Well, we can't go back now."

"What's to stop us?"

"I've got a pretty good idea what you were doing all that time in Beta house."

"Now *you're* speaking in riddles."

"Why'd you have to stop off in the first place? We could have just dumped Hoyt's car and picked yours up and taken off, but no, you had this mysterious business. I can imagine what the business was. You had to cook up some barefaced lie about why you couldn't keep your date and then arrange to get the message to this girl, wasn't that it? Well, it's done, Worth. It's wrapped up. You burned your britches behind you and now you've got to go down the lonesome road bareass. *Stop* driving with those invisible controls, will you? We're going on to New York, you and I. I'm going to show you a time, don't worry. All right. *Do* worry. Drop the gentlemanly reticences for once, what do you say, Worthington? Come on, tell me, what *did* Hoyt say about me? What did he really tell you about Varadero?"

"Well, he said he did a lot of skin diving. *Watch* it, you scraped that tree. Why are we stopping? We don't need gas."

"I just remembered, got to make a phone call."

"May I know to whom?"

"Man named History and some people. I've got to let them know we're coming. So they'll have some of that good and gassifying grass waiting for us."

"Grass? *Hold* it, you missed that gas pump by less than an inch. Grass?"

"Never mind what Hoyt told you about me and Varadero, Worthington. We could have had a fine time but he's got to examine every lofting and highlight thing out of existence. You're not the proctorish type, I can tell. We're going to have ourselves a time in New York, Worthington. You won't be sorry you came. I'll get my friends to light you up. You ever been tall, Worth, I mean *tall,* all the way to gone and without wings? We are booked for that Flight Topflight Top, you and me—the Flip Express, you know?—to where those out clouds *sing* it and the air's all *friendly* drums—some wear their muse sick—how hee the moo—"

8

THE WHITE phone gave a white shrill. It was lying in the Hardoy sling chair between the hi-fi tuner and the alarm clock.

Prosper was back on the bed, absorbed in what seemed to be a computation of his fingers by his fingers. He reached out a white, floating hand for the receiver.

"Yeah. History? Anything moving? What you laying down? No commotion in this pocket, no, man. Iceberg time. No cash and no concepts. I'm a nail-up with no visible means of suppose."

She was standing with legs apart now, doing the diaphragm pulses. He watched the belly button make its elliptical round trip with each drama of heaving.

"That much? Sure I can start you to the sooth, man. I'm sticking big, you know, yesterday was roll time and I went with Lewellyn all the distance. But there's no way to make a meet, I am fresh out of the mobility, man. I got to stick on the

38

watch here for the ample one you put me on to, you know, the Bennington pullet."

He listened some more. He watched dark Marga make a cave of her torso and then a boulder, insuck, outsock.

"Yeah? From around New Haven? Gass-*er*. If it shapes that curvy I am *in* it. Nine, I got you. A deal and solid, no backing and tracking. Waldorf-Astoria. You can faith me in this, History. Bring the best and most wherewithal, man. I got to have some of the folding and most pronto, we're clean. With it and with you. Nine. Consider it dug and dug."

He hung up.

"History for some?" the girl said.

"He knows we're in solid supply of the sooth and we need the green so we got to deal. He's playing a gig someplace. On the railroad tracks under the Waldorf, I don't know. He wants me there nine or in the neighborhood to turn him and the boys full on."

"It's straightening. Everything's straightening."

"The Penelope called him from like some gas station on the Merritt Parkway and said she got hung high temporarily but she was coming down and would without fail fall in over to the Waldorf for this blow."

"It's all in one carton now. We pick up on History for sure and on the Penelope maybe."

"You still got a dollar in the hold? We might could scoff back lightly, in the most minor way, before I uptown. My last meal was yesterday if yesterday was Friday. Let's count out the grass."

He rose, stretched his unendowed arms, and started across the room for the rear corner, past the refrigerator and the two-burner cooker. She followed along, saying,

"Listen, Prosper, see can you talk her loose from another sharp suit or dress and maybe a pair of high heels, her shoes come down on me like sensations too. Then maybe I could maneuver around and go back to the stores."

He said he would tip into it at the right and greasy time.

In the corner where he now stood was a set of wall bars and weighted pulleys, a contraption for arm and abdomen exercises. At right angles to it on the adjoining wall was another black-framed long mirror. He took hold of one of the horizontal wooden bars, his hands making quick turns in opposite directions.

The bar, made of two pieces socketed together, came apart at the line of junction. He pulled the left half through its hole in the vertical support beam. The inner end of this cylindrical piece was hollow. From this space his long and questing fingers drew several tied bunches of thin marijuana sticks.

"Twenty should cool them, many as they are."

He handed two of the bunches to the girl and returned the others to their hiding place, all but one. From this packet he drew four sticks.

"Two to damp us down, two to crawl up through the tight tunnel of the Sunday."

She went for the kitchen matches on the stove and came back to hold the light for him as he made deep sipping sounds through his laxed lips.

He filled his lungs with chugging takes. He did it a second time, waiting after each gasp with the large load in him, then letting the smoke out in dribs that he snuffled back up. Marga was doing modern agonized jetés in front of him.

"Now, yes, there, all the way and a mile again."

He felt it almost as a snap in his muscles, the joining moment. He and the other back in the partnership, components quick glued to make a work-possible whole.

He handed her the reefer and took hold of the two metal handles that lifted the pulleyed weights. He brought these loops close to his crimped chest and away again, over and over, arching his front out to maximum, watching in the mirror how his drumhead belly slimmed still more with the chest's paltry rises. Now no Proper eyeing Prosper from the distances. Proper and Prosper in the good overlap now, he wholed and gazing into his own full blend in the mirror image, all gaps closed. As he pulled the weights Marga, releasing and tensing her abdominal muscles, her haunches clenching to power the neck to pelvis peristalsis, held the reefer to his expertly pouted lips and asked again would he hit the Penelope for some suitable threads and soonest.

Sipping, ribbily arching, stringily flexing and unflexing, he said he would curve into it if and when the scene looked steady.

9

"YOU'RE *not* from Beirut? Then *what? Very* good steak."

"I am Swede, not Arab. Will you try a pickled tomato?"

"*Swede?* Just the crisped onions, thanks. Come on. Jet hair and cherry lips on the Arctic Circle?"

"Originally my people came there from a place of jetmost and cherriness. My father's work took him to the Middle East. No more onion for me. After he died I decided to stay on. In Sweden when I was growing up I discovered it is very hard to have free and roaming thoughts when the tip of your nose is always frozen."

"What line was your father in? More garlic bread?"

"Diplomatic. One slice, yes. They sent him to Palestine after the fighting to be on the U.N. Truce Commission. He was killed there."

"I don't remember any Truce Team man named Gasharid being killed."

"Our family name is Boergensen."

"Your father was Colonel Boergensen? He was doing a *very* good job."

"May I have a touch more wine, please? He was an able man but his success in Palestine was due to more than his ability. Our name, you see, was not always Boergensen. A hundred some years ago it was Bogenstein."

"We'd better get another bottle. Your people were originally German?"

"German Jews. Banking, spices, commercial fisheries."

"Full bottle or pint? Full, I think. Miss Gasharid, no, really, you're not Jewish?"

"In Stockholm, after a century, they forget these things. They would not have sent my father to Palestine as a neutral if anyone had remembered."

"The scrupulously objective Colonel Boergensen was a Jew? That's completely remarkable. Didn't the Israelis know?"

"They are alert people, they ferret out any little shred about those they deal with. Yes, they found out. When they put it to my father he said only that his sympathies for Israel came from human rather than racial considerations, and that by virtue of these same considerations he also felt extreme sympathy for the Arabs, particularly the refugees from Palestine."

"How'd the Israelis take that?"

"They knew the value to them of a Commissioner who was intelligent and also truly fairminded."

"Broccoli? Please, there's plenty. Go on about your father."

"He wished the state of Israel to have a chance. He knew its advances could mean something to the whole area. If, for example, they learned how to stop hoof-and-mouth disease, they would show their neighbors how to stop hoof-and-mouth disease. Not just out of kindness. So long as hoof-and-mouth disease was on their borders, their own cattle would keep getting reinfected. Epidemics sneak over the borders without passports. But what chance could the new state have with a million absolutely deprived refugees camped all around it, kept in a strong pitch of agitation? One way to help Israel, and at the same time the Arab refugees and all Arabs, was to improve the impossible conditions of the refugee camps. The Israeli officials encouraged my father in his private efforts along these lines."

"What could he do privately?"

"He was a man of some means. Also, he had excellent business connections in Europe. Without letting his name be used he founded in Beirut the East Mediterranean Development Corporation."

"Try the Escoffier sauce. East Mediterranean what?"

"Development Corporation. It is not too known. It does its work quietly. It is a non-profit organization financed by certain well-off people in Europe and now even in the States who wish to make some contribution, without publicity, without politics, to the life of the Arabs. But this is a technical matter."

"May I establish something? The doctoral dissertation I'm writing is called *The Thpectwum of Neutwalithm and Commitment in Miwwel Eatht Fowwin Powithy—*"

"Please? I do not—"

"The Thpectwum of Neutwa—"

"Why do you pronounce as with the tongue on crutches?"

"That's a technical matter too. It relates to certain premises in political philosophy which I can't go into now. The point is, I'm expected to take a position in the State Department when I get my degree. As an expert on Miwwel Eathtern Affairth. Two years ago I spent some time in Cairo and

42

Baghdad, doing research. I speak Russian and several of the Arabic tongues. Have you ever heard of Josephus Fairliss?"

"Samuel Josephus Fairliss, oh, yes. The American who worked so hard on the U.N. Partition Plan. The diplomat. You are related to him?"

"My nose is his nose. It runs in the family, forgive me. He's my father."

"How fantastic. He did many things to make the partition terms as fair as they could be."

"That's his specialty. Before Palestine he partitioned my mother right out of the family. She died in Caracas three years ago."

"They were divorced?"

"He had no choice. Imagine, he was practically the top man in State under Acheson, a founding father of the New Deal, and here was his wife two-timing him with a Liberty League America Firster, an industrialist who'd once gone on a sitdown strike against taxes and who at the moment was under indictment by the Department of Justice on seventeen counts for violation of the anti-trust laws. If mother had shacked up with an American for Democratic Action or a C.I.O.-v.p. the thing might have been glossed over, but she never learned to think politically. My father *had* to get rid of her. Politics can *un*make bedfellows, sometimes very fast."

"What are these potatoes? Hash brownèd? Thank you, I believe I will. Your father is not now in government?"

"Oh, no. One of the first things Eisenhower did was to clean the Acheson people out. My father's still in Washington, of course, he's got his own law firm, international law. Don't stint on the potatoes, we can get more. What about the East Mediterranean Development Corporation?"

"I will start with a question. You know what bilharziasis is?"

"One long chapter of my dissertation is about bilharziasis and its role in international relations."

"You know the life cycle of the Bilharzia worm?"

"It's a trematode, a blood fluke that lives in fresh water. It enters the human body when people drink water, or bathe, or do laundry. It lays its eggs in the veins of the bladder and small intestine. When the eggs hatch the baby worms fight their way out of these nests, causing multiple lesions, and exit in the waste products. Ready for salad? They are now very small forktailed wrigglers. Oil and vinegar? They swim about in fresh water until they find snails of a certain type, invade these snails and spend two generations with them, then swim out and look for a human body to colonize again. About fifty percent of all the poorer people in Egypt and nearby countries have these worms in their bodies all their lives. The symptoms are hematuria, sluggishness, loss of appetite, impaired capacity for work, constant fever, abdominal pains, intestinal bleeding, inferior I.Q., and early death."

"It is a pleasure to talk with an informed man. And do you also know what was and is wrong with the Aswan Dam project?"

"In detail. Nasser wants two billion dollars for a dam on the Nile that will supply power for industry and irrigation for farms. The trouble with the plan is that it doesn't take into account the Bilharzia worm with the forked tail."

"Because the snails go where there is fresh water and the worms go where the snails go. If irrigation ditches are cut through new lands and fresh water is pumped into them, the snails will spread, and with them the worms."

"But this can be prevented. Line the conduits with concrete, which repels the snails, and cover all sluice openings with special mesh traps. This would cost more millions, of course. The Egyptians don't include these extra funds in the Aswan budget because they wouldn't make headlines. The Americans did not include these millions when they offered to finance the dam—no headlines. When the Americans stepped out and the Russians stepped in, *they* did not offer any anti-snail moneys —no headlines. This has something to do with my theory that what we are dealing with here on all sides is not Middle East Policy but Miwwel Eatht Powithy, but that can wait."

"This is what my father saw. He quietly founded the E.M.D.C. to work out projects that will make few headlines but can bring more true benefits."

"Like what? Here, have the last pickled tomato, really, I couldn't. Like what, Miss Gasharid?"

"My father hired good engineers to develop an all-purpose dynamo which could be installed free of charge in villages that have no power. With it, electric light could be introduced into every hut. Irrigation could be arranged for the surrounding farmlands. Power could be provided for small factories. In this way, with one piece of machinery costing ten thousand dollars, the life of a whole village could be changed. With bulbs in their homes, people would spend their evenings learning to read, then reading. With irrigation they could grow the food they needed, with industrial power they could make products to sell on the outside for money. Of course, the irrigation would be planned so as to keep the snails out. There would be no saving of pennies on that item. Progress would not be bought at the price of universal worms in the bladder and intestine."

"Dessert? The baked Alaska is very good. The Israelis encouraged your father in all this?"

"Behind the scenes they helped him in starting the Corporation, they even contributed some funds. They understood that if the close-by colonies of refugees could be made into self-sufficient villages, the tension, the pressure to let one million refugees flood back into the country, would be lessened. Headquarters for the E.M.D.C. were set up in Beirut. Contracts for making the generators and other equipment were let out. Some thirty-seven installations were made, in as many dead villages, by the time my father died."

"How *did* he die? Nobody would talk to me about it when I was over there."

"Few know the story. Even I, who know it, cannot make much sense of it. Remember, please, this was a man who, being of Jewish origins, and known to be such by some Israelis, was yet encouraged by these same Israelis to keep quiet about his background and act with meticulous neutrality in border quarrels. More, he was encouraged by them to found a company to do positive things for Arab refugees. And in this the Israelis were not being altruists but were thinking of their own enlightened self-interest. This is the insane background for the bigger insanity that followed. During all this time, you understand, my father was busy with his duties as Truce Commissioner. There were many complicated border incidents to investigate and smooth over, some caused by Arabs, some by Jews. In assigning blames and exacting compensations my father was always strictly impartial, dedicated only to facts. This is the kind he was."

"I was told that many times. American coffee or espresso? They also have Turkish."

"Espresso, please. One night a very unclear event took place. I will see if I can explain it. No, not explain, only to describe it will be hard enough. There was a Jordanian Arab who owned a wretched little farm just over the hill from the border. Some nights he would put on the work clothes of an Israeli settler and sneak over the line to a small kibbutz to steal chickens. What he did not know was that in this kibbutz was a very young, very husky, very emotional sabra who was often on guard duty at the border post and who, looking up to

45

the hill, would often see this farmer's wife hanging up her laundry. The wife was much younger than the farmer, a buxom, hungry girl. She noticed the sabra guard too. Eventually he stopped being a Jew to her and became only a young man with broad shoulders. As yours. Yes. With very intense looking the clothes and languages tend to go away. At first she stared. Later she waved. The young man's hot blood became over hot. One day the wife seemed not merely to be waving but signalling. He thought he got the gist of her signals. She seemed to be saying that she would be most pleased to have his company this night. It was a foolish thing for the young guard to do, of course. It could easily have been a trap. But his blood was very, very hot. That night he crept away from his post, put on some Arab clothes, and proceeded on his belly up the hill. The farm wife was in fact alone. Her husband was across the border stealing chickens. The sabra enjoyed his visit. On other nights he enjoyed similar visits, whenever he read the all-clear signal in the wife's waving laundry. She chose those nights to invite him, naturally, when she knew her husband was going over to the kibbutz chicken coops. There came this bad night. The sabra had received his delicious summons. He had changed to his Arab clothes and crawled up the hill to his bliss. It must have been an unusually large dose of bliss. He started back an hour later than usual. There, very close to the border, he saw a figure crawling towards him. This man was dressed in the clothes of a kibbutz settler. It was the Arab farmer, of course. For once he had found the coops unguarded and had gotten his chickens very quickly, and so was returning home an hour *earlier* than usual. The Jew was astonished to see one of his own crawling *out* of Israeli territory. For his part, the Arab farmer was dumbfounded to see one of *his* kind proceeding in the *other* direction. The Jew stood up. The Arab stood too. For the moment each in his relief had forgotten that he was dressed in enemy clothes. 'Where do you think *you're* going, neighbor?' the Jew said, in Hebrew, of course. The Arab was completely overcome to hear Hebrew sounds coming out of a man in Arab clothes. He stuttered, 'Friend, compatriot, why do you dress in this peculiar way and crawl about here and there and talk ugly and strange tongues when you should be home in bed?' But this he said in Arabic. The Jew was speechless. At this moment, absolutely disorganized, the Arab dropped the chickens he was holding by the feet under his shoulder blanket. The birds began to squawk. The Arab was terrified.

Now it came to him that the man facing him was a Jew disguised as an Arab. The chickens he had just dropped were *Jewish* chickens. For all he knew, maybe they were speaking Hebrew too, telling on him. In his fright the Arab raised the knife in his hand and threw it with all his strength. It cut a bad gash in the Jew's arm. The Jew, too, was in a fever. The man in kibbutz clothes was obviously an Arab. The Jew had a revolver in his hand. Automatically he pressed the trigger. The Arab fell dead. All this racket brought the Israeli border guards running. The wounded sabra was taken to an observation post. At this point my father, who was on patrol in the neighborhood, was called in to investigate. From what the sabra told him he was able to piece together most of the story. But something altogether unexpected now happened. The young sabra had a fiancee, a worker on the kibbutz. This young woman heard that her man had been wounded and hurried to the observation post. She arrived in time to hear the last part of my father's interrogation. This was a *very* emotional girl. S.S. examinations, barracks rape, army prostitution centers, Belsen, one D.P. camp after another had not left her with the best of balance. When she heard what her man had been doing up on the hill with the Arab farmer's wife she completely lost her head. She had taken all the humiliations of Europe with a certain stoicism, but here was the last touch to ignite the whole hidden storehouse of hurt. To be betrayed by one of her own, a Jew, her lover, this was all the world's betrayal in one package. She snatched the sabra's gun from where it was resting on a chair and began firing wildly at the betrayer. She killed him with the first shot. Unfortunately she was not good with guns, also, she had her eyes closed. In her indignation she also managed to put three bullets in my father. I was in Tel Aviv at the moment, on one of my trips from Beirut. They flew me to the border. My father was still alive when I got there. This part, I think, you will not be able to follow. You see, my father was not in pain. His spinal cord had been almost severed so he felt nothing, only numb. Besides, he was a man with a larger than usual sense of humor. As he told me the story he began to laugh. 'A case of mistaken identity on every side,' he said, 'as in all international relations. With luck the rutting and poultry drives will yet cause enough traffic to smudge over the borders. It will help if people wear their own clothes and learn their neighbors' languages to avoid the most obvious misunderstandings. That they should stop coveting their

47

neighbors' wives and chickens is perhaps too much to ask, but they ought to overcome the costume and language difficulties at the very least. They will put me down as a martyr, of course. Incorrect. I am merely a spectator at an intensely interesting game who got too close. The most interesting things happen on the borderlines. Little one, my sweet girl, here is where the best and most instructive jokes come up. A Bogenstein become Boergensen and almost but not quite blond in the soul can see it better than some. No need to weep for me. I always had an appetite for the good jokes. Here they served me up the best, the cream of the crop, a vintage selection. I do not entirely mind that it kills me.' Just before he died he managed to say, 'Another thing. Listen, my girl. The work with the low-cost generators must go on. Please have your mind clear as to the reasons. It is not only for the food and the manufactures and the moneys. These are the most minor items, unfortunately made major by their absence. They must be provided merely so that people can forget about them and go on to the matters of interest. To bring electrification into the huts, to light up the dark, that is more to the lasting point. So that they can learn to read and go into politics and accountancy? Yes, for those things too. We must be absolutely modern. But there is better reason for distributing the Mazdas. They will make it possible for people who before were used to closing their eyes the moment the world closed its eyes, whose consciousness had no more staying power than the sun, now to look around after sundown and study the more shadowed things and see the big joke in the middle of the darkness. As I do now. The dark is frightening only because the very big joke in its middle cannot be seen. The best jokes are seen at night, if some light is provided and if you are near the important borders.' He began to laugh again, and he was laughing hard, laughing genuinely, when he stopped breathing. So, you see, this is why I continue with the work of the generators. Who knows? I may yet learn to laugh as loud as my father. It is my hope. First I must learn where are the truly interesting borders. My, how much I talk. My tongue has a motor. We have taken a very great deal of wine."

"Stop, Miss Gasharid. Enough, Miss Gasharid. It is too much for one head."

"The head can grow big enough to hold it."

"Can a dissertation grow big enough to hold it? That's my problem. A more immediate problem: brandy? Perhaps some

48

b-and-b for you? Yes? You've explained everything but one thing, Miss Gasharid."

"Ask, please. Oh, how I am dizzy."

"I see how Bogenstein might get Norsified into Boergensen. But how Boergensen gets Hebraicized into Shoshana Gasharid—"

"This is not for you to know, Mr. Fairliss."

"It is absolutely vital that I know."

"You have a face that invites confidences, reaches for them with begging teeth, no, it is dangerous for me. I have already talked too, how do you say, blabbermouth."

"Trust me, Miss Gasharid. You can't leave me dangling."

"You will never say a word to Worthington or any other living soul? You promise, absolutely?"

"On the beard of my father, Miss Gasharid. If you prefer, my pledge in mother's milk."

"Do not involve your parents' growths and secretions. Well. This also is hard to make into sense. I will begin with the founding of the E.M.D.C. When my father set up the headquarters in Beirut, the first officers were Europeans. Good men, the best technicians, but Europeans. They ran into the brick wall. Here they wished to give away to stagnating people certain machineries that would save them and the people totally refused the gift. Worse. They would not even talk to these Corporation men. It was clear enough why. They had a distrust of all foreigners. This suspiciousness was fed by propaganda, naturally. Nasser did not want these refugees to busy themselves with productive work and have a contented life. If their hardships were eased they would not be so interested in the holy war against Israel. The propagandists whispered, and the villagers turned their backs on us. Something had to be done."

"This is where you entered the picture?"

"I had finished my schooling in Stockholm and at the Sorbonne. My father had me come to his headquarters in Jerusalem. There he quietly explained the problem to me. He had talked it over with his well-placed Arab friends. His Beirut connections had proposed a solution. He had a daughter. They had seen my pictures. I was dark-haired and full-lipped, very much the Semitic type, amazingly so to these people who knew nothing of my multiple background. Very well. I could be of great service here. Nobody knew me in this part of the world. Nobody could possibly guess that I was the daughter of Colonel Nils Boergensen, the white-haired and blue-eyed Swede. Could I not *pretend* to be a Jewess? Let me proceed to Beirut. They, my father's Arab friends and well-wishers, would provide me with a passport and identification papers showing that I was Shoshana Gasharid, Jewess. I would put up in style in a first-class hotel, move around the fashionable places, be seen in smart nightclubs. They, my father's friends, would drop hints here and there that the mysterious Shoshana Gasharid, Jewess, was an undercover agent for certain Arab interests. Behind their fingers they would whisper that I travelled frequently to Tel Aviv and Jerusalem and other Israeli cities and there, through important contacts among my compatriots, stole important Israeli secrets."

"I believe I'll have to have another brandy. A double, yes. For you, Miss Gasharid? Another b-and-b?"

"If you don't mind. You must hear it all, Mr. Fairliss. If you mean to be a student of Miwwel Eatht, Middle East affairs you must recognize that the Miwwel, the *Middle* East is not Cleveland or Buffalo. The Middle East is full of intense night and with a great many borders. Where was I? Yes. I was made into a good facsimile of an Arab undercover agent. The word was planted with efficiency and I began to be treated with the utmost respect wherever I went in the Arab lands. I was the Jewess who stole invaluable secrets from those too damned smart Jews to be transmitted to my Lebanese and Iraqi and Jordanian superiors. Of course, my father's friends thought I was only *posing* as a Jewess. I made frequent trips to Israel. There I did truly gather vital documents."

"How could you do that?"

"These documents were not as unavailable as they seemed. They were actually technical papers and surveys and reports that the Israeli scientific institutes put out in multigraphed form. Oh, studies on the construction of generators, the laying out of irrigation ditches, the stringing of power lines, the setting up of small electrified manufacturing plants, the eradication of bilharziasis, and so on. All the things the E.M.D.C. was most interested in, in fact. But I did not bring these documents to Beirut in multigraphed form. That would have defeated our purposes. Some of my father's Israeli friends, who were in on the scheme from the beginning, had stenographers copy these reports on their typewriters. Across the tops of the typescripts they stamped big bold warnings in red, such as CONFIDENTIAL and TOP SECRET

50

and NOT FOR DISCLOSURE UNDER ANY CIRCUMSTANCES and BURN IMMEDIATELY AFTER READING. The Arabs were quite sure I was stealing for them the most prized technical secrets. My father's Beirut friends further circulated the word that these secrets were being turned over to the E.M.D.C. In fact, through the complicated grapevines of the area, the Corporation soon came to be known as the center and clearing house for my espionage."

"Miss Gasharid, you are smudging my borders, you are bulbing my nights."

"The shaking up can be a therapy. I am learning this. Let me finish. The whole climate for the Corporation changed. The Arabs could not accept offers of technical help that would seem to be directed at lessening their indignation at Jews. This they had to interpret as a subtle Jewish plot to destroy their holy-war unity. Now, suddenly, the picture was different. We were offering them aid based on secrets *stolen* from the Jews. This the most benighted driver-of-Israel-into-the-sea could accept, and eagerly. It seemed, indeed, to be part of the conspiracy *against* the Jews, and therefore in the best interests of Pan-Arab nationalism, to take these secrets and put them to full use. The refugees began to welcome us with open arms. The villages let us install our equipment and gave parties and dances for us. The Arab lands are full of whispers, have I said that? On the whisper level we, and I especially, became heroes to the worst off Arab peoples. Would you suspect that the name of Shoshana Gasharid, the Jewess, is known and revered all through the Arab refugee settlements? That they write songs and poems to me, their Semite Mata Hari and savior?"

"Who wants a frank and open gift when it's possible to get stolen goods? Isn't it human nature to reject the donor in favor of the fence? I see, Miss Gasharid. I'm beginning to see, in the back of my head. None of your Arab friends knows you really *are* Jewish?"

"None. It is too early to tell them the full joke. They are not yet ready to laugh at the jokes of the bigger dimensions."

"I'm not sure *I'm* ready, the laugh starts in my ribs but then I begin to choke. So. You were a Gasharid when you met Worthington, not a Boergensen? Certainly not a Bogenstein?"

"This too is somewhat devious. Worthington was travelling through the Miwwel, Middle East with a party of American graduate students, studying industrial installations. He

51

saw me at a nightclub in Beirut and asked a Lebanese businessman who I was. This man only repeated what he had heard, that I was a Jewess technically connected with the E.M.D.C. but actually doing confidential work for certain Arab interests. Worthington found someone to introduce us. He told me his father is an industrialist very active with electrical and hydraulic equipment and that he himself was studying management engineering at Yale so that he could take over some of his father's affairs. I was immediately interested in him."

"And he in you? Worthington, the world's foremost anti-Semite?"

"Anti-Semitism like his has two faces. He seemed to be pushed away and attracted too. I was dirty, yet he could not take his eyes or his hands from the dirt. I was not interested in his personal feelings. What I cared about was that his father had developed a certain kind of new low-cost water pump for use in irrigation systems, pumps that could easily be fitted with screens to keep the snails out. I began to talk figures and specifications with Worthington, I wanted him to get me these pumps from his father for cost plus little or nothing. At first he would not discuss business with me. I finally realized why. Oh, I am talking too much. He did not want to do business with a Jew, especially a Jew who wished so Jewishly to eliminate the profits. Though he was more than ready, in spite of his look of smelling something bad, to go to the bed with this same Jew."

"And did you, finally?"

"Talk business?"

"Go to the bed with him."

"I am a better businesswoman than that, Mr. Fairliss. First I swore him to secrecy. Then I let him see my real papers, to prove that I was really a Swede named Boergensen who was only *posing* as a Jewess."

"Ah. I see. Yes. Brilliant, brilliant. He immediately became very respectful toward your snow-white Nordic virtue. He began to talk nuts and bolts."

"What he suggested was that I come to the States when I could, visit him at New Haven, then perhaps go on to Detroit to pursue the matter with his father. He would lay the groundworks for me."

"He wanted to lay more than the groundworks."

"Hmm? He urged me to come. Now here I am, the false-face Shoshana Gasharid in New Haven, and apparently

Worthington Rivers is running around New York with a size thirty-eight, if your specifications are accurate. The jokes are not confined to the Israeli borders."

"He's a pig. He's a pig. He was careful to give the impression that he was spending the night with you. Not to talk pumps."

"I do not understand."

"He didn't get you over here because he's interested in your E.M.D.C. This was a transoceanic plot to try to make you on his home grounds."

"Again this make. My father made me. In Stockholm."

"It's an expression, Miss Gasharid, it means to wind things up, to bring matters to a head, to culminate relations. Worthington is very scheming with women because he doesn't feel sure of himself. He thought he'd have a better chance to storm your Nordic ramparts here. The pumps were just bait."

"Nevertheless I intend to get them. We need them badly."

"Enough to go to bed with Worthington?"

"You forget, I want *low*-cost pumps. This is a very *high* cost."

"Miss Gasharid, dear and astonishing miss, you are many things to many men. I put this question to you: do you know who you are?"

"I think so. Yes, certainly. I am the woman who assembles and installs generating and pumping equipment in Arab villages because my father asked me to."

"Other people see you as other things."

"Then they have not yet separated the jokes from the facts. They have had no training in how to see from both sides of the border at once, like a true truce commissioner."

"And that's the biggest joke to you?"

"Part of it. I am very far from completing my investigations, I think. I am also very far from sober, this I do not think, I know."

"Miss Gasharid, I have a suggestion. You don't want to spend two days visiting museums and art galleries. Come with me."

"To?"

"New York. Please, Miss Gasharid, it's no plot, I'm not trying to make you. I assure you, under other circumstances it would not be a hardship to have designs on someone so softly designed, far from it, you are made to memorable specifications, memorable, you are a full-lipped generator I would be pleased and honored to have installed in my stagnating village, but at this moment I have too much urgent business. You can have your talk with Worthington and go right on to Detroit. You'll save two days."

"You are sure you can find Worthington?"

"I know some places to look. We'll find him."

"I have business to conduct, yes. You have not said what *your* business might be."

"I'll put it in the most obvious terms, Miss Gasharid, though not necessarily the most accurate. There is a girl named Penelope up whose hill I have sometimes had the dubious privilege to crawl. If Worthington has the weekend with her, with no interference, he may very well make his way up the hill, rather, be carried up, in my place. I do not intend to let this happen, for reasons of my own. Maybe I am a dogged mountaineer. Maybe I just don't like to be used. Come with me, Miss Gasharid."

"Why do you want me there, Mr. Fairliss? How can I help you in retaking your hill, assuming I would want to?"

"You come to the crux of the matter, Miss Gasharid. This gets a little technical. One more b-and-b for the road, for the Merritt Parkway? I believe I'll have one last brandy, for the Major Deegan Highway. No, I'll take my own hills. But the hill is perhaps not the ultimate objective here. Perhaps it never was. This is a hill with too many slide areas, a man can get bouldered, avalanched. What I'm most interested in, especially now, after our enlightening talk, is learning to see from both sides of the border. You might be of immense help in that. Please. I implore you. I need a second pair of eyes along, I'm still in basic training in this double vision. You must."

"This drink is *very* strong. Fantastical. What means the name b-and-b, that it, mm, brangs and then blamps? Hm. I am not sure, Mr. Fairliss."

"Come along, Miss Gasharid. You'll see a couple of border-lines you may have overlooked. Say you will, Miss Gasharid. My affairth are very Miwwel Eathern in their overtones. Come, Miss Gasharid. Look upon me as a D.P. of the heart who needs some new pumps of hope that will filter out the more spleeny trematodes. We can be there in ninety minutes, Miss Gasharid—"

54

10

SAM'L, COUNSELOR AND FRIEND. Once more I take bane in hand to tender rebuts. On the Merritt Parkway passing the cutoff to Old Greenwich. Miss Shoshana curled up catching thirty-odd winks. Those legs, those legs. Excuse my not writing sooner but I've been busy. First had to fight this nausea down. It got bad when I climbed out of the bath. When I read Worthington's slimy letter to Miss Shoshana my whole digestive tract went into shock. Had to take four more Alka-Seltzers. It made me more nauseated still to discover that my condition was in fact nausea. You know how I balk at following the fashion, in my disabilities as in my clothes. Though I understand, not without nausea, because you can't win, that it is becoming increasingly fashionable to reject the fashionable. Entirely too much chic these days in working up and holding on to a medium-size nausea. Better the whimwhams or the meemies. Something behind the tepid times and with fewer bandwagons. Anyhow, about my nauseating shoulders. I have never, from Groton days on, been able to fathom why shoulders are reprehensible and to be concealed. I am against Chinese women binding their feet and I am against U's with non-U shoulders binding said shoulders. I somehow feel things with me and Penelope would be going better, at least going, if, one, I hadn't come into the world with big shoulders, or, two, I'd agreed in a spirit of U-solidarity to let J. Press naturalize my shoulders down to an unnatural U-ey toothpickiness. What the hell can she have against big shoulders? I know what I'd *like* her to have against my shoulders. Her. Her corresponding largesses. Once at the crucial moment she bit me on the shoulder. With a dedication too fulsome and too fanged to be taken for passion, much less fun. Listen, Sam'l, she's big herself in a couple of departments. Does she brang them, blamp them? Won't even bra them. Miss Shoshana does not seem that bloomingly endowed but those legs and so on. I feel I owe you an explanation re my behavior today. There is something about me drunk that the varicosed Sophies and simpatico grenade makers and acned

55

young townies don't see. When I'm drunk I'm not myself but Worthington Rivers. I have to watch and ward it. Ward it off watchfully. When Worthington drinks he gets more snotty-prankish. He snoots the lower classes. He digs at those without his polish. He stands on his pedestal of twenty million or whatever dollars and stares the world down. In short, he becomes more of the same. Drunkenness is simply a chorus call to all his possibilities, which are replicas of each other. I on the other hand loathe and abominate my possibilities. Because half of them are so much like his and the other half are against the law. Any rallying call to my innermost cisterns makes me panicky. When my skin cracks enough to let my less admirable syrups leak out I immediately slip on another restraining skin. Usually Worthington's, which is unconscionably thick and in abundant supply. Worthington Rivers is not a palatable thing to be but at least it's handleable. It dictates set gestures and calls out set responses so that nobody, neither audience nor actor, has to improvise. This son-of-a-bitch Worthington is all one piece, I won't say of what. He's predictable. He has continuity. He duplicates himself inch by inch and day by day. He's a unitary thing of class and breeding and manners and blood and genes and genealogies and so recognizable from any angle. If I ever let myself go when drunk the unWorthington things that came out would be minus labels and faceless and blowing in the top. They'd run all over the place like panicked bedbugs or lemmings sniffing the salt breezes. Messy. Nothing comes ont of Worthington Rivers, drunk or sober, but more Worthington Rivers. It proceeds with its thin umbrella down the main road. That's why when under the influence I have a tendency to put myself inside his skin. It stops up the holes in my own. Keeps my more berserker insides inside. Lets only the Worthington in me pass through. How do I manage the changeover? It's so little of a change that it scares me. I do it with an easy shifting of gears. I have so many Worthingtons in reserve in my back pocket, when I listen to them. I can't bring myself to listen to their well-bred accents unless I'm drunk, and not much then. But when drunk I'm still less ready to listen to the raspier yelpings in me. If you must know, this is why I hit the snide-playful Endicott on the bus. He was being so Worthington at a time when I couldn't stand myself for being so Worthington. Then the Sophies see the Worthington Rivers dredged out of me and pasted on as camouflage and take it that I am truly the son-of-a-bitch that he by definition is and they aim their dirty looks at *me*. That's unfair. I'm only the stage manager here. Maybe the clothes dummy. That's why I wear non-U clothes over my U-manque frame. To show them the U-Worthington in me is not me. They don't get the point. They never guess that I'm booing along with them at the smelly vaudeville. So I occasionally have to hit this or that Worthington to make my position clear. And separate myself from them because they're dangerously close. Miss Shoshana's dress is creeping and it looks like those sensational legs go all the way up. Sam'l, there's a missing of minds here. Misunderstanding is rampant. Consider the way I met Penelope. This was in Boston in the summer of Fifty-Five, right after I got back from Cairo. My leg was bothering me again and I was spending more time in the veterans' hospital, if you remember. We met at a party after an experimental dance recital. Penelope had been a fitful pelvis in the chorus and the party was in honor of the whole thrustworthy cast. I had admired Penelope on the stage for her contractile deftnesses as well as her robustious physique and I was more than pleased to see her across a crowded room. Her breasts were truly astonishing and inclined to reconnoiter on their own. The trouble was that after I saw her across the room the damned crowd was too thick to get through. In particular there was a breastbony member of the troupe with sheepdog bangs and expressive elbows who insisted on crawling all over me when I tried to edge away. A further complication, I was just then back on crutches, you remember they'd operated to cut some more of the irritated nerves in my leg. Crutches attract certain types of women such as modern dancers. They salivate over the lame and the halt. This may be why so many Worthingtons carry thin umbrellas. From where Penelope was standing it must have looked like I was another adorable cripple. She did not at all, she told me later, get the idea I was trying unWorthingtonly to get *to* her. It simply looked as if I was working to get *away* from this one with the aggressive elbows. She saw a man in what seemed to be hobbled flight from a woman and her salivary glands started to pump. *She* came to what she thought was *my* rescue. The sight of a Worthington in any way immobilized or trapped and so in need of saving can move her very deeply. I sensed this at the time and later events, as you will see, confirmed my impression. *She* approached *me*, the apparent cripple and therefore the desirable quarry. At this time, I should explain. I had not yet acquired my reverse-

English wardrobe from Giacomo D'Amici and so in addition to seeming an all-round casualty and captive audience I was dressed very Brooksly and bleakly. This no doubt added to my air of general debility. I seemed hemmed in on all sides, by clothes as well as circumstances. My crutches looked like ciliations of a moral infirmity, spines I had to buy in the truss and splint store. Penelope inserted herself between me and the tenacious one, who was anyhow too skimpy fore and aft and in the brain matter for my taste. Pretty soon Penelope of the generous beam and baft and I were talking in warm whispers in the corner. Her excitement level was high and rising from the first. I think her conviction that she had taken all the precipitative steps and was boltingly calling all the shots over a bolt-shot Worthington went to her head like wine. And of course my crutches were slobbermaking. All of this left me less than enchanted. I really do not, as I discovered long ago, like forward women. I have no big eyes for backward ones either. Let's say the shotcallers put me off as much as the wilting violets. But she was really fantastic looking and that body. I purposely began to make some Reich-tinted talk about culminations and the difficulties in arriving at them, I guess by way of hinting that I had my doubts about the genuineness of the erotic affidavits she was waving under my nose. She was not offended. It turned out she *was* a partial Reichian, had studied the theory of orgasm, had a friend who once owned an orgone box, was as a dancer intensely interested in the deeper body geyserings. She went on to let me know that she was a practitioner as well as theorist of the Reichian delights and furthermore was very good at it, one of the adepts. In ten minutes we were easing out of the party and in another ten harding into a room in a small hotel and undressing. It was her whimsy that she had maneuvered the whole bedbound operation. Her body was one of the wonders of the world. So was the total misunderstanding between us. I think she was from the beginning dismayed to discover that my game leg did not after all mean a total gameness. She had somehow set her sights on a basket case, that is, a Worthington. All her enthusiasm was geared to an image of my over-sized person deprived of its crutches and dewilled down to a percussion instrument on which she could play according to her own private sheet music. I would not be the xylophone to her hot fingers. I insisted on taking a hand in the concert, finally an even firmer and more authoritarian hand than hers. This was not in the slightest to humil-

58

iate her but simply to get the difference in roles and functions clear, the right and proper division of labor so promotive of those high and delicious unities. She took it, of course, as a struggle to get the *upper* hand, and she was very much against yielding any upperness to anybody. Yield she did because I weigh more and press my point unWorthingtonly. Maybe this is what she has against the bulk I did not ask for but which is irremediably mine. In this bedroom concert she had meant to be composer and orchestrator and maestro and virtuoso solist all at once and in her onesided terms she had been unceremoniously shouldered aside by my shoulders and made to play the ignominious second fiddle. This was when she bit me, finally. It got infected and some days later I had to go to a doctor. He was ironic about the inflamed teeth marks and said something about passion's tattoo being almost as neat as concentration-camp tattoos. He was a German refugee and a bachelor. The bite came at a supremely crucial moment. A moment of such cruxity as I had never run into before. Neither had she, and that was the wonder. I had had the good fortune to encounter responsive women a few times, among many who were not, but none of them, not one, had had such unambiguous and anatomically distinct responses. The physical evidences were so strong and so definitive as to rule out any possibility of play-acting. There are muscles you simply can't maneuver. Forgive the Aesopian language here, Sam'l. I suppose you got enough of it from mother. Or she from you. My meaning is clear, I hope. Her climaxes were not the vague and over-vocalized ones for which you have to take the lady's word and for which there are invariably too many words. They were all there in the deep muscles. They spoke for themselves and eloquently. The sound effects were not up and over in this performance but mere background ripples to the physiological mob scenes. There was only one thing wrong with all this splendor. It was remarkable, it was devastating, it was the first absolutely full and all-encompassing and proved beyond all doubt heave and let of everything I had felt in a girl. It made my head spin. But it did not take place at the time of my own high moment or anywhere close to it. Rather, once she'd been forced to yield the initiative and had simply given in, she had been more or less subdued during the thing, even inert. Up to the point of my own overboiling. Her own mobilization, it seemed, had to take place *after* that, and *slowly*. And without any discernible stirrings on *either* side.

The most unlikely place to look for a riot is in the morgue but there you are. But it took time. After some minutes of mutual rigor mortis I developed a sense of not belonging and decided to move away. Then she came to life. She would not let me go. She insisted on my hanging around for an indefinite time. She had need of me as a loiterer. Soon after *that* I began to sense this gathering in her. Then I began to *feel* it. Unmistakably. The first time I had felt such a rising to such highs in anybody. My reaction was natural enough, I thought. I was grateful for my own pleasure, no matter what a struggle it had been to get there. Though she had not been able to share it with me or even help it along significantly I wanted her to have her own, whatever the timing. My assumption was that I could make some contribution, even now, however modest, to *her* pleasure. I was ready to do so. But when I tried to fall in with this upsurging and give it courage, intensify it, all her trending to finality came to a full stop. My attempt to participate, it seemed, scotched the process instead of boosting it. Did she then want me to leave her? Not that either. She wished me neither to go away nor to take part in her intensifications. She only asked that I be *there*, among but not of. Maybe she wanted me as down with the trodden as she had mistakenly assumed I had trod her. Maybe it was an evening of scores. I don't mean that on this evening I scored. But to her own infinite amazement and even terror she was discovering that she had not exaggerated her capacity for reaching the farthest plateaus. For the first time in her life she was feeling it as she had read it and talked it. And with *me*. Why me? Mere fill has no name and no face. All it required was that I be there and yet on the sidelines. Both of us in a state of total freeze. It was a self-contained solo performance that contradicted its own logic in that it yet needed a silent and immobilized partner. This was a togetherness of the mortuary ice box. She insisted that I live up to my promise however belatedly and be now the man on crutches, the useful Worthingtonian basket case. When I stopped trying to participate and simply hung on the trapped thing came out again and proceeded to its culmination. Dazzling, it was. A remarkable way of taking pleasure from a man while excluding and eluding him. She was pantingly stunned to discover this retaining-dismissing technique and its big bonus payoffs. So was I. A complicated experience. Even a challenge, you might say. To find the rare one who can have the full thing and then to be shut out though bodily present is in many ways the ultimate slap in the face. It leads you to some wild imaginings. You daydream that if you press the matter hard and far enough, force things, *shoulder* your way further with her and to her, so to speak, this taunting time gap between two theoretically linked pleasures will be closed as ideally it must. You want, you *need* to reaffirm the linkage. You drive yourself in that lovely direction. But you are eternally stopped short. Because each renewed effort on your part freezes her, the gathering in her, which in any case began long after your own was completed and spent. She needs to use you as a space-filler but she does not want to acknowledge you as a being and presence and more or less prime mover. I kept trying, though. Never say die. Kid yourself you're Lazarus. Multiply your risings. At my insistence, and I had to insist more and more, we got together night after night. The gap remained and broadened. When the doctors said I could go on convalescent leave I suggested to Penelope that we fly down to Varadero for a vacation. Her classes at Bennington were not due to start for another month. She begged off from her dance rehearsals. She told her family she was going to sit in on a summer seminar in Afro-Cuban folk dancing at the University of Havana. She had heard that Varadero was dreamy. We held hands all the way, at 19,000 feet. She was too bright and chatty and already this battle between us for some undefined kind of dominance had reached several explosion points but to me just then, with my own vitality low and the funeral parlor smell of operating rooms with me still, the bubble in her was a tonic. She was becoming a talker. While she gave me professional tips on the techniques for pelvic loosening and plexal outgiving, like a master baker explaining how to get the best rise out of pastry dough, I admired her fine features and looked for words to describe the luring mix in them. The shooting shadows in her green, green eyes. Blarney stones chasing mezuzzahs? The vibrant undertones of her voice. Aili-Aili's brushing the heather? Idle couplings reflecting my wants more than her qualities. I looked for wild mixtures to echo my own mixing. She was eleventh-generation Boston topdog and so hardly a blend. Miss Shoshana is this kind of impossible blend but Penelope is all one piece and that full of fight and lecture. Only in one dimension is she a brew and that is where she comes through as lady and as hipster. But the lady-hipster is less brew than mishmash. You have to establish one fixed address in emotional space. There's no way to be simultaneously with it and above it. She would like to be gone and come too and there's no such way in any lee. I could find no words for her but she was lovely in her making and she talked too much about the vital centers. Because I was getting established in her mind as the examiner she was out to mock away the idea of examinations by giving more and wordier answers than were asked for. Varadero was fine at first but she kept talking and resisting my pushier and pushier efforts to keep her in bed and get our delights somehow lined up in a photo finish. How could a girl come to erotic blossom so effortlessly. The fact is that effort was ruled out. No small contribution however anonymous was allowable on my side any more than on hers and that was the damnable thing. I was to take care of myself according to my own time tables and then play dead but stay on the premises. She wanted no dramatic trespassings. Since I was pushing so hard for just the opposite condition, her more active involvement in my highs, my place in her sun, she began to resent me more and more and then to avoid bed with me. She never stopped her lecturing. Maybe this was a way to discourage me. She even took to talking in bed, in transit. She talked about the unlocking of the energy centers up to her own wild moment, almost up to it, as though the mustering was going on in another country, and she resumed the lecture a minute after, as though she'd just finished a massage or a gargle. Sex was a pause for breath in an impersonal running commentary on the body as instrument, as vehicle, as, maybe, utensil. The staggering thing was that this was the sort of chatter you might expect from an unreachably maimed and iced woman and she was not in the least that, at least, not in the usual sense. She had true and innermost orgasms and these were given the stamp of natural events taking place under their own power and self-scheduled, so that anybody who had wandered into the vicinity was to look upon himself as enemy alien and spy. The only thing wrong here was that you don't invite spies to make themselves at home in the parlor and serve them beer and sandwiches. But somehow she had found out that orgasm can be experienced as well as endorsed, event as well as slogan, and somehow it was essential that I be close enough to see that I was less the precipitator of the great flurry than a mere privileged bystander. Her upcomings had to be my comeuppances. So she talked. How she talked. "Dance," she would quote at me, "is the body's full language." Wasn't sex also its language, if you wanted, its Braille? "No. Sex gives you a hint of the body's possibilities. It's in the dance that the possibilities are drawn out and realized. The dance is a richer and more variable form." She may have been talking this little-magazine ideology to irritate me. On the other hand, she may have been a modern-dance nut who was building her own corkscrew esthetic out of Reichian bones. What she was really doing, I suppose, was making a pupil out of the examiner. With Martha Graham torsions of shoulder and abdominal centers, lying down in connubial laxity to show me the primitive roots and springing up to striving and sungathering poses to indicate the triumphal esthetic flowers, she demonstrated how the incipient mobilities get enriched by muscle art. These demonstrations usually came when there were signs of my ardor pushing up. "Not that I belittle sex. It's definitely helped me in my work, I want you to know that." Digs? Nose-thumbings? Side-trackings? It dawned on me all the same that her continuing professional babble was a device to lock out the personal and keep any partner from presenting emotional bills. She could stay an island in the closest emotional team, Johnny Over Donne and his twice tolled bells to the contrary. That way she held to her view of sex as dancing-class calisthenics. If you work out with a wall bar do you owe the wall bar anything? To her all objects were handles and all men objects. Big believer in private property, Penelope kept the deeds to her orgasms under lock and key. She wanted no clutter of any deterrent sort and no corporate ownerships. She was calling me examiner all the time. I began to spend the days away from her, skindiving around the coral formations off Kilometer 14 where the tropical fish that incautiously came up to make faces before my goggles did not present me with ownership deeds. She hardly noticed my absence. She was busy doing backbends and extensions, and, too, she was writing an article for a Paris magazine of the airier arts, a manifesto of the musculature entitled, "Dance: The Pelvis's Alpha and Omega." Do something was her motto, each minute and without collaborators. I came back to Boston with questions nagging at me as to women who need to clear away all the debris. What were these invasion fears of hers? Why the need to reduce the partner to a witness without simply giving him his walking, or crawling, papers? Such tornados in such total becalmments? It was in any case a variety of storm signal to run from. But women who can

63

come to the true eruption are not easily come by. Not to mention with. The challenge was spectacularly there. She the spectacle, I the captive spectator. Oh, to take these two fine nerve events so exasperatingly separated in time and establish some balming cause-and-effect between them. So that I might feel not simply a space-taker, bulk, filler, but somehow the precipitating agent too. I insist on some share of responsibility in the other's intensities. I want to be *acknowledged*, Sam'l. Make my presence *felt*. Well, I've been working at this desegregation project for going on two years now, whenever I can bludgeon her into another post-graduate try. She is less and less willing to be the examinee. Now weeks elapse between tries. Sometimes she goes off with other less examinative men. You would think that by now I would suspect the connection is not going to be made and give it up as a bad job. Not me. Not up and coming, uppity and sometimes coming, Lazarus. Tantalizing to be so near and yet so far. I suppose what I am trying to establish with and to Penelope is that I have more than a use value, a sidelines value. That I do not accept employment without being put on the payroll. If I am going to stand by I mean to be let really in. I must say the one result to date is a stronger and stronger feeling of being locked out. Call it test or whatever, the moment she's gone the more determined I am to have her again. Worthington has such obvious use value. She may decide to use him to the so-called hilt. The impossible thought is that precisely because of his lack of psychic as well as physical shoulders he may get to the connectedness that eludes me. Since such lack is what excites her most in men. This is why he must not be allowed to get to bed with her. I will not have this happen with anybody but me. If at all. You might say that in my doggedness I am really doing Worthington a good turn. I certainly hope to give him *some* kind of turn. It is his considered opinion, and, judging from mother's Aesopian hints, yours too, that all talk about explosions of any size or variety in women is a long ton of dream stuff. Worthington considers it physiologically, neurologically impossible, as I suspect you do. If Worthington were to be witness to Penelope's big moment, even if unrelated to his in any sense but the geographical, he might take to chewing the carpet. The worst place to have a theory disproved is in bed. I mean to spare my spare roommate this upset. As mother spared you when she thoughtfully arranged to have her high times with the Liberty Leaguer so that you might hold to your theory that in the ladies only lows are possible. Peculiar that an all but Fascist would have the requisite cojones rather than an American for Democratic Action. If there were any justice wouldn't the just also have the power? But that's a bad joke and I know it. The power is in the grand girls and the lack of it too. We don't really give it to them, we can just count ourselves lucky if we're around and they let us share it. I don't really believe that. Not that I *really* think I've got extra-special silver platters on which to hand Penelope extra-dazzling golden moments. Essentially what I do is want and want is black and nameless. Actually I don't know what I want. Just want. It's an intensifying ache and you don't like to sit back when you ache. Passing the New Rochelle cutoff. With luck I'll find Penelope at this Waldorf party. She has sharp teeth and has bitten me more than once but she is not going to take this biggest bite of all. I mean to do some counter-munching. Worthington may get gashed in the process and that's all right too. Good that Miss Shoshana's along. She is a neutral truce commissioner and from her point of vantage she may get an interesting view of the border incidents to come. Notably liquid person on the surface. Slips into whichever skins are at hand and momentarily convenient but I wonder whether she does much inside shifting. Miss Shoshana gives the impression that there are molybdenum constants down under. Memorable eyes. Those legs. Aili-Aili's nudging the fjords. Polar bears chasing the Blarney stones. You can see that there is too much going on at the moment for me to give due consideration to the Divithion of Miwwel Eathtern Affairth. More later, your everloving, etc., etc.

11

THE FIVE infectiously jolly Negroes were riffing along at "Muskrat Ramble" with fixed basement smiles but this was no ordinary basement. Rather it was a subterranean railroad spur for high livers who tripped here and there on private trains and did not care to locomote on their own precious two's even from Grand Central to the Waldorf-Astoria.

Cabaret in a subway station, it was. Here, three levels below the splashy shops and plush lobbies of the Park Avenue hotel, deeper than the silted beds of the East and Hudson rivers, snuggered in the city's rat nest of sizzling high-juice cables and glurbling water mains, submerged as sin, right dab here on the cement platform, surrounded by small tables with checkerboard covers, much cake to their walk, infinite blow to their blues, these Dixieland bust-outs were lilting up two-beat storms as at a cellar rent party. Since whites who can and do pay big rents have a steady taste for blacks who pass the happy hat for rent and scoff, provided only that they do it with incomparable rhythm and that grin-grained basement air.

Waiters in red toreador jackets twinkletoed here and there, serving champagne from magnums and jeroboams. There was a spiriting jiggle through the tight air of this city cavern, due to the happy chords blasted out by these Negroes playing as though rent was two weeks past due and the last meal a tattering memory. Couples were dancing in the open spaces with bent-knee lindies, unaware of the bland words the musicians spoke to each other in low tones behind their masking smiles.

"Nigra music, most hot," the drummer said.

"Exceedingly sizzling and with a gorgeous beat," the piano player said, making a whorehouse boogie run.

"Mighty lak unto jungle tom-toms," the bass player said, plucking a hot blue note.

"More like *Uncle* Tom-toms, massa," the trumpet player said.

"Ricky-tick and a fat um-pa-pa for the pale people," History Jones, the leader and saxophonist, said, extending his smile, in the style of his colleagues, to threaten his ears.

It was their custom when making very black and happy music for the very white and very hungry to exchange such musicological comments, footnotes to levee capers for which there were always so many caperous white customers. But their faces remained black and joyifying. The dancers were not meant to hear and they did not hear. They saw the smiles on the musicians' faces and assumed that as true Negroes they were toothy joy all through, very levee. Infected by the jollies made scrupulously to their specifications and wafted unerringly their way, the white folk smiled back in reflex and danced up two-beat storms.

On the track to one side of the musicians was a highshine silvery freight car happied with bright loops of bunting in the patriotic colors. Into its wide door ran a ramp with a red velvet carpet and inside the car were more freeloaders, around a bar on which champagne cascaded with a reassuring playtime hiss down a crystal fountain. A sign on the car's side said:

"Presenting—the freight hauler of tomorrow. The superstructure of this car is built entirely of aluminum and its weight, instead of resting on a bulky undercarriage, is suspended from an overhead frame, making possible considerable gains in stability and spaciousness. The Great Lakes Locomotive Company is proud to unveil this revolutionary cargo mover for the members of the press. This car and nine others like it will be shipped next week to the El Harrar Fruit Growers' Cooperative of the State of Israel."

History Jones, weighty, thick of neck and nostril, alive in the ample jowls, patted his tubbed front when he finished his quick-tongued grunting solo and nodded to the trumpet man to take it.

"Make it blasty and happifying," he said. "It's a treat to beat your feet."

As he lowered his tenor saxophone his eyes were still on the Locomotive Company's sign, whose words he did not understand. Who cares whether the hang-up is from the top or the bottom? He was not interested in the subject of hauling and did not see why the State of Israel should be, the Jews, those people used to bundles, peddlers to the world, having carried many hefty loads a too long way already. It was in fact his opinion, never yet developed to the point of concept or even word-possible thought, that the trouble with all states, including the various endorsed states of mind, was their orientation toward hauling, asses if nothing else. As for cargo, car could come and car could go. A man's blossoming head was enough heavy load. It was his philosophy that nothing should be transported from one place to another except the good weed and the soothful powders. He believed in traveling light at all times, so as to make a longer route faster. All he cared to carry was a tune. What he cared about Prosper carrying was some of the superior slimjims, his way, soonest. The pot was much needed to circulate down his personal sidestreets and ventilate his innumerable interior potholes. He was dragged with this New Orleans two-beat and much hung from overhead for some of the satisfactual soar.

This muskratbastard ramdamboling was never his true riff. His own tilt was for the cool and spooky, the flat today sounds, a music of mews thick and muse sick, but he was hired to play this hot way-back bubble by and for the Afro lovers who dreamed non-existent Africas. He did not know why these cooled white Protestants wanted Storyville heats from him and his levee-less blues-blooming stompers below the Waldorf-Astoria or any place but they signed the checks and therefore called the tunes. The why-surer and more Proddest-ant they were the goner they were for Afro. Even, at first, the Penny. When she first made the scene how she was cottoning overmuch to the cottonpicking. Why was cotton more fudgy to pick than fights or noses?

This Penny was a motherin' danger. He had arrived at this formulation by the following logic: she was a modern, modren, mutterin', motherin', dancer, damn-sure, damp-sir, danger. Hip to the mambones. One wild and too balling chiclet. In-a-tent to lean totalsome into the mamb and all the Afro-Cubano kick through Pros-the-per. Every day a Thirstday to this Penal-hoppy. But all the same she was learning to locate her curvier highs in the lesser temperatures. To throw away her bulky undercare and hang herself solid from a sky hook of sweet stabilizing grass, remaking all her overpoundage of center feelings in featherweight alum-minimum, with major gains in stop-ill-at-ease and spaceship-ness.

History generally twisted his words. When he was high, and he was always to a degree high, on anticipation or recollection when no elevating shit was to mouth or white stuff to nose or arm, the words came into his head sliced and slanty, but he had never known this mangling was worth much or had a market until he meeted up with Prosper-us and such po-wets of the po-whites. They chopped and sandpapered their language too, only by program, as a primary work, and they told him he had a special natural gift for making funky old words new. So now he often spoke as he thought, in the fogged syllables that before he had felt were throw-offs of the general fog in his head, words bobbing along in the stream of sounds like boulders and rubbing each other down, and the versers did not look puzzled but applauded and said he was the Adam of the apple of spoken language, the Cortez of the linguistic Pacific, a primeval maker of right and true sounds.

He hoped the Prosp would not jive the Penny for too much. She was carrying but not all Fort Knocksy-Us. Not just one more wide Proudestand to be pigged clean like cotton, that is, cut-down, that is, caught-on, and dumped with the chiggen faithers.

Blew more than gotten-pig, than guard-and-peek, than God-and-big, this Pain-holler-be. Learning to mamb it up from the left he the past years, that is, from the levee, the left-he, to cooler pastures, past-years.

Lipping his mouthpiece for the wind-up ensemble chorus, wondering when would Prosp show with the good grabbing grass, he saw Penelope coming down the far steps to the siding. Walking with a rock, eyes going from one scene to the next too questy.

Leanbone with her in hambone clothes. Study in pinch and skimp.

"Who's gonna sound when the rent comes round," he said just before he started to blow, smile on almost straight.

"Go, Poppa Pigfoot," the piano player said.

"Make it very whoryhouse," the bass player said.

"Serve up the poke chops and a side of chitterlins," the drummer said.

Jowls ballooning, eyes on the prowl, History Jones began to make that feisty must-krap ram-bull round the feasty-day railroad siding some shivaree-bob more. He was watching Penelope switch down the steps and he was speculating, as he had more than a few times, that he would like to have him some of *those* shitterlins if any was up for grabs, if any of those why-test and most Prowed-distant jitter-links was on the sweet market *this* sweet grabbacious season.

12

SHE WAS beginning to feel sober. Put it: more sober than drunk. Moving with reasonable uprightness from step to step with the feeling that she was nailed still while the platform bellied up toward her level, the scurry of redjacketed waiters rising by surges to her eyes, the heave of seersuckered and gabardined dancing fools, the burble of shuffling Dixieland chords with their nowhere studied stridencies, she felt in herself what might in certain quarters, quarters she would go a considerable distance to avoid, a vast discontent.

She had only lately become aware that the younger black boys who gave out with this Louie music of foamy ferment would prefer, if allowed their heads, a more jelled and just-so sound, that in themselves they felt less perky than cavern-hollow, that marketing themselves as ecstatics they held to a private image of their persons as iced and inheld, that they were brought bottom-scrape down by the ostentatious prance of their fathers and wanted to demonstrate a cooled side-lines looking around, some capacity for a paralysis like that they saw or thought they saw in whites, but that this less heady and most head-formed art, this more structured math-ematical sound of the Dizzys and Birds and Mileses, being too white in spirit, was not so much in demand by whites and therefore not to be hawked in festive places where dancing was in progress and paraded up spirits were temporarily the white go. She did not understand why these dark friends of Prosper Merrymake were so gone for the freeze-out over the boil, having herself come to their submerged world of hipness for the hot let and loosening traditionally attributed to them and their fathers and traditionally the black negation of *her* tight-assed father, but it had been brought home to her that such was their thinking and she needed to be in the know and all the way with the knowing.

Now, descending into this cavern that vibrated with the bounce of moldering rambles, this pit slapping toward her face in pulsed assaults, hearing instrumental yelpers she knew would much prefer to be murmuring drawled and dissonant questions under their held breaths, she suddenly felt bad and cornered by evil shapes, not the least of them being Worth-ington Rivers. Not only was oncoming sobriety going through her head tissues like a brown stain and strain invading her muscles with its inching needles of ice. Here alongside her Worthington was taking the steps two at a time with his spider-hook excuses for legs and saying in his high-bred accent that was designed exclusively for complimenting the help, "Say, that's a *wonderful* band! They really *go,* they have that jump!"

She was filled with a shame and an anger of which she was through a guilt by association, to the extent that she shared any least thoughts and tones with Worthington, a partial target. Hoyt would have been hard enough to explain to her blowsy-blowing friends. But Worthington? This speaker of encouragements to the hired help to make them worthier of their hire and more helpful? Hoyt they might have taken as an oddball, an eccentric dancer who tapped his own offbeat softshoes. But Worthington? The neat sliver from the topmost of the top crust whose every feeling and attitude had been plotted on the slide rule and laid out with T-square?

She saw immediately what it was about Worthington that was beginning to make her squirm. It was his predictability. He was a bundle of the recognizable. All he had in him was built in according to a tried, trued master plan. He derived from a known mock-up shaped by the powers and the interests. Throw a "Muskrat Ramble" at him and his synapses snapped back with the cut-to-pattern "Say, some jump!" Meaning: those who congregate on the bottom are so flamboyantly unlike us that they obviously deserve to be where they are though they do have an interesting set of enthusiasms. Hoyt at least came at you from unexpected corners. He was a source of unannounced sorties. His chin-leading oddnesses kept you on tiptoe, with hands up to protect the face. You said, "I'm not going to your apartment, that's final, I'm going to New York with or without you," and he said, "No, Penny, you can't wear my balls for earrings," and half-carried you to his car and drove to the apartment; he came at you hard and kept you off-balance. She was especially sensitive to cornfed insipidities of the Worthington Rivers variety because only recently, under the deadpan needling tutelage of her with-it friends, had she come to see the square core in herself and to guard against it.

She had lately, on sidewinding research grants from Prosper and History, been doing postgraduate work in spotting the inconspicuous but lovingly honed jeer within the made-to-order jiggle. Here she was now with a prize advocate and devotee of bottomdog jiggle at her side, going to meet her jiggle-for-money most hip and cool friends.

Going down the platform toward the band, she said in answer to his glad-eyed questions, "Yes, it's a press party, no, it's not a usual place for a party, right, they're showing this new freight car what's-it to the public and the man in charge of arrangements, this public relations man from Princeton, he's got tastes like yours, Worthington, he likes the old jump so at my suggestion he hired my friend, my friend History, to make a lot of jumpee-jumpee for the occasion. History's a good musician. Very professional. Customer's always right. He'll make his jiggle as old as he's paid for. Play his rambles on a lute and a clavichord if they meet his price." Worthington said without a ruffle, "That public relations man knows his stuff, this is a band with a *sound*." She said, "Correct, a creak, the creak of bones, Brother Bones. This man went to

71

Groton, he talks very much like you and my father and F.D.R., and something else, he enjoys an oldtime bash, he does like a good bash of the long-gone type."

Then they were close by the band and History was chiming in with his men to put the finishing embroideries on the musky rat, making that mildewed old fur-bearer sashay some for the paying customers and the freeloaders too. The band opened out to maximum with its final blare and at the top of the full give cut it off. The dancers made their last afterbeat hops, came to rest like marionettes when their strings go slack, applauding, faces lit high. History inclined his round cuckaburred head to acknowledge the standing ovation for a music he wouldn't care to give away but gladly overcharged for, mopped his forehead with a silk foulard handkerchief, slid his saxophone away in its stand and came over to Penny.

"The scene," he said, fat face unsending, "is to be seen and not heard," carefully not looking at Worthington, "with much of musk in the rat and that's all," never giving Worthington the benefit of a direct meeting of eyes but all the while taking his cramped measure dimension by dimension, adding easily, "There is that fay-belled and lessened-airy street called Basin and there are cats who work both sides of it," the inventory up and down Worthington's one-way streets continuing through strategies of avoidance, to see would the live one dig or come on know-nothing.

He was reacting, she knew, to Worthington's heather gabardines and rep stripes, his side vents and shaved lapels, his pleatlessness, his right-rolled buttondowns, his Madras belt, his wing-tipped cordovans, his head-hugging blondness, his skimped nostrils, his white-on-white face, his lips meagered to a smile he did not in his cocooned life owe anybody. Just as Worthington was putting on his overapproving smile in reaction to History's loudmouth plaid jacket and dove-gray slacks and blue suede shoes, his style of the indomitably hot and florid, his damp mahogany face, his air of headwaiter with satiric napkin over funning arm. She knew from the immediate clash of wardrobes and melanins that she had made a bad mistake to show with Worthington. She was well aware that when he did not have to fool with the muskratty tip History tended to tog exactly like Worthington, all the J. Press subduing way. There, of course, was the joke that Worthington would not see and History would not admit to. This was a joke she did not want to be around but it had been arranged under her own auspices.

72

Worthington said as though slipping the maitre dee a five, "I like the way you play, it's enormously groovy."

History said, "That's good and fine." His face was sober as he added, "They're sending this freight car to Israel. To carry fruit."

Penelope said, "History, Worthington Rivers, Worthington, History Jones."

The two men shook hands with the air of diplomats from opposite camps of a cold war meeting on neutral grounds at a third-force embassy reception.

"It's a good-looking freight car," Worthington said. Puzzled eyes travelling from the aluminum car to aluminum-calm History.

"For carrying fruit," History said without commitment. "Grass is something else."

From the way his eyes deliberately said nothing she understood this was a message for her.

"Prosper?" she said. "Where's he?"

"Be here in like a hour."

"Carrying?"

"He ain't empty."

"I suppose," Worthington said questioningly, "the Israelis might be transporting grass in freight cars too. Hay, clover, alfalfa, they're grasses, you might say."

But he was not going to be invited into this coded conversation.

"I'm not waiting an hour when my solar plexus says right now," Penelope said. "Where's he at, home?"

"Was when we set the meet," History said. "Said he'd show here and be bringing."

"Then I'll cut for down the town and load up in front." Her eyes indicated Worthington. "This chorus I take myself, the other half is Squaresville." History was getting the message behind his barricaded face. "See can we tip it for the single-o."

As she was turning to Worthington he opened his mouth to make another try for a complimentary ticket into this dialogue.

"I suppose," he said, looking from one to the other for recognition of his presence, "the Jews have developed *some* kosher grasses over there in Israel. You know the soup they, the Jews, eat, schav? That's made with sour grass, so maybe, if grass gets sour enough, not sour grapes, sour grass, why, I guess, it must be kosher." Nobody acknowledged his attempt to warm up a too cool Negro with feeling-out innuendos about Jews. It probably never occurred to him, Penelope speculated,

73

that when he made digs about Jews in front of a Negro he was only proving himself capable of making digs about Negroes in front of a Jew. "You've heard about the advertising slogan contest the Manishewitz Wine people are running? The first prize is one week in Israel and the second prize is *two* weeks in Israel." The world was sitting on its hands. "Listen," he said with a creep of irritation in his voice, "what are you two talking about, exactly? Maybe I'm not hearing correctly, every other word just about seems to have been left out."

"Look, Worthington," Penelope said, "I've got to leave for a few minutes. You're to wait here for me, I'll be back."

She realized something. Hoyt was given to making bull-headed charges and generally she just backed off, ducked, dodged, making neat veronicas and snapping her cape deftly. But this Worthington, he was a charter member of the do-nothings, Mr. Passivity, and with him *she* was somehow encouraged to do the charging. She had the urge to rough him up, slap him down, and so she found herself saying, "Worth, my love, tell me, do you play any instrument?"

"He said a little testily, "Not really, I used to fool around with the drums in prep school, nothing much, a little brush work."

"That's great, Worthington, boy. Here's something you might get a kick out of, I could get History here to let you sit in on a set."

"Oh, come on," he said. "I couldn't do that. Besides, I didn't come all the way to New York just to——"

"If you dig the beat you got to have the beat," History said, taking no sides but in the scrupulous process backing him into the worst corner.

"Really," Worthington said, "what an idea, I couldn't."

"We go at it very rhythmic, ching-a-ching," History said. "You just catch the beat and fall in."

"I can't do stick rolls," Worthington said with loser's down tones, looking around at the freight car as if for an escape route. "What I do, mostly, is a little easy riding along with the brushes."

"You come to the right place," History said. "We got rhythm and we got brushes."

"Go, Worthington," Penelope said, pushing him toward the bandstand. "Make a big ching-a-ching for the peoples."

She knew she was setting him up as a patsy for the all-too-ready History and his boys and it was all right with her, she loved to see those of her own too snooted clan put down all

74

the way by these subtly relentless blacks whose faces never let on to the warfare in the cool play. Worthington was an offering she could afford to make.

Before he knew it he was being led off by a neutrally firm History and Penelope was heading for the stairway. As she started her climb the band began its next number and she turned to see.

The tune was "Won't You Come Home, Bill Bailey." As if by prearrangement all the musicians had started off with a few ensemble riffs and then lapsed into a kind of chuffing, making a pulsed chordal curtain against which Worthington was to stand out strong. They were now as one backing up their guest drummer, all of them with hospitable eyes turned helpfully in his direction, those with free hands finger-snapping as though in full approval. Worthington sat behind the snares in a private bog of embarrassment, face sunrise red, body starched with unease, shoulders hopping in parody of Krupa excitements while his hands agitated the steel brushes across the skins in irregular jumps, an incorrigible half beat behind the band. The musicians were in the mood of unwavering permissiveness, their fingers were snapping not the right beat but Worthington's laggard swishings and on their lit faces was nothing but admiration for the white man who had so thoroughly mastered that levee footloose jog.

It was, Penelope thought as she crinkled her nose, like a scene in a schoolroom for backward children, the teacher maintaining her steady smile of encouragement in the face of the retarded towhead's awful gum-tongued mistakes.

The instruments around Worthington went on contradicting his nervous hands while the accept-all faces behind and over the instruments told him and the world that he was right with it and past master of this tricky art.

Worthington humped, shivered, swung a hand out to strike the cow bell, missed it completely. His left foot went spastically at the bass pedal. Striking in the direction of the cymbal, he hit it on its rim and almost knocked it over.

The black fingers about him continued their glad accompaniments, the black faces went on feeding the white man elaborate compliments, History's bulging head nodded its solids, its gones, its too-muches.

Penelope's fingers were just now unhooking from the dash down the Connecticut thruways but the tensions were only being redirected toward her shoulders and neck muscles, her cheeks, even her wrists and ankles. She had a dancer's awareness of her body, she knew her Reichian catechisms, she understood that these hot clampings and tightenings along crucial stretches of her musculature, these selective armorings that made her body a hot burden, a recalcitrant mass she was stuck in, were due to the many trapped orgones in her, the smothered sobs and tantrums, all the howls that had been sat on. In dodging Hoyt these past months she had neglected to find a substitute for him and now she was tight with festering energies. She knew she was going to need a venting before the night was over, an all-the-way letting go, the pot would see her along for a while as a gassy poultice on the upstarting plexus but this was only a postponement. It was past time for somebody to take Hoyt's place. In this kind of foot race you automatically lost by staying consistently ahead of the field. To forget the joys of being overtaken is the occupational hazard of the congenital front runner.

Going up the stairs to the freight elevator that would take her to the Waldorf's 49th Street exit, she faced the fact that she was going to bed with somebody before the night was over, had to, but *who* was the question. It would have to be slim pickings before she would let it be Worthington, that dragger of beats and misser of bells, that eternal passenger, and she had cut Hoyt all the way out of the running. Who in this town of eight million blanking faces was going to wind up in her bed tonight, giving her, no, helping her to give herself and her too hard muscles the needed let?

For all his pimp threads, his bullish prancing and pawing, she almost regretted Hoyt.

13

"Lo, Mar."

"Hey, now, Pen."

"Missed the mamb lesson, sorry. Naturally I come up with the gold allee samee."

"Everything's cool."

"Prosp around?"

"History let him know you'd be trending toward the Waldorf so he cut out for there."

"Screw, thought I'd catch him. Lewellyn score this week?"

"Much and heavy. I can turn you on some if you're marketing for some appetizer jolt. Come on in, girl. Bed you down and I'll light you up lightly."

"Deal and done. I'll rest my wearies here on the kip. Hey, is that where he stashes it, there in the exercise bars? Cleh-ver. Screw, I never guessed."

"He don't show his places. He says cache as cache can and don't mumble bout it to the people. To his thinking, what they don't know they can't buzz in the narcops' wide flappers. Here. Ease some of this Guadalajara superior down the ready lungs. This shit ain't the supreme end but it takes hold some solid. Gasp it backwards and forwards, girl."

"Mm-*mm*. Cray-zy. Takes hold, yeah. Of your scalp. From the inside. Scratches your everloving head from the *in*side."

"I feel it more like in my fingernails. Like worms under the nails. You know?"

"Mm. Inching and switching their saucy bottoms, fat, hot worms, all over you know where. Here, you finish the roach, I don't like roaches, they catch me in the throat. Light me up another stick, huh, that's right, I'll come forward with the appropriate gold, you don't have to ponder it. Mar. Listen good. You know, I've got like steel ribs all over me body, I'm not dancing enough, you know, that's one reason, I think, me muscles knot up. I ought to be dancing more, it would help dissolve the tensions, relax the tight places. What about your group, the Movements of Tomorrow group, they going to be giving recitals this summer? That one last year, the one up in the 92nd Street Y.M.H.A., that was a gas, it knocked me out to be dancing with your people, maybe if there's a recital this summer and I'm around I'll come down again and re-hearse with you, get more in shape, maybe you could get them to let me go with them again. Oo, getting a right friendly buzz. Message, get through to me. You think that would be possible, Mar? Here, you finish it, it's getting me in the throat, screw, I hate roaches. I feel, I don't know, all crawly. Too much bunching up here in the shoulders, up through the neck here, the crying and sucking muscles. And down there too. Got crying muscles down there too, want to wail. Sucking muscles want to sock. Itches where I can't scratch at them. Mar, listen, I've got this problem. I came down here with this fellow, see, he's waiting for me now at the Waldorf, he's with History. This man, he's from Drag City, he's the mayor of Nowheresville, if he's on my neck all night, after the boys get through at the Waldorf, I mean, later when we're moving around and balling, well, I won't be able to

77

operate, you know, he'll be all over me and I got no eyes of any size for him. Listen, Mar, you could do me this big favor, you could keep him busy, see, stick with him and sort of keep him out of my hair so I can move around some, I'll make it worth your while, if you like I'll lay another suit on you or any kind of outfit you like. All right? Mm-uh. Head's on crooked. Funny, my right ear weighs seventeen pounds. So you come back to the Waldorf with me and take Worthington out of the play so I'll have room to agitate some, pick and choose, all right? You'll do that for me, won't you, Mar?"

"I would but all I got to wear is what you see on me, just this sweatshirt and these jeans. That's why I didn't go with Prosp, no togs."

"Where's the suit I gave you the other week?"

"Well, Pen, I guess I never told you this but I got this kid sister, seventeen, cuter than ticks, that bunny, she lives up in Harlem and last week was graduating from, uh, beauticians' school only she said she couldn't go to the graduating because she didn't have anything to wear, she was feeling low about it so, uh, I let her have the suit. If it wasn't for my kid sister I'd still have the suit and could go with you easy but now all I got is on my back and I can't make the Waldorf in a sweatshirt, you know that."

"Drag. That's a drag."

"Me in my beatific generationist's cutaway. Tell me a thing. How comes it we beats wear sweatshirts when we're against all forms of sweat?"

"I'll tell you, honey, you wear sneakers too but I don't see you entering any races."

"Oo, my fingers are falling off, plop, plop. Look, Pen. Here's a way. You said, would I help you out with this square and then after you would give me one of your outfits? Well, could we like *reverse* it? Could you maybe give me the outfit in *front*, and then I could go with you and take this cat out of play for you?"

"It *would* work, Mar. Under other circumstances it would work. Trouble with that is, we drove down, see, I did the driving, and by the time we got to the Bronx I was so tired my eyes were closing and I wouldn't let Worthington take the wheel because he was still too drunk so I made him park the car on Fordham Road and we came down to the Waldorf by cab. My luggage's up there on Fordham Road, all my clothes are in it, I just took what I needed in this bag here, underwear and diaphragm and such, it would need hours to go up there

78

and back, we'd miss the boys entirely. Damn. Screw it all."

"Don't know what to say, Pen. I don't picture myself going to this and that place in a lousy sweatshirt and being thrown out every place. Me being much spook and down front in the eye already, you dig. Hey, I'm rising and shining, I'm a chocolate float."

"I'm a raspberry flip. Listen, Mar, this is Saturday. Aren't some of those shops on 14th Street open late Saturday?"

"Sure. But breadless as I am I can't buy me a whole new outfit or even a shoelace."

"Dam, bam. I don't have enough cash on me, I figured I was going to be with a man all weekend and wouldn't need it. Didn't even think to bring my checkbook. Here's an idea, Mar. You've got the gift in the light fingers, you've tipped me about you and the stores. Maybe we could like sneak a couple things and get you elegant?"

"You don't plumb to my meanings, Pen. I was explaining it to Prosp before, you can't go on the lift in these stores togged sloppy. They give you big looks when you come in with a uniform like this, they watch every least slightest move you make. Me being so deep-dyed and worthy of note already, you know?"

"Mar, you're overlooking something. The main thing here. There are *two* of us, remember? At least it was two at last count. They're not going to watch *my* moves, are they? I'm moneybags in their eyes, Uptown Ursula, they won't give me look one. *Together* we could do it, Mar, all we have to do is work out a little of the old strategy, you know? What say we give it a try? Hey, wow, I'm *on.*"

"Don't know, Pen. I don't feel right about it, dressed in sweatshirt and pants the way I am. I get to feeling self-gawky, you know, being of much color and all, and that slows me up, slows me down, slows me up and down and makes me spady and awkward, kind of stiff. Hey, yeah, I'm upping."

"Come on, Mar. Do it for laughs, all right? This could be real kicks, wow, I'm going, going, *gone.* I'll do all the work if that's the way you want it. We'll have a ball. I'm all keyed up, you know, and want to spin like a top, hit the turf, you know, topsy, turfsy. I need something like this to unwind me and my kinked bones."

"This could unwind you right to Fuzztown with no return ticket, Pen."

"Come on, we'll beat them for a real nice outfit, we'll get

79

you the gonest outfit on Union Square. Say you'll do it, Mar.
I'd appreciate it and we'll have a ball in the bargain. Let's go,
Mar, come on, get with it, it'll be flippy, dippy, huh?"

14

FLYING THOUGH she was, Marga held to her position that
she would be asking to have her privileges taken away if she
tried any hauling today. It would be, she insisted, like sound-
ing sirens for all the precincts to so much as walk into a
place of business in these blues and sneakers, she being of the
high-visibility spook camp and therefore a magnet for eyes.

She repeated the case for her curving around this trippy
scene as Penelope led her across Washington Square and up
University Place to 14th. By the time they arrived at a
likely looking dress shop she had the Penny convinced that
she, the Penny, had to go in alone and do the snatch and skip
alone. The best she, Marga, could do was patrol the curb
outside and keep a sharp watch for noseying fuzz.

But Penelope was confident she could nab the needed
threads on her own and have the salesladies and floor-
walkers bowing as she switched out holding heavy. Marga
had given her the five-minute review lecture on how to make
the snatching hand faster than the proprietary eye.

"Watch me get you a head-to-foot wardrobe while they
make with the rubby hands and the oily smiles, wow, I'm
bumping into chimneys," Penelope said as she examined the
cotton prints and summertime silks in the bright windows.

Marga was worried over the Pen's flip attitude. She felt this
too-cocky Pen needed some last-minute instructions to knock
the sneeriness out of her:

"Pen, don't look at their faces, that makes them sus-
picious, keep your eyes on the dresses, act like a shopper
thumbing through the goods. You know? There's too much
sass and dare in your eyes, never mind the dare, case the
goods like a honest little shopper."

"Wow, those chimneys keep lunging at me, free lunge."
Penny said, and walked briskly and high-shouldered into
the store, swinging her large leather bag by its thongs.

Marga leaned against a water hydrant and watched the
Pen ankling her queenly way down the main aisle. A minute

later she could see how the Pen was fingering garments critically in the dress racks, cocking head and narrowing one eye as she held various numbers up in front of her before the wall mirror, examining price tags with a frown.

Then Marga forgot about the Pen. Coming along the sidewalk toward her was a tall young man with curly blond hair, dressed in antiqued loafers, thin-cut white twill slacks, and a V-neck red cashmere sweater, one of the Village pipe smokers. He drew her attention because the leash in his hand was attached to a small, roundish, furry animal with delicate feet, it went along with toes-first ballet minces.

Marga was interested in small animals because of the way they moved and their quick straight-on eyes. Often she stood in front of pet shop windows an hour at a time, holding staring contests with some parrot or ocelot.

She said to the young man as he came up, "What's that bundle of nothing?"

"A raccoon," the young man said, stopping and taking the pipe out of his mouth.

"Why you have a raccoon instead of a dog or cat?"

"So girls will ask me questions and then I can ask *them* questions. I make a lot of girls through Wilbur. What, come to think of it, are you doing tonight?"

"I'm going to the moon and eat a tuna fish sandwich."

"I've got a telescope at my place and some cans of tuna, fancy white, flakes. Also, there's a stereo hi-fi and all the Miles Davis records. What you say?"

The raccoon was trying to tip the fire hydrant over, maybe to make the foundation for a bridge.

"I've heard all the Mileses and why do you call him Wilbur? If I had a raccoon I would call him Tuna Fish."

"He's called Wilbur after his father, whose name was Wilbur. The next time *you* get a raccoon you can call him Tuna Fish, all right? My place is just a couple blocks from here, on 11th. I've got some great Tuoca demi-sec milk brandy."

The raccoon was trying to eat the fire hydrant.

"You see the liquid so economical way he moves?" she said, trying to put the important thing in words, grabbing in all directions, at all the dance recital program notes she had ever read, for words. "They all move the same way, all the different kinds, sure in their minds, no false starts or hesitations, all in simple lines, the line is the ultimate gas, you know, like the world was all eggs and they have to cross the

81

eggs without breaking a one. Wilbur, Wilbur, you do fine toe work and you're a gas, you have directness and compactness, you know where you're going and how to get there, you live right there in the pelvis, you radiate out from the pelvis, you're Martha Graham and Katherine Dunham and Balanchine, you know that, you Wilbur?"

"Why, yes, sure," the young man said tentatively. "Listen, you in your green sweatshirt, you're a good-looking girl but are you a Bellevue outpatient or suffering from a concussion or something?" He considered her with saucered eyes.

She had forgotten all about the Pen. Flying as she was, it was hard to dodge the chimneys, and now here was this furry, hydrant-nibbling, clean-eyed Wilbur with his dancer's coy feet.

Penelope followed Marga's instructions to the letter. First she browsed around in the racks, telling the saleslady she just wanted to look, holding the suits and dresses in front of her until she found what she wanted, a simple two-piece pink Shantung suit whose top was cut low without sleeves or bulky frills. That was the important thing, Marga had insisted, that the top be cut low and without sleeves or frills that would bulk.

Next, Penelope nodded casually at the saleslady and took the suit to the dressing rooms. She found an empty cubicle and pulled the curtains fast shut, slipped out of her Bergdorf Goodman pima suit and put the Shantung on, then put her own cotton suit on *over* the Shantung. Marga had the answers, all right. With the Shantung skirt rolled over a few times at the waist it did not show below her own skirt, and with the blouse cut low and sleeveless the way it was it was completely hidden under her own high-necked and long-sleeved jacket.

She came out of the dressing alcove and examined herself carefully in the full-length mirror, turning left and right, running her hands over her buttocks. Looked as though she had put on five pounds, that's all, not enough to attract any salesgirl's lazy eye.

Pink would be a fine color for Marga. Penelope nodded approval at her image in the mirror, saying "Fatty, cut down on those meringues," and turned to go, her pouch bag in her hand again.

So far she was following instructions. But as she approached the archway leading to the front of the shop she saw something on a chair that interested her. It was a sensational fingertip-length off-white summer coat, collarless and trim-lined, made of loosely woven fuzzed wool.

The thought came to her like a dart of acetylene flame in her misted head that Marga should have a coat to complete the outfit. This particular coat would be sensational with the pink Shantung. This was just the coat, the right coat, the perfect coat, for her friend Marga. Marga was going to have this one right and fitting coat to sway snazzily into the Waldorf with.

There was a challenge here. Penelope liked challenges, she felt her heart begin to thump faster as she faced the delicate problem.

A daring idea came to her in another white dart. She didn't have to *hide* the coat, she could simply *wear* it out. Not try to be sneaky about it, not do what Marga had warned her against, not stuff a whole garment into her pouch and make it bulge suspiciously, no, just bold as brass and cool as dry ice put the thing on her back and switch out as though it had come down to her from her maternal grandmother.

She knew she could pull it off, she knew it. She was well aware that when she turned on the great lady style, the to-the-manor-born look, the lesser and shakier ones backed off to make way for her.

She had supreme confidence in her ability to brazen all impasses out and away by the easy device of lifting her nose a little higher and icing her cool green eyes down a few more degrees.

Her heart making urgent paradiddles against her rib cage, she put the coat on, got a firm grip on her leather bag, and swung out into the store.

The saleslady who had directed her to the dressing rooms, a bony, spatula-nosed woman in a flowered blouse, with planking legs that did not bother to thin at the ankles, was standing before her. Penelope raised her head high as she went by and looked Fifth Avenue scorn.

"I've decided against it, it didn't fit well across the shoulders," she said in her flattest boarding-school tones. "Thank *you*." She kept going toward the door. Nobody said boo or even ho-hum.

But as she was about to reach the doorway and the refuge of open space there was an agitation to her left. A woman standing there, a butterball with breasts like squashed pillows, the one holding a bathing beauty's minimized swim suit against her massy frame, forlornly facing the old poser of the camel and the needle's eye, was looking Penelope's way and gasping at her, lips flapping.

The swim suit dropped from this one's outraged hands.

She raised both hands toward Penelope, pudgy index fingers going like upset moths.

"What!" she boomed with something like a baritone. "Ha! Where you think you're gone hey! That there's *my* coat, that's *mine*, thief, stop, you thief!"

The whole store froze as in a stop-action trick movie effect.

Penelope froze by reflex. She considered the stout lady of the fluttering fingers. She shook her head, trying to get it clear, and looked down quickly at her coat sleeves.

There was no ticket on either sleeve, no price tag.

She had had the exquisite taste, the gorgeous instinct, to choose the one coat in the whole mother of a store that was not on sale but belonged to a customer.

Damn! Screw!

The butterball was squirming her way toward the door, fingers agitating, mouth letting out rasping cries: "No-good thief you! My beautiful new coat that Matty give me on Valentine's Day, you dirty thief!"

At the rear of the store the manager, a stomach-ulcer type in a silvery raw silk double-breasted suit, was starting toward the door, here and there a salesgirl was coming to life and moving forward.

Penelope turned to look assessingly toward the street. The way was clear, nobody there but Marga and some slim fellow.

She bolted outside. In a split second she was at Marga's side, tearing at her sleeve and hissing into her slack face, "Fast! They're yelling for blood! Go, for Chrissake!"

Marga started to say, "Wha—"

The young man, who seemed to have some puffy animal on a leash, began to say, "Look, a minute, I was just—"

Then the message got through to Marga's vague head and she was hurtling down the street with the Pen, saying, "That fellow's got a raccoon with the wrong name." They tore through the crowds of shoppers and window browsers, darting in and out, then broke wildly across the street through the heavy traffic.

Behind them, trying to keep up but slowed by disadvantages of age and weight as well as by his flat feet, clopped the store manager, puffing distractedly, "Hey, you! Who do you think! Come back, you!"

Behind him, a loose quiver in the doorway of the store, the outraged fat lady was spattering low cries at the astonished strollers: "What a snip! What a rotten! My coat, my lovely, and she walks out like she was queen of the goddam May! You ever see such a filthy no-good nerve like that! Bum! You hear! Lousy bum! Police!"

The young man in the red cashmere sweater looked down the street after the highstepping girls, then at his raccoon, who was again trying to muscle the fire hydrant over into a more usable position.

He said when he was able to speak, "Wilbur, see that line, their line is a gas, those two raccoons've got directness, they know where they're going and how to get there. After this, Wilbur, you Martha, you Balanchine, do me a favor and don't speak to kookie girls in green sweatshirts, all right? What you suppose her name was, Tuna Fish?"

They went at top speed down Fifth Avenue, turned west on 12th Street.

"That's no name for a raccoon, Wilbur," Marga gasped.

"Go into it later," Penelope managed to get out.

As they neared Sixth Avenue Penelope noticed a modern building with bands of window running its width. Something was going on there, people were rushing their way inside carrying books and briefcases.

Penelope slowed down, reaching to brake Marga.

"New School," Penelope said. "New School for Social Research. Did a dance program there once. Wait."

She stood with Marga across the street, looking carefully up and down the tree-dotted block.

A squad car came in sight at the corner of Sixth Avenue, going along slowly.

"Cruising the neighborhood for us," Penelope said. "We better get across the street and do us some quick social research."

She led Marga over to the school, into the crowd around the lobby. People were moving along in a line, buying tickets from a grey-haired woman seated at a little table. Those with tickets were heading for the main auditorium just to the rear of the lobby.

Penelope eased her way into line, holding tight to Marga. In a minute it came her turn and she fished out the bills needed to buy two tickets.

"How much you guess a raccoon would cost?" Marga said as they were going in.

"Thirty-seven-fifty plus sales tax," Penelope said, looking over her shoulder as she steered Marga to the far aisle.

They took seats on the aisle, near a rear exit. After a time a small, emaciated man with wisped hair came onto the platform, arranged some papers on the lecturer's stand, and looked out at the audience, clearing his throat and blinking. The room grew quiet.

"Ladies and gentlemen," the speaker began in a tight voice that seemed poised for the falsetto, "our subject for tonight is, 'Beat and the Poetic Muse.' As you all know, a clattering new spirit is afoot in the esthetic back-alleys of the land, as in the community's hidden deeps and on its outermost fringes. Everywhere the deliberately raucous young and the voluntarily dispossessed are gathering in odd social and esthetic pockets to thumb their collective nose at the standards and stances of the square ingroups. Their rallying cry is hipness. Their new manna is pot and peyote. Way-outness is their credo. High on their list of enemies, indeed, first among their targets of choice, are work, sobriety, ambition, the gray flannel suit, nine-to-five enterprises, programmatic heterosexuality, congenital optimism, the armored musculature, science, the atom, government, patriotism, manners, the daytime, sunny weather. Their primary sound effect is the rattle of bongos. Their favorite meeting hall is the paddy wagon. Their field of operations is the night and their M.O. is total anarchy. All their transactions are carried out in the coffee house, in the shadow of the espresso machine. Their emblem and badge of merit is the scraggly beard. Their one place of refuge is the county asylum and their best sleeps come after the administering of insulin shock. For uniform they wear the blue jeans once a sign of the laboring man but now made the costume of the dedicatedly unemployed. In this jet age they prefer to transport themselves by motorcycle, the rods, and unrhymed iambics. For the most part, though, they so dislike going anywhere on their own power that when rising they prefer to be *sent* and when descending to be *brought down*. Under their aegis cool jazz has become a way of life, the hypodermic needle a quill and a brush, the gangshag an art form. They hold their soirees in cold-water flats and for hymn these antagonists of all forms of labor choose to sing the West Virginia coal miner's work song and the New Orleans levee stevedore's loading chant. They toil not, except at the daily scrounge for a connection, neither do they spin anything beyond floating marijuana tales. Washing perfunctorily as they do, they are everywhere in bad, gamey odor. But do not dismiss as spiritual hoboes these sandal-wearing barbarians who hold themselves holy and from their beatness fashion a Zen beatitude. From their disheveled ranks has come a wild surge of poetry, an inspired, battering babble. . . ."

Many people in the auditorium were nodding and taking notes.

"Is his name Wilbur?" Marga said. "He looks like a raccoon but he moves like a praying mantis with much arthritis. Is he talking about me? Wilbur walked like he was on eggs and he didn't talk."

"Shh," Penelope said. "The professor is making us into a movement, I could puke. Fuzz must be gone by now. Let's make the Waldorf."

She helped Marga up and guided her toward the exit, past the rows of busy note-takers.

His beat being more or less The Village and his view on life being sour-apple liberal, the cabbie did not raise any eyebrows when he turned into Sixth Avenue from 11th and saw this number with the big ka-nockers and white coat flagging him, even though she was holding on to a colored number in something a sweatshirt and blue pants. He did not turn a hair or a blackhead when the colored number said as she was climbing it, "I'd like to buy me a raccoon but thirty-seven-fifty is too damn much."

He wiped the cigar ashes off the front of his plaid shirt, adjusted his black leather cap, and said without attitude, "Where to, ladies?"

"The white article said, "Get up to Central Park and drive around a while. I'll give you the address later."

Nothing so front-page happened on the way up Sixth. Once the colored article said, "Gassy coat, Pen, but you're a flip, you got too much of the doodely dare." The white article said, "At least you can wear it and look like somebody. What would you do with a raccoon, put it on your head and go as a zoo keeper?"

All right. A person *could* wear a raccoon in your hair.

Him, he was mostly bald, it would have to be a small-size type raccoon.

But when they were in the Park, curving around there by the skating rink, the white number said, "We can do it now, nobody'll see. Just scrunch down there on the floor. I hope you like pink, it's the only one I saw that looked like anything." To him, the nothing special at the wheel, she said, "Never mind us, driver, you just keep your eyes on the road, huh?"

Where would he keep them, in his pocket?"

Next thing he knew all two tsatskillehs were both sunk down on the floor where the fold-in seats were, all he could see in the rear-view mirror was their heads and upper parts going higher and lower.

His first thought was to stop the cab right then and there, stop short altogether, because him he didn't want no dirty stuff going on in his hack, not on these premises, he ran a good clean cab, everything was so-what to him but the dirty stuff, yet and still their heads stayed in sight in the mirror so it wasn't too dirty unless they had some new wrinkle he wasn't up on. Or maybe being a couple Village tsatskillehs they just like better sitting on the floor like at some artists' party.

He saw the white coat being thrown on the seat by the white item. Then it looked like the colored item was pulling the sweatshirt over her head and for a long-drawn second he could see her absolute naked right down to the ka-nockers, tsa-tsa-tsa, ai, Mr. Adlai Stevenson, she was made nice.

This colored one more or less sat there as she said, "Pen those chimneys keep hitting at me."

But by this time the white item had *her* clothes off, her blue suit was thrown likewise on the seat. Only she had a something else on *under* this, some kind from a *pink* type suit, and this garment also she was taking off.

Altogether not to be believed.

One party dressing for two?

Then the white number was saying, "Mar, pink should be a great color for you, you'll knock that Worthington stone dead."

Now *she* was naked like a newborn all the way down, it looked like, and ach, gewalt, Mr. David Ben Gurion, what a pair of somethings *she* had, they were a pair ka-nockers to end all ka-nockers, they belonged in a magazine a grown person would be positive ashamed to buy on the stands.

He almost ran into a lamp post.

Then the colored number was slipping the pink blouse over her head and wriggling into the skirt, it looked like, saying,

"Sure, the color's fine, but what about those chimneys that keep coming at me?"

Then the white number was similarly wriggling into a skirt and buttoning up a jacket, putting on the blue garment she herself had took off in the first place. Saying, "Sure, you're a knockout, Mar. Worthington'll cream."

Then they were both back up on the seat and the colored number was saying, "Oh, but listen, listen, Pen, all I got on is *sneakers!* We forgot about *shoes,* I can't go anywheres in *sneakers,* my galloping God!"

And the white number was saying, "Cool it, Mar, I've got some spares in my bag here, brought them because the ones I'm wearing pinch a little, here, put them on, they're white, be a gas with that suit and that coat." Then saying some more: "This Worthington, you can make it with him or not make it, that's up to you, any riff you're on, just keep him busy, you know, give him the idea he's going to get in and that'll put the stars in his eyes. All right, Mar?"

Then the colored item was bending forward like she was putting on shoes, and at the self-same time saying, "Driver, can I ask you a question, is your name Wilbur?"

Then the white item was leaning forward and saying, "Driver, you can take us to the Waldorf-Astoria, not the Park Avenue entrance, around on the 49th Street side where the freight elevator is?"

Why not? A couple lady freight handlers, all right. Probably two lady dock wallopers on a night off.

"Right away, anything you say, lady," the driver said, adjusting his leather cap. "Waldorf, freight elevator, you say, I go. Only my name ain't Wilbur, it's Maximilian, Maximilian Schmantz."

And the colored article was saying, "That's a gassy name for a raccoon, Maximilian Schmantz, almost as good as Tuna Fish."

So tomorrow morning first thing he would go to city magistrate's court and fill out forms to change his name to Tuna Fish. With lettuce, also mayo.

He wondered, as he curved around the fountain across from the Plaza, did the U. S. A. supreme court have any kind of a halfway idea what a mishymashy this desegregation could bring to pass into the world?

Did those nine smart brains foresee all the full consequences when a black lady stevedore and a white lady stevedore got together for a party on the floor of a respectable cab on their night off?

15

WORD MUST have gotten around that here in the town's lacquered and festooned bowels there were free champagne and dancing to a rocking band. Close to five hundred people were now at this affair, many crammed into the freight car, others clumped at tables and around the dancing area, all kinds of people, columnists, nearfamous actresses, press agents, writers of television commercials and other representatives of the creative arts, men in bow ties, a prizefighter who had once held the light-heavyweight title in three West Central states, a Hungarian lady who specialized in giving parties and had recently been in some trouble with New York customs.

Time had become a pleasant ooze for Worthington Rivers. The waiters kept pouring champagne for him and the band's sets jaunted by. He was quite drunk again and had lost most of his self-consciousness about playing the drums, he was back at them after an interlude and beginning to take real satisfaction in the chugging way his hands made the brushes go over the snares, now when he swung at the cow bell he usually connected and when he missed he didn't care. He had not had so much free fun since the time he had sat in with Blue Barron's band at some Groton spring dance or other.

He was letting his shoulders rock free and smiling broadly to himself when he raised his eyes and saw Hoyt Fairliss standing two feet from the bass looking like a thundercloud about to open up.

Worthington's face imploded. He half rose, holding the brushes out like offerings.

"Hoyt?" he said. "Oh? I would advise." Then his eyes wavered to the girl at Hoyt's side and he stood up straight and shivered from head to foot. "This is hardly," he said deep in his throat. "I would never." Beyond that all he could think of saying at her composed face was, "Imagine. Nice. How have you been?"

"Imagine, nice, quite well, Worthington," Shoshana said. "If you're going to ask how things were in Beirut when I left, we were having a heat wave and another cabinet crisis was looming. You have concluded your business with your father satisfactorily, I hope?"

"I'll tell you about that," Worthington said with stricken eyes. "Something came up in Detroit at the last minute, yes, my father's catching a later plane, exactly, late tonight or, let's see, tomorrow at some time."

"So you decided to play drums and live a little," Hoyt said. His eyes swept the platform and came back. "Where is she, you turd?"

"Where's who?"

"Penelope, you shapeless turd."

"Hoyt, if you cannot remain civil, if you refuse to address me with some civility, this conversation is at an end. I warn you, I will not tolerate your rudeness and your coarse insults—"

"You'll tolerate my fist in your sniveling teeth unless you tell me where she's at, pal. I tolerate your coarse insult of a face every time I look at you, don't I?"

"Penelope is a free agent, Hoyt."

"Not free to you, you scummy sneak. You're not doing any free loading at *her* bar. For the last time, where is she?"

"There's no reason why I should tell you this, I've every right in the world to turn my back on you and your gangster manners, but she had to go somewhere, she said she'd be back." Worthington looked sidewise at Shoshana and said, "I trust you did not find New Haven too disappointing?"

"With all the goodies at the Peabody Museum and the School of Fine Arts Gallery?" Hoyt said. "With those unusual prehistoric specimens and that yummy collection of French Impressionismists? You offal."

"So you also stoop to reading other people's private correspondence," Worthington said, the brushes twitching in his hands. "You will even go that far. It is entirely in character."

"I'll tell you something else that is in my character," Hoyt said. "I dumped your clothes down the incinerator, all of them."

Worthington stared.

"All? You?"

"By my estimate," Hoyt said, "your gorgeous wardrobe was worth about three thousand dollars. I did some adding up and according to my figures the loss of Penelope's company for a weekend was worth exactly that to me, three thousand dollars. You've got to pay your way in this life, Worthington, you detritus."

"If, if I get home and find one, one thing missing," Worthington said, "I intend to see my lawyers about it. I will have the fullest legal recourse."

"You will have the fullest cowflop and in your withered face," Hoyt said. "Do you have any idea what the penalty is in the state of Connecticut for stealing a car and a girl? One peep out of you, you refuse, and I'll have you up on the Mann Act. Do you know you transported a girl across a state line for immoral purposes? On a weekend when my purposes with her were entirely immoral and I had no intention of crossing any state lines? You tainted piece of faecal matter."

"Gentlemen," Shoshana said, "if I may say so, I think this conversation has stopped being profitable. I suggest you table the remaining business and adjourn for a cooling-off time."

"I'll table it on his head," Hoyt said. "I'll cool him off so he stays cool."

"I am not impressed by your ruffian's threats," Worthington said. He turned to Shoshana. "I'd like you to know, Shoshana, one reason I was so anxious to see my father was, I wanted to take up the whole matter of those pumps with him. I mean to go into every aspect of the pumps when we meet."

But Shoshana had heard none of this. She was staring at the sign on the aluminum freight car and saying, "El Harrar? How very strange. El Harrar is the kibbutz near which my father lost his life. They are now considering a proposal to change the kibbutz name to the Nils Boergensen Fruit Growers' Cooperative."

"I'm afraid I don't understand," Worthington said, furrowing his forehead. "Your father? Why should some key-boots people in Israel—"

Then he was not talking. He was standing there with the metal brushes near his ears, looking at Penelope come down the stairs in a regal sweep, arm in arm with the most sensational, most fabulous, most strikingly unwhite girl he had ever seen, a vision in pink flame.

16

At first she was stunned to see Hoyt's hulk there by the band.

Then she felt a burst of positive pleasure.

As she hurried down the stairs, arm linked with Marga's, eyes on Hoyt's clouding face, quick thoughts trained through her head. They had to do with men and the classifications they fell into.

Group A, the most sizeable group, consisted, of course, of those who did not believe that women were capable of orgasm or in any case needful of it and oriented toward it, and who therefore dedicated no percepible energies to that elusive end, their theory being that females came more under the category of services and were not constituted so as to be served. These men, whose name was Legion, Tom, Dick, and Harry Legion, were to be side-stepped like the plague and watercress sandwiches. Group B, also of some dimension, was made up of those whose bed instinct was more charitable and equitable but whose knowledge of anatomy was very spotty, in other words, those who felt that the ladies should have big bursts but could have them only in that highly localized surface nodule known in the trade as the vestigial phallus, or button, or boy in the boat. Ready though they were to devote considerable time and energy on behalf of the lady's pleasure, these misguided citizens were in their often exclusive concentration on the button decidedly off the button. In any civilized society, Penelope was prepared to argue, the erotic illiterates of both Group A and Group B would be required to wear identification badges, since it was as important to a girl interested in saving time and cutting a few of the less lustrous corners to know a man's bed habits as to ascertain his blood type and the results of his last Wasserman.

Worthington Rivers was undoubtedly such a know-nothing. Possibly of the Group B variety, more likely of the Group A.

Hoyt Fairliss was a more slippery fish. He belonged to the much more exclusive fraternity of Group C, a category made up of those educated few who had been made to understand that a woman's deepest parts are or at least can be more than mere backstopping to the over-publicized clitoris, more than a bit of irrelevant stuffing designed to take up some anatomical slack. The members of Group C were the promising bed partners whom you tried every way you knew to flush out of the overpopulated thicket of lusting and have extended dealings with, because, whatever quirks they might have in other departments, a taste for Italian pimp clothes, a tendency to lead with the too-big shoulders, they were at least straight and in the know as regards the true innermost seat of a woman's, at any rate certain women's, topping highs. They at least grasped the cardinal fact that a woman is made the way she is not simply to provide a receptacle, not to be a mere quiescent and insentient surround for pulsating maledom, a spiceless watercress sandwich or, practically as bad, a push-button dollie.

In her extended dealings with Hoyt Fairliss she had come for the first time to know the true potentialities of her innermost nature, her furthest possibilities for sweet riot, had, in strictest accuracy, come for the first time, deeply, centrally, in the early days with some outrage over being so inundated, so carried away, so taken to the core, then, as the weeks passed, with a growing sense of delight in herself as she bloomed the Reichian all-through way, taken with herself, taken, finally, *by* herself.

So, learning that there were richer foods than watercress, she had been pleased to know Hoyt Fairliss.

But Group C was tricky. Hoyt Fairliss was especially tricky.

She was not sure exactly how it was with other women but Penelope had come to know one sure thing about herself, namely, that there had to be a sequence, a time lapse, first the man's high, then, much later, infinitely later, and in the midst of complete unstir, with a fabulous lingering immobility for both parties, then, and only then, her own high.

Now there were troublemakers in Group C, amoks like Hoyt Fairliss, who agreed with the promise of mutual pleasure and understood the vaginal as against the clitoral emphasis but who all the same took strong issue with this idea of the two-peaked, his and then hers, highing chronology.

Men like Hoyt Fairliss, makers of exasperating trouble, were opposed to the spread in time, they insisted on what they called a simultaneity, a blending of times and elevations, an all-at-onceness, as though all good things had by definition to be socialized, all central happenings communal.

This Penelope found impossible and not even desirable. She wanted the man to be over with it, long over and left motorless and unstriving, before the lovely storm began to gather in her, and with this in mind she would even try to hurry the man along. The man's unwound finality, in fact, was the necessary condition for any gathering in her, it was an emotional seesaw. But the Hoyts were supercharged with their need to sweep the girl up in their own gushings and kept driving away at her even after they themselves were spent, in the joykilling effort to prove that they were the makers and molders of her top-up. Hungry for bylines, they were compiling credits, these self-appointed pile drivers. This driving and storming when only a stillness was called for made everything inside her stiffen and freeze, put binding clamps on her own deepest muscles, brought her to a dead, dismal stop. Why were they, the members of this rambunctious subdivision of Group C, this band of troublemakers, so huffy about taking a back seat once in a while?

They had to feel responsible for and swarmingly on top of everything.

Why did they have to *push* their way into everything and so throw dry ice over all the woman's inner flows and flutterings?

So she was increasingly edgy about Hoyt Fairliss too, avoided him more and more, and though of two minds about it most often tried to steer him away from the bed where he was so set on pushing things his most male-ego way. She insisted on choice privacies at choice moments and saw no reason why he had to be *acknowledged*, to use his word, every second. Some neural items were hers alone and she insisted on clear title.

Admittedly her first reaction upon catching sight of Hoyt at this party was pleasure, almost a sigh of relief. If Hoyt was back in the picture at least she could be spared the drudge's work of looking for a bed partner somewhere in this city of eight million, of throwing her baited hook out and hoping against hope that the fish she came up with would not be a drag of the Group A or Group B variety. With Hoyt she was at least assured that she would be taken as needful, and deep-needful at that, some of her big needs would be faced and catered to. He would make his big-shouldering fuss about wanting to get them together, would crowd her with his simultaneity line, his bed communism, but she could finally manage with him and to hell with his residue of sulkiness. A Group C man like Hoyt for all his shoulder work was better than an A or B type who had to be taught all the facts of life from scratch and then might not believe them or buddy to them. It would be far better, of course, if Hoyt had been obliging enough to belong to another subdivision of Group C, a less embattled and more cooperative subgroup, those ready to be quick-spent and long-stunned. But at least he was a charter member of Group C, that fine but hard-to-find minority.

If only he were more inclined to fold up and not make such fusses after it was over for him.

If only he would let her go the way she had to go, without so much good and enthusiastic fellowship from him.

A belonger, that one. A joiner.

Had to apply for membership, and more than honorary membership, in all flurries.

All the same, he belonged to Group C. Blessings were to be counted. Tonight called for a Group C man.

So her features were beginning to mellow up in a smile as she steered Marga toward the band and Hoyt. But there was no answering welcome in his face when finally he turned and saw her. Blacknesses welled in his eyes. That dammed obstreperous jaw went out still more. His too-big shoulders actually swelled, he was making fists. His weightlifter flexings.

She had been ready to make up with him. He was such a down-home sight at this point that if he had cracked his feeblest smile she would have forgotten all the nastiness of New Haven and let herself go to putty in his arms. But she was not going to take that kind of glowering and glooming from anybody. That setting of jaw and thinning of lips, that air of outraged accusation he could work up, always made her bristle. Him and his jutting face that said, me, me, *my* way. Well, if he wasn't going to meet her half the distance, screw him.

She bristled now, her own chin going out and high as she came up to him and Worthington.

Volumes had been exchanged by their faces, five-foot shelves spoken between their hungered and angered eyes, without a word being formed.

"Hello, examiner," she said. "Hello, simultaneous."

"Hello, car thief," he said. "Roommate thief. May I point

96

out at this time that who steals my roommate steals trash. Some might say rich white trash."

"I won't take this from you, Hoyt," Worthington said.

"You'll take it," he said. "You're one of the big takers of our time."

"So you came all the way to New York to advance the good cause of simultaneity," she said. "You just won't quit, will you?"

"Only when I'm ahead," he said. "Shoshana Gasharid, may I present my footloose hill, Penelope Gissings."

The two young women nodded cautiously at each other.

"Marga Countryman," Penelope said. "Shoshana Gasharid, Hoyt Fairliss, Worthington Rivers."

"How d'you do," Marga said. "How do, how do."

The others inclined their heads at her.

"A distinct honor," Worthington said, narrowing his eyes in an effort to unfuzz his luring image of this dark queen. "A very great pleasure, Miss Countryman. You live in the city or are you just visiting?"

"Been passing through for going on twenty-three years," Marga said. "I'm visiting permanently. New York is a great place to pass through forever."

"Well, that's nice," Worthington said. "Good for you." He smiled experimentally.

"Worthington," Hoyt said, "does a lot of passing through. He passes through other people's lives without leaving a trace."

"That will be just about enough of that, Hoyt," Worthington said.

The band was beginning to play the bouncy strains of "When the Saints Go Marching In."

"Will you excuse us?" Penelope said. "I'm going to dance with Hoyt if he'll ask me. Shall we dance, Hoyt? That's one thing we might manage with some degree of simultaneity."

"You know how you'll be remembered?" Hoyt said. "They'll say, Penelope Gissings, who was a genius at all the lesser forms of togetherness. All the ones that don't count. Come on, if you want to dance."

As she turned to follow him she said over her shoulder, "Miss Gasharid, why don't you make yourself comfortable at that empty table? We'll join you in a minute. And Marga, be very, very nice to Worthington. He feels much better w̶ when he knows he's wanted."

"By the authorities," Worthington said. Penel

vacantly at him. He added more slowly, "You know, wanted by the authorities? Joke?"

Penelope said, "I see," and went off. These three took seats at the nearby table, almost directly in front of the band.

"This party seems to be in honor of a freight car," Shoshana said.

"A freight car to carry sour grass," Worthington said. "Uh, have you heard about the contest the Manishewitz Wine people are running?" He was eyeing Marga.

"I've heard that joke before, Worthington," Shoshana said. "From you, when you were in Beirut. I didn't think it was funny *then*."

"I think it's a damned funny joke," Worthington said. "There's nothing wrong with it, it was *told* to me by a Jew."

"I can imagine that you would be expert in picking anti-Semitic Jews out of a crowd," Shoshana said. "I guess I never told you about my father, he was in Israel for a lot more than a week, he'd been there for close to two years when he was killed, there by El Harrar."

"What was he doing in Israel, growing sour grass?" Worthington said. "I don't understand, a girl like you, doing espionage work and all that against the Jews, with a father who was on a key-boots? What was he doing, stealing secrets for you or something? That why they killed him? Besides, let's see, if they killed him why are they naming this key-boots after him?"

"My father was a Pullman porter for thirty-one years," Marga said. "He stole mostly silverware."

"I couldn't help noticing, Miss Countryman," Shoshana said, "how beautifully you walk. You carry yourself with your shoulders back, everything balanced from the center of the pelvis. Are you by any chance a dancer?"

"I've been dancing for more years," Marga said. "See?" She stuck one leg out and flexed the muscles. The heavy medallion of the calf sprang up like a shotputter's.

"I'll bet you're a very good dancer," Worthington said, looking at the bare leg. "I'll bet you're a simply marvelous dancer."

"Dancing is a very nice and good thing," Marga said. "It keeps a person from being a waitress."

"Worthington," Shoshana said, "didn't you get me all the way over here from Beirut so as to lay seige to *my* fortress ¤n *your* home grounds, was that not the plan?"

98

"Ah," Worthington said. "You've been talking to Hoyt. There's an entirely new note in your voice, Hoyt's been filling you full of his nasty niggling thoughts, I might have known. Well, look, Shoshana, if you've lost interest in the pumps, if you really don't care about them any more, if you're set on making some kind of lark out of this whole business trip, why."

"Pumps?" Marga said. "Stomach pumps? They had to pump my stomach once at St. Vincent's, took an overdose of bennies, I was like dancing up the walls and I don't mean the waltz."

"I am still interested in the pumps and I mean to get the pumps," Shoshana said. "If you have changed your mind about which fortress you want to climb, that suits my plans perfectly, we agree for the first time. Make your seige plans as you see fit, Worthington. Siege away."

"Would you care to dance, Miss Countryman?" Worthington said stiffly.

The members of the band were now standing with their heads close together, singing in spatters of words about the great day when the saints, when all the saints, when every last saint on the heavenly roster would go marching in to some unspecified but most heartwarming place.

"I won't have you following me around, Hoyt," Penelope said as they danced.

"You won't have me, period," Hoyt said. "At least that's your current strategy, I've got my own ideas."

"You'd better give it up, Hoyt. It's no soap for this weekend or any other weekend from now on henceforward."

"You're not spending this night or any other night with Worthington. My express purpose in coming down here was to prevent that."

"This trip wasn't strictly necessary. I have no plans to spend even a plugged nickel with the gentleman in question."

"No? Then who's to be the lucky man?"

"I'd tell you if I could, Hoyt, but I can't. I haven't met him yet."

"I see. You're planning a night of mad adventure. You're open to any and all suggestions."

"So long as they don't come from you."

"Let's get my position very clear. I had my mind set on spending a weekend with you and I still mean to do just that, what's left of the weekend anyhow. We're several hours behind schedule, due to your tendency not to stay put."

"I'll tell you what's wrong with you, Hoyt, my bullish friend. You're congenitally incapable of being nice to a girl."

"You'd like me to woo you a little? That's a new twist."

"Isn't that what any girl wants from a man?"

"Penny, my footloose hill, I know that when the soggy years set in most girls miss the initial wooing period and complain that they can't recapture its gossamer ecstasies with their men, but you have less cause for complaint on that score than most. We had a highly compressed wooing period, if you remember, it lasted about three minutes all told. Five minutes after we first set eyes on each other we were talking about going to bed, twenty minutes after we *were* in bed. At your instigation as much as at mine. Maybe *more* at your instigation."

"Do you have to keep throwing my bad judgment in my face? I thought you had some capacity for niceness."

"You're dodging the issue, Penny. You came down to New Haven with one idea in mind, to say no to everything I said, to cut my privates off, and I don't mean to allow that."

"You call them your privates but you think of them as your lieutenant colonels at least, with a brilliant combat record and up for promotion. I came down with one idea in mind, yes, to be nice to you if you were nice to me."

"All right. There are two nights left to the weekend, two nights for you to be nice to me. You're going to be nice to me, very nice, whether you like it or not."

"Now *there's* a typical Hoyt Fairlissism. That's our Hoyt Fairliss through and through. You're going to love me no matter how much you hate me. Damn you, my love, my leper, open up. My distinguished lieutenant colonels await without."

"I don't think I'm making myself clear. You're going to bed with me, tonight. There's no need for more discussion, that's it."

"Thanks, but no, thanks, Hoyt. Examination time's over for me, Mr. Much Shoulder Simultaneity."

Black, very black, in any case demonstratively unwhite, was his true love's hair, along with the rest of her person.

Blackness to Worthington Rivers was more a mystical shimmer, an emanation, than a color. It was, actually, a big dancing no—a nay-saying to the quality and the aura of the true whites, whose numbers were quite limited, embracing as they did only those peoples of the Anglo and Nord strains. Of

100

all the millions of souls of the European countries, Worthington was unreservedly convinced of the whiteness only of the English and the Scandinavians and the Germans, the Latins and Slavs were definitely beyond the pale of the acceptably pallid and even the French were suspect, a bit swarthy in more ways than the skin would show. The epidermis did not have to be bronzed or mahoganied in order for the more devious tarrings to be there.

The suggestion of these slightest shadings in another person, especially in a woman, most especially in a young and attractive woman, aroused intense feelings in Worthington. Unwhiteness, anti-whiteness, was for him a sure sign of second-class status in the human family, a mark of lagging merit, an affidavit of precious few Grotons and nice tea things in the background. But in drawing away his eyes all the same dwelled with bubbling speculations on such a shadowed person, especially if it were a young and attractive female. The urge that was born in him when confronted by a fresh bloom of a lady of his own station and hue was for a staid, proper and subdued sort of sex, but when facing such a one of the duskier strains he felt runaway impulses, he wished to do all sorts of things thrashingly and shriekingly, mob actions stirred in him. Darkness, the hint of any least smear in the woman, branded her as inferior, yes, but it also was thick with the promise of ultimate, abominable, fine riot.

He had felt this quickening and churning in himself when he first set eyes on the raven-tressed and bituminous-eyed Beirut beauty identified for him as Shoshana Gasharid. She was definitely on the charry-tarry side, spiritually speaking, and therefore most certainly had terrible, enticing chasms in her, dankly delightful caverns to challenge the most intrepid spelunker. When he was informed that this flashy, lush person was a Jewess his head had begun to swim. Jews were decidedly on the darkmost side, filled with the most tainted and tarantellaing blacknesses, from which it followed that nothing you did or tried to do with them could with any justice be called illegal. Shoshana suggested much thrashing to him, many neck-swollen shriekings, all the improprieties set free.

But she had produced papers to show that she was a person of impeccable Swede-white origin, a product of long lines of unblemished alabasters, only for the moment masquerading as a Jewess, that was to say, one of the alluringly tainted. Immediately his ardors for her diminished to the staid, more accurately, the *stayed*, the toned-down, the rigorously held.

101

He still wanted very much to have her, she still gave out the darker wave lengths, he had indeed invited her to the States with the idea in mind that the conquest would be easier over here, but his images of what it would be like, of how far he would allow himself to go, were drained of their steamier excesses. He had even been ready to abandon her for the weekend in favor of Penelope Gissings, who, improbably enough, was white all through, had the amplest papers to prove her lack of tar and tarnish, and yet gave the promise of an unparalleledly thrashing, shrieking blackness if and when you could get to her. The fact that she went after Negroes for friends only pointed up this buried blackness in her.

Now he was ready, even eager, even salivating at the prospect, to turn his back on Penelope Gissings in favor of this Marga Countryman. The fact was that, for all his imaginings as to the erotic possibilities of and with a girl of color, he had never actually held in his arms, never been in bed with or even shaken hands with, an undeniably colored partner. From Southern classmates at prep school and college, squirts who had had colored maids in their homes and tasted them to the full in linen closets and storage attics, he had heard a good and titillating deal about how these anything-goes blacks could be. Grinning tales of much shrieking, infinite thrashing. But until this night, here many levels below the Waldorf-Astoria, here alongside the improbable aluminum car and the inexhaustible Dixieland band, he had never held to him a colored girl. The conditions of his life, the altitude of his position, had imposed on him a total segregation which socially he took as a working out of natural law but sexually filled him with gnawing ache.

Wants in mobs were ascending his spinal column. His mind was fixing on perspectives of riot, to be inaugurated, if humanly possible, before the night was over.

Marga, this one inconceivably in his arms, was all the unwhiteness in the world for him and therefore his new true love, all the abominable promise.

"Miss Countryman," he said tightly as they danced, "I'd like you to know, you may be the most beautiful girl I've ever set eyes on."

"May?" she said from far away. "You giving me the permission?"

"Ha, ho, that's very good. You have my permission. Be as beautiful as you want. I'll put it in writing."

"Listen," she said with no question in her voice, "you on one of them spook kicks? You one of them?"

"Am I on one of what?"

"You got eyes for the dark meat? You want to rub some kink hair for luck?"

Dimly he made out her point. "You ought not to think such things, Miss Countryman. What I admire, yes, admire very much, is you, not your color."

"Well, I down mire yours. What's white but a whole gang of nice-shaved nothing? You white when you got no color. It an absence. Comes from taking away. They put you in the ground and you grow some high color fast nough, you turn cheesy soft and black like the rest. Death the big damn Man-Tan." She had a tendency, when talking to his cornfed kind, to cut the grammatical corners and work up a mammy-much Jo-ja slur. Much of this style she had picked up from History Jones, whose English, when he chose to express himself in English, at those rare moments of sobriety when he had some choice, was actually as good as hers.

"We're getting off on the wrong foot, Miss Countryman," he said agitatedly. "You've too much of a chip on your shoulder with me, really you have. All I think about you is that you're a marvelously pretty girl, and you're right, of course, in the grave we'll all be dark and worm-colonized. Death everybody's Mau-Mau." He added, almost as a verbal tic, "I read somewhere that death is Nature's way of warning us to slow down, hm."

Feeling that he had made a concession big enough to placate her, he was emboldened to press the small of her muscled back, flattening the whole lush terrain of her torso against his. It was a way he had never before danced with anybody.

Speaking to his crewcut, his buttondownness, his nopleats, his whole lot of barbered nothing, she said, "I know you, you after a change of luck. All right, Mister Man, I and my permanent flush gown help you change your luck. There gown be big changes if that how you want it, you blob of no."

Addressing himself to the black hair, the swirling blackness of her presence, feeling a spurt of wild black hope in him, the most taboo doors opening, and at the same time throbbingly aware that he had never spoken in just this blackened and blackening way to any live woman, that what he would not have dared say to a girl of his own kind after a full month he was about to voice to this dusted Marga after hardly five minutes, he announced in feature writer's dramatic lead style, strangling on the words, "You're incredibly beautiful and I want, if you don't mind my saying it, I want everything with you, all the things and fast, fast."

The band took off on yet another chorus of "Saints," he pressed her harder against him, he felt the fine breasts mash wonderfully into his ribs, he could hardly breathe.

History Jones finished his solo and signalled to the band to continue stompilating the saints around. He put his sax away and stepped over to the table.

"Excuse, miss? Did I hear you telling to my friend Marga there about how your pa was washed away in one of them kye-boatses?"

"That is correct. We were not introduced, I believe? My name is Shoshana Gasharid."

"They call me History, History Jones. You mind if I set me down here? All right, then." His appetite for modulated S-curved attack had been whetted by the first scapegoat served up to him this night, Worthington Rivers, a fine meal. Now here was another white smelling of the far outside and therefore more fair game. She had not appeared here under any auspices that said hands and needles off and so she was presumably a right target for some of the dead-panning jive, which he sometimes liked to pronounce *jibe*, thinking he was only giving it the handkerchief-head sound and but dimly aware that he was speaking another more accurate word. He said: "How come he was in that kye-boats, was your pa a Jewish man?"

"This is not easy to explain." She looked at him hard, trying to read in his bland eyes the intention that was too carefully draped in his words. "History? I have not heard of such a name."

"They, my friends, po-wets and such, say history is what came before. They say I came before, or should of, long time past, cause I make the talk like the first people. What was he doing in that kye-boats, missy? If he was with them people why they wash him a-way? He say or do something to make them Joosh peoples sore as boils at him?"

She looked at him still harder and said deliberately, "So, then. One more whiner."

"No'm, missy, I don't mess round with the wines. I don't hold with the winos nohow. Wine ruin the stomach and give no kind of bigger buzz a-tall."

He gave her his most innocent and full-open eyes.

104

"You're a whiner," she said. "You whine. When you begin to, how is it said, put the needles in people, strangers to you, about anything and nothing, this means only that you are whining about your condition in life and cover it by being a needler. If at the heart of you you were not constantly fussing about what the cruel world did and does to you you would not feel such a need to make fun and hash of the world every time you think you can get away with it." She leaned across the table and looked deep into his unsending eyes. "I know about those who whine. I have made a study of them in certain places. Shall I tell you something? For many centuries the Jews were whiners too. They covered it with deep sighs and jokes told with the lips twisted, but underneath they were miles of whines. Not that they did not have good cause to complain. It is just that complaints and the jokes and needles built on the premise of complaints don't get you anywhere, they only intensify your bad mood. You listen. The Jews stopped their whining and learned how to shoot and got themselves a state."

"I don't want no state, ma'm, lady," History said, staring. In his entire life no woman had ever spoken to him in terms of such ultimate putdown. "Onliest state I want to be in is the state of totable confusion and no matter. Listen, you tell me to get a gun? I can't buy no gun. You got to have a license to go out and buy you a gun. I would have to have a gun to steal me a license."

"I'm not saying you ought to buy a gun," she said steadily. "My point is that it does not accomplish anything in the real world, except to make other people's tempers as bad as yours is underneath, to form guns and needles out of your words. You will refrain from making further sarcastic reference to what my father was doing in Israel, please. He was not whining. He was working with people who were learning there are more efficacious ways to handle the world than to look it up and down with narrowed eyes and whine."

History Jones looked away with narrowed eyes and watched Penelope moving around the dance area. He reflected that *this* one was a gunner, an artillery spotter, a bombsight, but that Penelope now, he would like to have himself a taste of *that*, that was a fine bundle of nice dressy eats. He actually felt the saliva springing up under and around his tongue, and swallowed hard.

A little troubled by the surge of appetite in him, sensing tensions everywhere that were somehow equated with and radiating out from the sudden boulder of appetite in his stomach, he said worriedly, "Plenty of your whiners on the scene this eve, missy. They gown reach for their guns and needles any minute now. We should all go away from here in different directions. Big trouble in this shaky place."

She saw how his eyes were following and following Penelope, the grope in them. She watched as Worthington went on socking it in systematically, pelvic-bold, with Miss Countryman, and how Mr. Fairliss and Miss Gissings danced with a foot of stern space between them, watched all the faces, she saw in them the want and the shutdown. She was worried too.

"Yes," she said with a thoughtful heaviness. "There are troubles here. Enough for everybody's needs."

History shifted his attention back to her and blinked, to avoid a gulp.

17

SAM'L, SIR, POP, PROP, PROD. Another bulletin from the front. Somewhere in no man's land *below* the Waldorf. Hostilities going underground. In the shadow of a high-sheen freight hauler that is going to El Harrar people are lindying more and more unsteadily to the spiked champagne music of some unannotated History surnamed Jones and among them are a motely few preparing to do battle that must bode ill. We questers are at the moment sitting at a table near the bandstand and playing ping-pong with our inflamed eyes. My eyes glare at Penelope. Hers flare at me. History sits back eating said Penelope as he might a barbequed sparerib only with his eyes. Eat of me only with thine diner's eyes. When said History shifts his attention momentarily from his redheaded meal it is to consider with cool reconnaissance behind which Mau-Mau's convene our friend and neighbor Worthington, who is nudging this dispersed girl Marga from head to foot and back again with *his* eyes, all the while said Marga lets *her* eyes go scouting and table-hopping. Pingpong? More like ninepins. Bowl me, as over as possible, only with thine kegler's eyes. No good can come of this building tension. Everybody is preparing to make an entree or a bowling alley of everybody else. Miss Shoshana taking it all in with no comment and no pleasure either. When she looks over at me it is as though to say that armed frontiers are being established here with no nations to back them up. Not so sure any more that Worthington is my proper enemy. Not even easy in my mind about Penelope being my rightful quarry. Frankly I suddenly don't know what I'm doing here because Miss Shoshana's presence keeps posing questions as to why I am not elsewhere engaged in more productive work. I would like to insist that important issues will be decided by these mottled misfits this night but I can't think what they might be. Getting very, very hot by this railroad siding, take my word. Hotter than the thermometer and the barometer would indicate. I am sweating in the manner they call profuse. Seems to be a sprinkler system under my collar and my shoes feel as though they're filled with lard. I know this feeling. It's what I call my Korea feeling. The way I used to feel in Korea each and every time we were instructed to fly to some area where they were shooting at each other. I may as well finally confess that I am not the combative type and the smell of battle makes me want ardently to go away to another less odorous place. Sam'l, I have never made this clear to you but the fact is that I let you down badly in Korea. I know you felt strongly about the issues you and those like you presumed were being fought out in Korea and therefore would have swollen mightily in the chest had I come through those indeterminate skirmishes with flying colors. I was in the Air Force, yes, but the colors I emerged with were less than flying, though I did not display them recklessly enough to warrant a court martial, which takes another, no more palatable, kind of bravery. The crux of the matter, Sam'l, is that in Korea as in so many other exclamatory places I was a distinct though hardly distinctive or distinguished misfit. Let me make that clearer. The others were no more enthusiastic about being in the helicopter rescue teams than I was but none of them had my minority reasons for disenchantment. The others, I mean, were Worthingtons. They were obliged to fly undramatic and unstatused eggbeaters when all they wanted was to be with the elite jet pilots. Class struggles everywhere. I did not wish to be with the jets. I did not have the slightest interest in being airborne in any manner, shape or form. I wanted to be permanently on the ground, attached to no service other than the care and feeding of my skin, at the greatest distance possible from the shooting. I was oriented toward other continents altogether. One reason, no doubt the primary one, was, of course, this Korea feeling, which consisted in about equal parts of crawling sensations along my spine and heavy refrigeration in my stomach and an itch in the feet to break the world's record for the mile. There was a very wide streak of cowardice to my thinking in and on Korea and make no mistake about it. The first part of me that got mobilized over there and remained uppermost in my mentality was unquestionably the craven. Still I would like to submit for your consideration the proposition that other parts of me were in operation too. The fact is that I had no abiding interest in the happenings in and around Korea because I could not see what the hell anybody was doing there outside of the natives working the rice fields. I am not good at charades and I never take part in them when I can beg off. Korea, it occurred to me early, more specifically, the moment my feet first set down on its uninspired soil, was only another of the charades that public affairs are tending increasingly to turn into in our posey times. The charade in Korea, I need hardly point out except to those like you who stubbornly refuse to acknowledge the existence of these transoceanic charades (even when you are among those who set up the ground rules for them), was that we (on both sides) were fighting for the inviolability of a certain unprepossessing tract of land whereas in reality we (on both sides) were rather putting up smokescreens behind which the two great powers could go on stockpiling and counting their triggerable atoms. So it occurred to me that the basis for patriotism had abruptly been yanked out of the world, if, in fact, it had ever been there in more than slogan form. I did not feel like being patriotic toward the atomic stockpilers and counters on my side, and I saw no reason why the people facing us on the various fronts should feel any warmer sentiments toward *their* atomic custodians. It then became intolerable that while I was not in any way interfering in the world's affairs the world should have decided to interfere so spectacularly in mine. The truth is that I don't trust any group of men enough to place the disposition of my person in their hands while they go on conferring in private about how many atoms to do up and when and where they might be triggered. Their mistake is that they don't stop to consult me. I am surprised that they have not recognized this oversight. If I were taken on as a consultant with some real say in policy I might, I just might, feel a shade patriotic. I am making no promises but it is a remote possibility. They will not take me on. Because it's not feasible? All right. Just my point. *Patriotism's* not feasible. I therefore am oriented toward transporting myself as far from the Koreas as possible. I am tired of offering my services as smokescreen when there is a good chance of my being dismembered in the process and when I don't approve of what's being screened anyhow. This non-Worthington attitude, though conveyed by eye rather than mouth, *was* conveyed, and it did not make me popular among the many Worthingtonian 'copter pilots who felt like second-class citizens because they were not jet fighter pilots. But this attitude might equip me for a policy-making post in State. What State needs first and foremost is a personnel that has lost faith in the idea of a national team and looks askance at all formations such as State and even state. I suspect that I could make a real contribution along these lines for about twenty-four hours, assuming it would take them that long to find me out and throw me out. I am not saying that I won't apply for that job. I am merely raising the question at this time as to whether there will be a shimmering career in the Department for a man who believes that all the atomic inventorists and custodians ought to be dispatched to a remote planet with instructions to drop their triggered atoms on themselves. Must cut this short, Sam'l. Much crawling along spine, deepfreeze in stomach, itch in feet, etc. Bad enough when Penelope was looking daggers at me and History was looking seven-course meals at *her* and Worthington was looking tin cups at Marga and Marga was looking rooms-to-let at all and sundry, not to mention Miss Shoshana surveying the shrinking buffer zones between us like a truce commissioner about to give up and go home. Now there has appeared in our disorderly midst a person claiming his name is Prosper Merrymake and what *he* is making with his oystery eyes is not in the least merry. In fact I incline to the theory that his eyes have been turned inside out and the more he stares the more he sees of his own shrunken brain matter. He seems to be wearing belts everywhere. He is standing alongside us squinting studiously into his prefrontal lobes as Penelope makes the introductions and I feel he bodes this assemblage no good, no good whatsoever. Smell of battle becoming a stench and again I don't know what the shooting is to be about. Should get up and start to sprint but suddenly all the exits seem closed and we are doomed to party forever with our eyes snookering off each other and the band huffing "Wish I Could Shimmy Like My Sister Kate" just behind us. Sister will no doubt dislocate her hipbone soon and this will be the signal for all of us to stand up and begin firing point-blank at each other. Your devoted frontline correspondent, feeling mighty like Korea and wondering can there be the least Prosper in this cadaver-eyed Merrymake? Respectfully, forebodingly, etc.

18

PROSPER MERRYMAKE was wearing his party suit. Made to his very particular order with the first moneys he had realized from the pushing of Lewellyn's highly pushable weed, the material in it, gray flannel, was standard enough, but the concept behind it, the spirit imbuing it, the aura wisping from it, would have caused riots up and down Madison Avenue, assuming its dedicatedly downtown wearer might ever have had occasion to invade those mamboless and unbongoed uptown precincts.

In designing this garment Prosper had followed the same esthetic that inspired his Whitmanesque, mail-order-catalogue poetry: isolate the thing that smacks of quality and reproduce it in swamping quantity.

With tailor as with muse his creative impulse was directed toward uncovering the element of accepted excellence and then setting up a breeding farm for it, on the theory that you can never get too much of an undebatedly good thing.

It had come to his attention that Ivy League trousers were often fabricated with an adjustable belt sewed just under the rear waistline. He understood that this device was for the purpose of making the tight garment still tighter and he approved, believing that good things come in small, trim, even cramped packages such as he felt his own skin and skull to be. (What he had against the sheathing of his own person was not its compactness so much as its tendency to fissure and leak its contents; much of the time, even when more or less sober, he had the worrisome impression that his best substances were oozing out from various faults and rents in his easily lacerated surface and forming small spectacular puddles around his feet.) Taking adjustable belts as a mark of heightened style consciousness, fashion hipness, and also endorsing them as anti-leak aids, he had had several of them spotted at points on his suit where they might do their work and in addition be immediately visible: on the sleeves to replace the unfunctional buttons found in squarer jackets, to the rear of both trouser legs a bit above the ankle. These latter, it turned out, had little use value because the legs were already so slim that the tailor had had to install zippers along the seams to enable Prosper to get into them.

On his feet he wore salmon-colored suede desert boots of ankle length. These, too, were equipped with small belts over their rear seams. On his head was a black leather cap with a very small Scotch-plaid visor, and this cap had a plaid belt in the back. He had for a time considered attaching a belt at the rear of his jockey shorts but when he could find no way of displaying this extra style touch he gave up the idea, believing that invisible and entirely self-consumed hipness is the winding route back to squaredom.

Very central, focal, *in* people, he had observed, had their jackets cut with three and sometimes even four front buttons rather than the one or two he had grown up seeing in his home neighborhood on the Lower East Side. (When he was still Prospero Mario Maggi, before he had come across a volume of Prosper Merimee's and realized that given names are only raw material for the forging of gone and grabbing personal labels.) Concluding that the road up from the slums led through levels of more and more buttoning-in, and on the general premise that multiplication is enhancement, he had had his jacket made with six front buttons. The top five he kept closed, the bottom one he left unused to indicate his at-homeness with richesse.

Each lapel was further distinguished by the presence of *two* small notches rather than the usual one.

Orthodox people had their jackets made with either one rear vent or two side vents. Prosper's was vented both at rear *and* sides, giving it tails that fluttered uncoordinately in the breezes.

Under the form-hugging jacket was a red and gold brocaded vest with shawl lapels. His shirt was an orthodox pink oxford buttondown but instead of the ordinary rep or foulard tie he had hanging from the collar a sort of Las Vegas cowboy adornment consisting of two leather cords strung through holes in a silver dollar. Sentiment rather than materialism was involved here because this dollar was the first he had ever earned from pushing reefer, back in the miss-meal days before he had begun to give mambo lessons. His attire also contained a reference to his mamboer's life in the form of a paper napkin with a border design made up of miniature

111

bongo drums, a memento from the Palladium Ballroom. On the night he won his first mambo contest and thus found himself launched on a new career in the twitchy realm of body poetry, teaching youngish West End Avenue matrons the art of forming fractured iambs with their feet and hips, on that turning point of a night he had stuffed this napkin into his breast pocket, never to take notice of it again.

Tight though his pants were they always, on his hipless frame, this body that seemed incapable of sprouting even a wart, let along a true bulge, had a tendency to fall down. He did not like to wear belts because they gave him the eerie sensation that he was being cut in two *crosswise*, which, added to his steady impression that he was already spiritually split down the middle *lengthwise*, produced in him the overall conviction that he had been neatly quartered and was being held together only by his tight suit. To get around wearing a belt he had his pants attached to his brocaded vest with safety pins. The unified vest and trousers had a tendency to start moving a fraction of a second after he did and to come to rest just a bit in retard, as though he were making his way fully clothed under water.

His pants were cuffless. The cuffs had been displaced rather than eliminated, they were now on his sleeves, made with several folds to provide a lush proliferation of flannel out of which his pale thin wrists budded feebly, as though they had fought their way down from his underfed shoulders during a blight.

Having noticed that among smart dressers, real pacesetters, it was all the go to wear leather pads over jacket elbows, Prosper had had large oval alligatorskin patches installed on the elbows of this suit jacket. The tailor had induced him to drop the idea of treating the trouser knees the same way only after patiently explaining that people of quality seldom engage in activities which might tend to wear out those areas.

At this moment, standing at Penelope's table and nodding to her rhythmic syllables with sage egret head dippings, hearing the separate sounds she was making as she introduced him around without being able to string them together into meaningful sequences, aware chiefly of the slow and almost audible swirl in his head that was the result of the two more reefers he had consumed as he made his way uptown, he felt he was in imminent danger of leaking away entirely into a puddle on the floor if he did not plant himself and somehow firm up

112

immediately. So he raised one foot and placed it hard on an empty seat to keep from melting down and for balance.

His brick-red ribbed socks were at the moment serving a purpose they had never been intended to serve by the woolen mills supplying Brooks Brothers, each of them being receptacle for ten neatly packed reefers.

When he lifted his foot to the chair his tight trouser leg slid up almost to his knee and here came into view, jutting out from the sock, an indubitable, indomitable, incorrigible, brownish stick of tea, there for all to see.

It was Marga Countryman who saw it first.

Her itinerant eyes having completed yet another circuit of this table, from the elbowy hoverer of a Massa Rivers, who was inching his way toward her in what seemed a determined effort to install himself in her lap and/or down her dress front, to the big and scrappy-faced one, the one with the bulldozer shoulders, the Meestah Fairliss, who kept shooting looks full of poisoned darts and garbage at the Massa Rivers, having gone this route once more, they, her hoboing eyes, now lit on Prosper's desert boot, then on the red sock above it, then on the top of the sock, then, doing a doubletake that shook them into quick focus, on the errant reefer that had worked its way up blowing shrill whistles all the way.

She was pretty far gone herself but she recognized that they were in something approximately like a subway station and that in places of public congregation wares such as these are not put on display for the casual passerby.

She would have liked to reach all the way to the truant reefer and push it out of sight but at this moment she did not have enough coordination. So she raised both hands and waggled all the fingers lobster fashion, hoping to make a general commotion in the area of the trouble that would alert Prosper.

She said, "Hey, uncool, the sock, Prosp."

Worthington Rivers had his arm around Marga's shoulder and was saying into her ear with all the insinuation he could muster, as his starved eyes scurried over her half-out coffee breasts, "I mean it, Miss Countryman, I really do, I think you are the acme, the pinnacle, loveliest honey, and I'd enormously like—"

Through his drink-rippled eyes he saw her fingers crawling without destination in the air. He watched them for a while, frowning.

It dawned on him that somebody, very possibly Marga, had said something about a sock. It did not seem an appropriate answer to the riding greed he felt and was trying to find adequate words for, but in a moment his eyes drifted and he saw that she must have had reference to a real sock, the bright red one that he saw now poised above the chair close by.

At first it was only a pulsating blob of color. Then it took on a distinctly unsocklike attribute. It had something thin and yellowish protruding from its top.

He looked more closely, squinting to cut through the blur. A cigarette, an undeniable cigarette, was rising from this sock where no cultured damn cigarette that knew its place and wasn't trying to butt into people's business had any right to be.

He reached waveringly, saying, "Rotten upstart, downstart cigarette, getting out of hand, going for your foot, got to watch them every—"

He never finished the sentence, if sentence it had been meant to be.

Prosper had been watching Marga's fluttering fingers with no comprehension. Her code words about his sock registered with him as nonsense syllables. But when he saw a hand reaching out for his leg from this tall drink of gabardined and crewcutmost and obviously top-drawer water, a seam opened in the dingy cavern of his head and sunlight bolted explosively in.

He saw the reefer half out of his sock. He saw this hand going for it, the hand of an obviously instyled though fundamentally square stranger going for his sock.

He knew one thing, and supremely, that strange hands should not be reaching for his all-purpose sock.

He was ever ready to defend his inviolable socks from the fuzz and all their proliferating everywhere representatives.

With a reflex motion that flicked with unbelievable speed out of his general flab, his lips trying at the same moment to form the words "You got no cause to go fingering up people, not without search warrants, bud-boy," he clamped his hand over Worthington's wrist and flung it away with all his brittle might.

Worthington was in no condition to arrest his hand in its fast-propelled flight.

He watched with startled eyes, like an aficionado at the dog

114

races when the whippets streak by, as his hand flew past his face and continued on in Hoyt Fairliss's direction.

Now Hoyt had been paying no attention to all this byplay. At this very instant he had his head turned to Shoshana Gasharid and he was saying to her, loud enough for Worthington to hear, "One thing you should know about Worthington, he adores the girls. He can't afford not to, he's got to go on adoring all of them, all without exception, until he finds one backward enough, not to adore him back, that would be asking too much, but to more or less tolerate him, one stunned and nerveless enough to close her eyes and not make too much of a face when he—"

Something crashed into his face.

He whirled around, blinking.

It was a hand. The hand was attached to an arm. The arm was attached to Worthington.

Worthington slowly held the hand up and considered it as though it were a prodigal just returned from an ambling world's tour.

Worthington let his disastered eyes go to Hoyt.

"You hit me?" Hoyt said with undeviating evenness.

"Now, Hoyt," Worthington said, "forget how it looks, just ask yourself why would I want to do a thing like that? Ask yourself if by any conceivable stretch of the imagination I would be so asinine, so juvenile, so downright, well, I don't know what, as to—"

"You raised your hand." Hoyt was speaking very, very slowly, in a monotone. "You moved it. You hit me. In the face."

"I did no such thing," Worthington said still more hurriedly. "For heaven's sake, Hoyt, don't go reading all sorts of things into this, I was just sitting here—"

"In the face," Hoyt said. "With your hand."

"If you choose to believe," Worthington said huffily, "that I would ever rise to your cheap insults in such a primitive way, that I would let you pull me for one instant down to your childish brawling level—"

Hoyt reached across the table, placed his palm on Worthington's forehead, and heaved him away with a thrust into which he put his all.

Worthington's chair tipped over backwards. He went sprawling onto the bandstand and did not come to rest until his head had punctured the skin of the big bass drum and the top half of his body had disappeared inside this drum.

115

History Jones was just then joining his band for the final chorus of "Wish I Could Shimmy Like My Sister Kate." All the musicians stopped playing.

All the dancers stopped dancing.

The drinkers had no intention of stopping drinking but they held their slowed glasses in their hands musingly.

The drummer sat with his sticks in his hands, looking down at the flailing legs his drum had suddenly developed.

"Hh-*rmm*," he said reflectively. "That white boy sure like the drums some. Look like he can't get him e-*nough* of dem dere drums."

History Jones crossed the bandstand unhurriedly. He reached down to take hold of Worthington's hips and helped him get extricated from the drum. After that he helped the shaken young man to stand up.

"Tell you one thing in front," History said into Worthington's pale face, "that the best damn drumming you done here tonight. Right *on* the beat, drummer man."

He reached over to straighten Worthington's collar.

"You better not!" Worthington said in a sudden sputter. "You keep your hands to yourself, you!"

What he had in mind was, first, this colored man obviously did not like him, second, he had busted this man's or his drummer's drum, third and most important, he had been working up to wild passes at the colored girl and so, obviously, inevitably, this colored man, because they all stuck together, they were like Jews in their clannishness, they hated outsiders, would be resentful and take advantage of any slightest opportunity to hit him. Absolutely certain that History's hands were coming at him with intent to cause damage, he leaped back and away from the bandstand.

But he had not reckoned with the long step down to the platform. His foot was unprepared for this drop and when it landed he lurched sideways, colliding heavily with a very big, very ugly, very drunk man in a salt-and-pepper raw silk jacket.

This man narrowed his eyes under brows piled high with scar tissue. He pulled reflectively at one of his thickened, meandering ears. He laid a beefy finger along his mashed, flattened nose. His massive shoulders began to inflate some more.

"Fooling around," he said in a beerily hoarse voice. "Big clown. Go around making punk trouble."

His puffy, humped, irregular lips were twisting in a parody

116

of a smile as he took hold of Worthington's very Ivy League lapels with one enormous hand and began, systematically, as though fanning flies away, to slap his face with the other.

Worthington could not move. He was suspended from the man's imprisoning hand as from a meat hook in a slaughterhouse. His head jerked right and left as the man's great streak of a palm went rhythmically at his face.

Hoyt Fairliss was instantly on his feet. He crossed quickly to this big man and put a restraining hand on his free arm.

Hoyt's feeling at this moment was something like that of a cat that has been playing desultorily with a failing mouse, losing interest in the game steadily, until a real killer calico from the alley stalks in and takes over the prey. His sentiment was that he had every right to go on clawing at Worthington's dragging tail for as long as he pleased but that no interloper from the alleys was going to take the game away from him.

"Better lay off," Hoyt said to the big man. "You've got fifty pounds on him."

The big man released Worthington. He regarded Hoyt with interest. The scar tissue gathered in hard buttes over his eyes again.

"All right, jack, now," he said with elaborately lazy good humor. "I tell you what, jackie, boy. You take say twenty-five pounds off of me and put them on him, all right? That way it be nice and even all the way, all right? You do that?

Saying which, he threw a lightning left hook in the precise direction of Hoyt's liver.

Hoyt could move fast when he had to. He parried the punch and let his own fist go in the big man's face. The man was staggered, but only for a moment. Almost before he had regained his balance he was swinging lustily at Hoyt and Hoyt was swinging with still greater zest back at him.

There in the shadow of the aluminum freight car destined for El Harrar, to the accompaniment of the gentle hiss of champagne flowing down the fountain inside, they fought as though at their moment of truth, as though after a lifetime of searching they had finally found their true occupations, their predestined callings, in each other's beckoning nose.

The total absorption with which they went at it was infectious. Before long dozens of men around them had squared off and were pounding at each other. The platform was suddenly overrun with unsteady but most exuberant apprentice light-heavyweights.

For all his conviction that he was not a combative type,

117

Hoyt found himself fully engrossed in his sudden campaign to cube this stranger's face into a flat and raked expanse of meat. The sense of chuckling involvement which he had never experienced for one moment when working on his Ph.D. dissertation he now suddenly discovered in himself as he set about to mince and rearrange this bruiser's unsavory features. His knuckles sang with pleasure each time they found the chunked bones of the other's physiognomy.

It was not happening with the regularity he would have wished, though. Through a peculiar and complicated chain reaction, a process which all in all had taken about ten seconds, beginning with the runaway reefer in Prosper Merrymake's sock and ending with Worthington Rivers flying in terror from the Negroes whose drum he had just shredded, Hoyt Fairliss was now, three stories below the Waldorf-Astoria, sweatily trying to connect with the features of a man he had never seen before, the pugilist who once for a month solid had held the light-heavyweight title in three West Central states.

Nearby stood Shoshana Gasharid, her face registering total disapproval. Not far beyond her two ladies, inspired by the spirit of jolly mayhem, were tearing at each other's hair, one of them the Hungarian partygiver who had lately had some run-in with customs, the other a Madison Avenue copy supervisor who in her spare time, when the need to be immersed in significance came over her, locked away the singing commercials in the back of her head and wrote campaign literature for the Committee For A Sane Nuclear Policy.

Of course, it was the Hungarian playgirl who had started the fight, not the Sane Policy lady.

Hoyt Fairliss was so busy trying to hit and not be hit, and Shoshana Gasharid was so engrossed in watching the progress of one more border skirmish of the kind she abominated but apparently could not altogether avoid, that neither of them noticed the furtive exodus taking place up the stairway, History Jones leading the overwhelmed Worthington, Penelope and Marga hurrying along close behind with Prosper Merrymake floating between them in his party suit.

Under one arm History Jones had his saxophone, under the other a suit draped neatly on a hanger, a gray flannel suit.

19

"LOVE IS a termite in the beamery of my so-whole," Prosper Merrymake said tonelessly. "Love is an acne on the face of my come-pose-sure. Love is the razor the wrist seeks out. Love is a lysrgic acid of your own gall's make. Love is an ingrown toenail of the mind. Love is a fixed roulette wheel on which the bouncing ball is your adrenal. Love is a typewriter with all the lower-case letters missing and only the exclamation point for punctuation. Love is a prefrontal lobotomy you do to yourself every morning with the cornflakes. Love is a giggling Chinese laundryman who knocks off all the buttons on all your shirts. Love is a jockstrap lined with itching powder. Love is a traffic light that blinks go go go when all the traffic's against you and all the drivers are driving drunk and blindfolded. Love is where you hang your neck. Love is a fast mercury. Love is a slow leak. Love is a bad asbestos." He raised his hands and considered his fingers as though counting them. "Love is a inebriated dove you got to shove."

History Jones was leaning against the wall just behind Prosper, eyes closed, saxophone to his lips. From time to time, as Prosper spoke his slowed and evencoursing lines, History would back them up with scampering runs on his horn, random spasms of sound, cool, sharped, barbed. Uptown he had had his full of blowing hot and now downtown he was blowing cold, letting out a spray of iced yips, trilling up and down the scale in frozen, handcuffed dementias, a most deliberate and programmed cackle, a showering of tinkly precise icicles of sound, delightfully abstract and carefully robbed of rhythm.

They were gathered now at The End, a hangout on Thompson Street between Bleecker and Houston where poetry-against-jazz chantings alternated with flamenco guitars and folk-sings and Congolese drum recitals over the hi-fi. The spectators, those in St. Marks Place sweatshirts and those in Sutton Place cashmere pullovers, leaned low over their espressos and capuccinos as they followed Prosper's elegiac prose poem.

Penelope and Marga were braced against the wall close by Prosper, making curt, draggy, boppish Martha Graham movements with their hips and shoulders in time with Prosper's accents.

"Wonder if that damn Hoyt Fairliss find us here," Penelope said without turning her head.

"Wonder we gone find ourselves here," Marga said to the lamp above her head, a huge red Japanese paper sphere. "Looked everywhere else, about."

Worthington Rivers was seated near the girls in a listing slouch, looking up at Marga with effortful eyes as though trying to see her outlines through consomme. They had smoked several reefers in the cab coming down to The End, Worthington too, under History's tutelage, had taken his share of deep lunging drags and now a marijuana vagueness was seesawing with his alcoholic ferments. He was trying to see Marga, the object of his brimming desires, and frustrating pea-y smog kept getting in the way.

His eyes wandered to the abstract expressionist paintings that lined the walls, paintings that were neither abstract, being very concrete and specific imitations of *other* suddenly fashionable abstractions, nor especially expressive, unless what a lunger does when it is spat with full force against the wall is taken for the last word in eloquence: these "action" canvases all looked like finger dabbings by hyperthyroid children in a progressive school where uncontrolled outpourings, which in other quarters might be taken as a sign that tranquillizers should be administered without delay, were applauded and encouraged as therapeutic, a wholesome release, a bowel movement of the spirit.

Worthington blinked in dissatisfaction. These paintings seemed to be running too, dripping away, like Marga. They appeared to be one more maneuver in a vast plot to convince him that his eyes were rippling and going fast.

"I sure hope that damn Hoyt doesn't catch us," Penelope said. "He's in a bitch and a funky hyena of a mood."

"Like something or body to catch *me*," Marga said. "Take hold where I'm giving way and tell me what kind of a mood to be in and donate the solid shape where I need it."

"Listen to me you atom bombastards," Prosper went on in his unlilting low-keyed way, without comma hesitations. "You with your big mushroom comes. You got to have your U-235 ejaculations with your names written on each and every one.

120

Got to autograph all your uppings and outings and into the oo-ee ecstasies you introduce your armies of uh-uh certified public accountants. You have in our boom-boom times made of love an exercise in bookkeeping and of Whistler's mother a whoremonger. I am here to tell you that with your countdowns and blow-ups and signatures on all the wow you have turned the swim soft state of loving fluxing into a cartridge-nosed space probe with a scared dog in it. Well we are the palace guard of be and am against the sneaky acids of come and go. The with we shall yet put on the throne above the over. The trip is better than the destination and grope cuts goal. Done is the word to be purge-urged from the vocabulary of the seeker. Seek and you do not hide. We will make a rich sideways something of our hours on the un-me looser plane and shit on you and your going somewhere in a hurry and getting there me-first to nowhere. Go fuck yourselves you come-earlies come-alls you followers of maps and crossers of t's. Listen I have been touched by the finger of Hieronymus Bosch outside N. Y. U. on the left groin where I have the mole. You come. We your nemesis your snare your pratfall we just go go go on on on you bomb-dastards. When the fox terrier climbs out of the space missile we have instructed him to bite you all in the soft balls."

They were all listening with rapt, rigid faces.

"Yeah," somebody breathed.

"You *know* it," somebody else said.

"Tell *all* the dogs," a third listener said. "Sharpen their teeth. Get them snarling."

History Jones' fingers were posed on the saxophone keys, waiting for Prosper's next phrase. It did not come.

History opened his eyes. Prosper was standing absolutely still, with *his* eyes closed.

"You the tellingest man," History said.

"I know and I tell," Prosper said without awakening.

"You gone tell them some more?"

"I *told* them. I told them good." Prosper opened his eyes and without looking at History, without focusing on anything in particular, addressing the close air, said, "Now *you* tell them. You dig back to the first dancer words and you tell them right and true."

"Togged like I am? In the threads for shouting out coony and blue-jorous and not speaking with the pulpit tongue?"

Prosper did not hear. He was trying to adjust his eyes so as to make out the faces in the dim room.

"Folks and friends," he said, "we got a real telling man with us. We got History Jones who goes back to the first true tellers and who knows how to put it so you hear. This seeing and talking man here this History he is going to bear us some fine and straight witness he is going to get up here and speak some sharp pieces so you listen."

"I am *a*-tired in these most cooniac and blue-istic garments," History said to the audience. "I can't do me any true out and front telling in such a blue-coon garments, they is for damn-sure too blue-gy and coonerous. I gone take me five and put me on some true-telling items of right Harvard-ashery and then I gone put *you* on, so you wait, you listeners to the straight, I be back and give you the big damn talk-to."

"Do it good," somebody said.

"Speak it out and make them *know it*."

"Tell *all* the people."

"Go, go, go for the corners."

History put his saxophone on a chair and reached for the suit that was hanging from an 1880's copperish wall lamp. He went away to the men's room.

The place buzzed unhurriedly. Some played chess, some read Casablanca papers. Penelope remained against the wall, snapping her fingers and bobbing her head to some tune she alone heard. Marga was making slow-motion movements with her arms as though doing the Australian crawl through buttermilk. Worthington licked the saliva off his lips and reached out with one hand in an apparent effort to take hold boldly of Marga's bold thigh, but it was too far away.

The members of History's band picked their way lazily to the performing area and took seats there, ready to fall in with a held-down background rhythm for their leader's exhortations.

When History came back he was wearing a slimming Madison Avenue gray flannel suit, a fitting and proper one with just the right number of notches and buttons in just the right places. If they had no openings for such a one at B.B.D. & O. it was because of his hue and not his hand-me-ups.

He took his place before the musicians.

The room grew quiet.

"Now you listen to me good," History said. "I gone tell to you the what of the what. This the telling-out time and I gone to spell the *en*-tire kitch and flap-doodle out."

"*In*-form the people," somebody said.

"Go and come back," Prosper Merrymake called without intonation from the side.

"Hear me tell it," History began. "Before I come down here to straighten the customers I was up the town blow-jangling some righteous blow-me blues, making the bluesies for the floozies and boozies who pay up the major cash for a black man's jump-a-jump. Hear me good. I made the mussed-cat rammable and the good red scents go margining in and system Kate, sewer Gate, sizzler Crate do her shim-sham-chemise some too, there by the frayed-car gown to El Horror over in Is-raw-eel where the Joosh peoples got them a new jumping nay-shunning nation. Hear this all the way. Now why the Joosh peoples, after they tote all them bales down all the sinning centuries they want a mother of a state weighing down their backs way down some more, and freighter cars for to haul round more heavy loads, why they make a new life out of the old crating and freighting, hold tight to them bales, want more dry goods and kitchen knives humping on their already too long bent backs, I ain't the one with the answer. Keep your ears on this tight. We don't want no more states and such making mothering pressures on the bruising back because a man got to stand up straight with his totable assets in his pocket and the load on the back just pressure him down with his face to ground and the blues is all you blow when your widest how-rise-sons is down round your feet. Listen to my words as they come. . . ."

They did not understand and yet they did. They sat nailed to their seats listening to History's spiraling statement of his position against loads and the employment of human beings as dray horses and the creation of state-nations as adding to the general load, and since they too were devoted to travelling light, to moving along with no valise other than the skin, they listened with careful ears and nodded, nodded. They thought, many of them, the black man has a heavy load in his blackness, and therefore he is the first authority on the bent back, and therefore we have to listen in humility, and besides, who among us wishes to be a dray horse that is the essence of square?

Behind History as he spoke out his indictment of the cluttered scene in measured risings and fallings, the members of the band plucked and tapped a slow, jolting rhythm. And they began to chant in low voices, incanting a background out of their leader's theme song.

Some air their mews thick,
How feign the tomb,
Some wear their muse sick,
How hee the moo.

"Muse sick and getting sicker!" Prosper cried suddenly from the shadows.

"Hear the death rattle in hims funky throat!" somebody called loudly.

"Kill him dead, History!" somebody else shouted. "Step on his windpipe! Cut his dicty entrails out with those sharp oldtime knives!"

"Mew it louder!" a third person exclaimed. "Preach it out thick till it chokes them all!"

"Now I'm gown tell it all," History said. "You let this here absorb into you good. What we colorated and kinky-coony black folksies got is not no kind of a nation because there already too much damn nation I mean *damn*nation round here and it all rest on our down shoulders so we don't want no more and no big loads of stuff to cart around in them freighter cars and slow the people down. Pay me attention now, you who want to find out. What we of the much color got is no overweight nation but the drum and it weigh plenty damn tons too. We got us a big bass drum and the wide Prouderstands they admire to think that this drum is where we dingerous blue-blowing coonish peoples lives, right there inside the big wailing drum with a big supply of chitterlins, and the only place we want to live. They come up on the stand and beat away at the drum because they think we inside it taking a nap and they want to wake us up so we make more nice damn blues for them. Follow this drift because it go right to the source. They admire to desegregate themselves right up on our bandstand and kick some at the big bass drum where they think we holes up with our musky rats and shimmying sisters and all the big jump. . . ."

He was talking to Worthington, who was sitting with his head and hands hanging, preaching hard at him, but his eyes were all over Penelope.

"That damn rotten Hoyt was nasty as a bedbug tonight," Penelope said, pumping her shoulders in time with the band's pulse.

"I never slept in no bass drum," Marga said, jogging her hips in tempo. "Sleep in a bed like anybody else and hope they won't crowd me too much."

124

The members of the band made their percussive sounds and sang low,

Some wear their muse sick,
How hee the moo. . . .

20

LEWELLYN PERIOD was moving across Bleecker Street on Thompson, heading for his home away from home, The End.

He wore a bulky thick-ribbed sweater without a shirt underneath, wide-waled corduroy pants, canvas shoes. All his clothes were unrelieved black except for the slabs of rubber on the shoes, which were white.

The shiny leather coat which he now wore hanging open, the ends of its heavy belt trailing behind, was black too. He wore this coat in winter and in summer, as though to make the point that though he would not follow any eye-soothing fashion in his appearance he at the same time insisted, shrilled at the top of his voice, that he was opposed to being seen and meant to rebuff all eyes.

His black hair was not cut or combed in any particular way. It was long and it went exactly where it wanted to, not trying to make any case for itself, just going, being itself. This was Lewellyn's whole program for himself and for the world at large except where the world's tendencies and inclinations cut restrictingly across his own, which in his scheme took top priority.

Lewellyn Period refused to wear any of the current costumes as he refused to speak any of the current innercircle tongues. Anything that smelled of a shared uniform or lingo he automatically turned his back on. For example, the hippies in his circle peppered all their choppy, laconic sentences with the word "like," as though they lived in a world not of events but of similitudes, as though there was no reality for them but reminiscence. Lewellyn did not introduce such curves into his language. He spoke a simple, direct, unmannered English. He did not appreciate anything that was in the slightest "like" anything other than itself, he was opposed to comparison because it led inevitably to imitation. He would accept no models for speech or general behavior, believing as

125

he did that all personal plays and ploys should originate and terminate on the home plate of each man's brain matter.

He was so determined to act without precedent and pattern that he had even dropped his last name, first from his vocabulary, then from his thoughts. When he was obliged to give a full name he usually said, Lewellyn, Period, which in time became his legal identification on library cards, driver's licenses, hotel registries and census reports, the comma having gotten lost along the way.

The family name which he had abandoned along with the family bearing it was an earth-moving if not earth-shaking one, a distinguished label in the world of American manufacturers, one which could be found on half the tractors and bulldozers and other earth-movers at work on the unsatisfactory hills and dales of these United States.

Lewellyn was hardly five-six but very stockily built, with banded swells in the pecs and abs that were the result of intensive weightlifting. He worked hard at his regimen of bodybuilding because he understood that powerful muscles were needed to defend his right to be mussed and everywhichway in his life, in keeping with his hair style or, rather, lack of style.

Thanks to his dealings with Prosper Merrymake and such, Lewellyn was aware of the muddier currents on the hip literary scene. For the most part, what he heard from the mouths and pens of the beat esthetes made him laugh.

When a histrionic young poet memorialized the best thinkers of his generation, who it appeared were forever buggering each other in paddy wagons, Lewellyn laughed because it was obvious to him that smart buggerers, devoted buggerers, ones who wanted real elbow room for their buggering exercises, would wise up enough to steer clear of cramping paddy wagons. When an advanced and angry novelist stated his conviction that no American can become a writer until he has had one homosexual relationship and spent a year in jail, Lewellyn doubled up with laughter. The people he had respect for were the ones who were too busy having homosexual experiences to write about it, all kinds, in all directions, and who pursued all the other fringe allurements that attended on and developed from this homosexual adventuring no matter where they led, and stayed meticulously out of jail, where the opportunities for everywhichway experimentation were by definition somewhat limited. Enthusiastic openness was what Lewellyn looked for rather than dogged program. He did not

126

like fads of any sort, including the faddist romanticizing of places of constraint and confinement. The challenge, he felt, was to be everything that suited your fancy, everything, all the time, a cornucopia of fresh possibilities each and every sun-up, and to dodge the coppers' squelching hands.

This, he was ready to admit, took considerable doing. Lewellyn was a very busy man. He had broken some five dozen laws but he had never once been taken in, much less booked, on any charge listed in any statute.

Blackly, bleakly, very much his own stunningly-biceped man, he made his way along Thompson Street toward The End, to listen some to the exclamatory poets and novelists and have a couple more laughs.

Nine pairs of eyes watched him as he came.

These nine young punks from the tenements of Mott Street in Little Italy, some in sweaters, some in blue-and-gold zip-up basketball jackets, were hanging around on a stoop a few doors below Bleecker Street. As they watched his squat, heavy-torsoed frame come their way, they talked:

"Here's a one."

"Shut up, how you know?"

"I smell them a mile away."

"You smell shit. This one looks like he got muscles."

"Sure, this is a one. He's a tough and he's a dearie one."

"You got your eyes up your asshole. This one maybe works around the docks."

"All right, he works on the docks and he's a dearie one. I smell them, I smell them."

"You smell shit. You couldn't smell a dead rat if he was up your nose."

"You got two dead rats up your nose and you go round smelling roses. This is a dearie one and he's mine."

The last speaker got to his feet and moved lazily to the middle of the sidewalk. As Lewellyn came up this young punk took a step to bring him directly in the walker's path and planted his feet wide apart, watching.

Lewellyn stopped.

He made as though to step around the young punk.

The punk moved sideways to bar Lewellyn's path again. Once more his feet were planted wide. His hands went to his hips. He waggled his shoulders in a girlish way, humorously.

The eight young punks on the stoop watched with absorption.

"What do you want?" Lewellyn said.

"To ask you a question, sir," the punk in his way said.

"Ask it."

"Sir, me and my friends here would like to know, sir, are you a dearie one?"

"Am I a what?"

"Are you a fagola, sir? My friends and me, we got to know. Are you a whoopsie? You know? You do those bad and dirty things?"

Lewellyn studied the punk's face. He took his hands out of his pockets. Otherwise there was no alteration in him.

"Is it important for you to know?"

"Very important, sir. My friends and me, we beat up fagolas. We come up here to The Village specially for to knock fagolas around. We punch their eyes inside out and knock their teeth down their throat. We wouldn't like to beat the shit out of you and then find out you wasn't a real darling cutie, sir."

Lewellyn turned his head to see the other young punks on the stoop. They were all standing now. A couple of them had come down the steps and were almost close enough to touch.

"You're right," Lewellyn said. "You should know who you're beating up. You don't want to waste your time on the wrong ones."

"So tell us, do you do those dirty things with other pieces of dirt? Don't keep us in suspense, sir. Me and my friends, we're dying to go to work on you and begin taking you apart."

"I'm sorry," Lewellyn said evenly, "I'm really exceedingly sorry, but I'm afraid I can't let you and your friends take me apart. That goes against all my principles and if you're interested I'll tell you why." The other punks were coming down the stairs now, forming a semi-circle around the two talkers. Lewellyn's hands came up until they were resting easily on his upper abdomen and that was all the movement in him. "The idea I live by, you see, is that there are different parts to me and I'm not truly me, not the full person I was intended to be, unless all these parts are kept together and working. Let me make that a little clearer. Basically there are two main sides to me. My name is Lewellyn, and I like to think of these two sides as, one, Lew, and the other Ellen, I mean, to be me, entirely me, I have to be Lew *and* Ellen, Lew-Ellen, both sides of me, hyphenated. That, by the way, should answer the question it's so important to you to have answered. The answer is, yes, the Ellen side of me does homosexual things, and for a simple reason, it likes to do homosexual things, that's its nature. You see that the matter isn't so simple after all. Because while the Ellen side of me does homosexual things I will not agree to let you call me a homosexual, period, because there is also the Lew side of me and that side likes to do many different kinds of things, some even with girls. Now do you see why I can't let you take me apart? I insist on the right and the capacity to be everything all at once and it would be a violation of myself if I let you put me in one category as one monolithic thing and strip away all the other contrary things in me. What you are interested in doing, of course, is beating up the Ellen side of me, the side you like to think of as doing dirty things with disguised pieces of dirt like yourself, but I regret that I can't let you do that because you can't beat up Ellen without beating up Lew at the same time, since they are so close, which Lew would most certainly not like, and in addition, your approach to this project would mean you would be favoring one part of me over the other, which is a kind of discrimination and a refusal to recognize me in the overall which I can't permit. Follow?"

All nine punks were staring at him with their mouths open. Finally the one confronting Lewellyn turned to the others.

"I told you he was a bugger," he said. "He talks like a goddamn bugger. His lips keep moving and nothing comes out but bugger noise. This one's mine. I saw the dearie one first and he's all mine, see?"

The others nodded, still stunned by Lewellyn's peroration on the whole man and authenticity. The punk who was trying to bait Lewellyn took a wary step in his direction.

Lewellyn looked quickly up and down the street.

"No cops around," he said in almost a friendly way. "Good. That's as it should be."

The punk did not understand.

"You want cops?" he said. "You ain't going to find no cops around here to protect your bugger skin when I begin to rip it off you a foot at a time."

"You don't get my meaning," Lewellyn said. "I'm not afraid of you and the other pieces of dirt you call your friends, I'm afraid of the cops, just the cops. I didn't explain my whole philosophy before. The first half of it is, be and do everything all the time, and the second half is, don't get caught. It's the cops who do the catching. I think we're safe now. You can begin any time you want to."

The punk's mouth was open again, bewilderment was creasing his forehead.

"Listen," he said, with something like a plea in his voice, "listen, just exactly what the shit are you talking about?"

His hesitation was his undoing.

With the speed and grace of an eel, a dartingness and pouncingness nobody had expected from his burly person, Lewellyn had reached for one of the punk's wrists with both hands. He spun the punk around and with one quick judo flip, using his own shoulder and back as a fulcrum, heaved him into the air. The punk landed on the pavement ten feet away with a sickening plop.

The others stood and watched.

Lewellyn was at the punk's side and bending over him almost as he landed. He took hold of the punk, one hand at his throat and the other between his legs, and raised him high over his head like an exercise bell. Carrying the punk in this position, he walked back to where the others were standing still as statues.

"He's your friend?" Lewellyn said. "Then take him. Friends should stick together."

And he threw the body of the half-conscious punk at the eight other punks.

It was like a bowling game with human bodies for ninepins. Under the weight of this flung body, several of the others went down.

Lying, sitting, standing in poses of total confusion, they watched Lewellyn.

"You ever hear of rough trade?" Lewellyn said. "I'm rough trade, very rough. The next one who moves in this direction is going to get both his arms broken."

He stood perfectly still, waiting.

Nobody moved.

He turned and continued on his way without looking back, heading blackly, bleakly, barrelingly, stunningly-muscled toward The End and a couple of laughs.

21

DEAR SAM'L, Omnipresence, Scourge of the Law, Quintessence of Sam'lism. I am obliged to register a protest in the strongest terms. A few minutes ago you kept me from getting arrested and I don't like it, I resent it, I deem it an infringement on my rights. Just as it is my unique competence to decide whether I wish to be locked up in State so it is my competence and mine alone to decide whether I wish to be locked up in the municipal cooler. Let me give you the pertinent details on this outrage. I was going along there baiting Worthington but taking less and less pleasure in it. It had reached the point where I was insulting him more out of habit than conviction and this is not the way great insults are born. The trouble was that I was beginning to see the source of my bad temper with this termite. In point of strict fact I had been wanting to hit him only because so much of him is unavoidably an echo of me. When you want to hit a man because he looks too much like you, like the side of you you'd like to disown, the logical thing to do is drop your belligerence and go home and pound your fingers with a hammer. if hit something you must. I can't in all justice commit violence on good comrade Worthington because circumstances of birth and training have made us uncomfortably, disgustingly, stomach-turningly alike. Worthington is my nausea only because I am so nauseated with myself. So I was taking rather less joy in the harassment of Worthington and I think one reason for this was that I was taking considerable less interest in salvaging the weekend program with Penelope. This is hard to explain but it has in an obscure way something to do with Miss Shoshana. Miss Shoshana has been letting me know with her eyes that she regards me as a demonic violater of borders whereas the civilized and intelligent attitude would be to survey all borders with a truce commissioner's impartial eye. What she doesn't know, of course, is that there is one border, one last and crucial front, that I have never even been able to push toward with Penelope and which I must cross at least once before I can develop any commissioner's impartiality. Except that during this devious night I have begun to wonder if that coveted outpost of outposts can ever be approached in Penelope's company and if, conversely, another traveling companion might not have somewhat greater mobility and, incidentally, travel better. In any case I was getting around to the idea that I might abandon this chase altogether and leave Penelope and Worthington to their own devices, though I sincerely hope that to reach their respective hearts' delights no devices of any sort will be needed. Do not misunderstand. I had not come down to any specific thinking

131

about recruiting another traveling companion in this largely uncharted frontier land. It was just that I was aware of Miss Shoshana's disapproving eye on me and I was considering her stunning legs and other attributes with unqualified approval. My thoughts have not entirely jelled on this subject. At this point I can only report that Miss Shoshana has served to remind me that there is a range of possibilities in this world and that some ladies may approach examination time with a less embattled attitude than others. All this I have to establish to explain my reaction when, after Worthington stove in the bass drum, through a sequence of mishaps I could not in this life make any sense of, he was catapulted into the mitts of a mug who turned out to be an ex-pug and at the moment out for blood. I felt obliged to step in and stop the slaughter. Maybe I had given up the idea of hitting Worthington and maybe I hadn't but I found it intolerable that anybody else should be hitting him. You develop strong instincts of private property about the better punching bags. Well, it was a superior fight that started then and I was more than holding my own, I might even say that I was acquitting myself with some distinction, until the police descended on us in swarms and carted a baker's dozen of us off to the precinct house. What appalls me about this situation is that while I take considerable satisfaction in acquitting myself more or less well I do not in the least care to have the police acquit me too, and for reasons that have to do with you rather than me. That is exactly what has just happened. The sergeant here is strongly inclined to book the ex-pug for creating a disturbance but he has decided to let me go scot free, although my contribution to said disturbance was, I insist, far from negligible. The reason they are so eager to get me out of here, as you may have gathered by now, is that they remembered the name of Samuel Josephus Fairliss and prefer not to book anybody who shares this illustrious name. I protest, Sam'l. Miss Shoshana is at the moment in the ladies' room tidying up and I thought I'd take this opportunity to register my strongest protest. I don't want to go through life being acquitted of charges because of the magic of your illustrious name. I insist on the right to get heaved into the calaboose when the occasion arises without your splendid name coming along to grease all palms and open all doors. If such a basic right can be suspended so cavalierly then where is the famous due process of law the Constitution guarantees us all without regard to degrees of eminence and

Sam'lism? When the first Sam'l affixed his signature to the document in question I am reasonably sure he did not have in mind that the scion of the eleventh Sam'l should be able to contribute notably to a public disturbance three floors below the Waldorf-Astoria without getting pinched along with the other contributors. Of course, neither did he have it in mind that the same scion of the same eleventh Sam'l should have a career automatically set up for him in State in which he will have very little opportunity to make any notable contribution to any significant public disturbances. That we can go into another time. What I wish to take up with you now is the matter of tradition. I think it is safe to say that our family and our whole line reeks with this commodity. Our name is magic, a command to attention and a key to all doors, and what's in a name like ours but tradition? This struck me with especial force tonight as I sat in this police station and saw how the other brawlers were treated as potential Jack the Rippers whereas in all official eyes I was clearly a Little Lord Fauntleroy who had somehow taken the wrong turn on his way to church. My noble heritage seems to go on dancing in the gleam of my eye and the cut of my ear and the jib of my nose no matter how much I try to disguise myself in wop clothes and dull the overall topdog effect with too much booze. It is a peculiar and attention-arresting shadow that always precedes me wherever I go. So let us look into this matter of heritage, at any rate until Miss Shoshana comes out of the bathroom. You used to say that it is something like a relay race that never ends. Now the thing about relay races is that they can go on indefinitely but somebody has to start them. In the beginning there's no packaged and embalmed thing called Tradition whose shivery capitals make people take their hats off and bow their heads in automatic revery. The very first runner in the very first race is in a difficult position. He has to provide his own baton somehow, there's nobody coming up from behind to hand one to him. There isn't even a starting gun to get him moving. He has to fire his *own* gun. After he *makes* it. The stick he starts out carrying is almost anything to hand, anything he's been able to pick up, anything light and homemade. What was the object in the hand of the first runner in the All-American relay? Oh, a sliver of a pine log, a corn stalk, a hoe, a leatherstocking's ramrod or flintlock, something definitely light and useful and close by because there weren't any other kinds of objects around to make a clutter. *You* might say it was something more ephemeral, a rolled-up piece of parchment with some words painstakingly scratched on it, the Declaration of Independence, maybe, or the Bill of Rights, back in the borning days when these things were the echoes of living hungers rather than the easy slogans for political speeches. But the American relay has gone through a lot more than a dozen runners now. In the case of our own clan, eleven, there have been eleven generations of Fairlisses since the first half-literate one signed the papers that made of this disorderly place a republic. Now the thing about this kind of race is that as the baton is passed from runner to runner it tends to go bloated. It swells in too rapid succession into a bathtub, a mansion with many gables, a seat on the Exchange, a black Cadillac, a factory, a bank, a library, heavy things, heavy. By the time it gets down to somebody like me it's not a bit of a log or a simple scroll any more, it's tons of what from many points of view must be regarded as elaborate junk. No longer a token weight, a simple device to establish continuity between one runner and the next, but sacred property to be handled with care. This can have only one effect, to slow the runner down. Especially on a fast track like the American one, where the only tradition, originally, most originally, was to travel light. I have inherited all sorts of estimable goodies from all the Sam'ls and the chief feeling I get is the sensation of being overloaded and therefore a slow starter. Try running a race that way. The race is certainly to the swift, provided they don't carry any important baggage. How much junk did the frontiersman carry? What was he, a foreigner? Yes, he was, in a way. He was a foreigner to baggage. Where is that arms-free-and-swinging-loose part of the American tradition now? But we seem to have gone most solemn. Let me make my point another way. There is the story about the Jewish boy from the Bronx. One day when he's grown up he says to his mother, "Ma, I'm a big boy now, I'm going out to Hollywood to become a famous star and make my fortune and as soon as I get that done I'll call you long distance and tell you you don't have to worry any more." The mother gives him her blessing and he sets out. After a time he calls his mother from Hollywood and says, "Ma, I'm famous, I made a fortune and you don't have to worry any more." The mother says, "Sonny, hang up! This is costing you money!" He says, "All right, ma, I'll hang up, but first I want to tell you that I'm sending you two fine presents, a Picasso and a Jaguar." A week passes. Again the

134

son calls from Hollywood and says, "Well, ma, did you get my presents?" She says, "I only got one, sonny." He says, "Which one was it?" She says, "I don't know." Twenty years of the most expert education have been devoted to the job of making me acutely aware of the differences between Picassos and Jaguars in all their nuances. Fine. All I feel is too stuffed. I have reached the point, this young, where I count off these differences as a form of cultural exercise and wonder if there are not equally important *similarities* that may have gotten overlooked in my circles. The Picasso and the Jaguar are certainly the same in respect of having width and depth, of being heavy, of being expensive, of belonging to the clutter that is slowing everybody up. It would be nice to be able to make a clean sweep and come back to the bare landscape again. Not that I am trying in any sentimental way to set forth here an image of the unencumbered Noble Savage we all allegedly were before Culture got its deadening hands on us. I know that the only things savages are liberally endowed with are lacks and hungers and itches, which mean *more* pitchforks in a life, not less. What I am talking about is only the mythical time when a man could swing his arms and not keep bumping into things. Mythical, yes. It never really was like that. Even stout Cortez finally met up with Indians. So here you see the difference between me and Penelope's hip friends. They think they can slough off the stultifying layers of culture and get back to a fine and free natural state. I share some of their disenchantment with this clutter but I know there's no noble disrobing to get back to. I suppose this makes me a bohemian manque but that may be better than being a bohemian blindfolded. I will tell you one thing that has been disturbing me all along. I somehow can't get rid of the uneasy suspicion that the State Department, and by definition all state departments and proliferations, have as their central function to contribute to the clutter. That will take some more thinking about. I must say, too, that some of Penelope's friends seem to be somewhat confused as to whether they want to be Noble Savages or on-the-double Sam'ls. This Prosper Merrymake has his suits made with *six* buttons on the jacket front and *two* notches in each narrow lapel. What relay race is *he* trying to catch up with? Is that the way back to the loincloth? Not much of the nobility of stripped-down savagery in *his* perspectives, I daresay. He may turn out to have the biggest hunger of all for the full clutter in all its stylish forms. In which case the

135

laugh would really be on Penelope, who is trying very, very hard singlehandedly to burn the entire American landscape over so we can all make that lovely fresh start. Here comes Miss Shoshana, Sam'l. Off on the next leg of the relay. Speaking of legs I must say hers are something to write home about, which, come to think of it, is precisely what I am doing. They don't make legs like that any more. They threw away the mold when they made those legs. She is otherwise painstakingly constructed too but I believe I have already established that. I wish she would not look at me with such total disapproval. We're all after pumps of one sort or another. You will hear from me again, Sam'l. In future do me the courtesy not to interfere when the long but easily dissuaded arm of the law reaches out for me. There are custodies I should be eligible for or this American relay that once was a self-perpetuating sprint has slowed down to a walk and is in danger of petering out altogether in a morass of Picassos and Jaguars. Let us all look for lighter batons to pass down the line. Yours for the race going to the swift, if such there be, if such there ever were, as ever, etc.

"What do you propose we do now?"

"We're going to Greenwich Village."

"Oh, no, Mr. Fairliss. No, definitely. I have a headache and my feet hurt and I have seen enough for one night of strangers giving each other bleeding noses. I am going to take a room in a hotel and sleep."

"Just when the night's getting lit up so interestingly? You can always sleep."

"Where, exactly, in Greenwich Village?"

"West Broadway. This Prosper Merrymake has some sort of studio down there, I just found the address in the phone book."

"What do you hope to accomplish there?"

"Miss Gasharid, I can't let Penelope slip through my fingers just like that, can I? I'm going to find Penelope."

"For what purpose?"

"Don't raise ontological questions at this stage, please. The practical problem is to find her. The metaphysical problem of just what she's good for I'll face later."

"May I suggest something? I do not think you have the slightest interest in Miss Gissings as an entity, a being."

"I have the most profound interest in her as an irritant, an

136

exasperant. All right. What do *you* think I'm up to with the lady?"

"My impression is that you are a tourist who is ashamed of just going here and there and looking. You have to pretend you have a mission."

"You feel Penelope is my mission?"

"I think, I have a certain preliminary suspicion, that you have been trying for a long time to use this girl not as a true partner in your affairs but rather to rescue yourself from extreme unemployment. It does not seem to have worked very well. Now, suddenly, you smell a big, troubled, explosive situation close to hand and you have high hopes to occupy yourself spectacularly with *it*. The fact that Miss Gissings is a component of this situation is, I would take it, accidental and quite irrelevant to your purposes."

"Miss Gasharid, surely you're not against the idea of employment, a busy girl like yourself?"

"I have a certain reservation, as perhaps you can understand, about the types of ersatz employment that can lead a man into subway massacres and police station roundups."

"Miss Gasharid, I make you a solemn promise. If you will come with me, and you must, you simply must, I need your perspective on these events, if you will come along I guarantee, I give you my unqualified word that I will not hit any other human being for the rest of this night, neither friend, foe, nor casual passerby. Come along, do. The Village on a balmy spring night is a lovely place.

"Mr. Fairliss, allow me to ask, are you a whiner?"

"A what?"

"Do you under your elaborate surface of parody projects hold grudges and nurse grievances against the world in general? Is that why you parody the world and its works? The Jews, the Negroes, the Arabs, all have been whiners under their very different surface styles. If one with your many privileges should also turn out to be constructed around a thick core of secret complaints. . . ."

"My complaint is very simple, Miss Gasharid, I don't have enough to keep my hands busy."

"Perhaps it is because what you reach out for and put your hands on has a tendency to drip away."

"Precisely. That is why I must now make a close study of hands and their possibilities. Now, in this connection Penelope's friends, not to mention Penelope herself, are extremely interesting. These people fascinate me because I get the impression that their hands have never closed on any object or enterprise in this world, they strike me as being the idlest hands I've ever encountered, totally and chronically idle, and very much worth studying close up. A busy person like yourself could find much in these lax and unenthusiastic hands to make notes about. Come with me to The Village, Miss Gasharid, we'll track these congenitally retired hands down and study them. Who knows? Among other things we may find confirmation for an old theory of mine, namely, that very clenched fists from exceedingly limp wrists can grow—"

22

THE DRUMMER in History Jones' band, a man of wide-ranging interests who on his nights off audited lectures at N.Y.U. on existentialism and the different schools of Zen, had just finished reciting some of the more arithmetical-anatomical outbursts from one of Jean Genet's man-exclusively-to-man prose works and the room was alive with clapping and cries of "Gone!" and "Too much!" Penelope was applauding louder than anybody though her vivid green eyes seemed to be on an indefinite sabbatical.

Lewellyn regarded her with amusement. He had seen enough of this ready girl in and around The Village to know that she had catapulted herself out of an elite camp very much like his own with her sights set on any and all stumblebum camps that promised to put down the idea of eliteness. What amused him, the anti-belonger, the non-joiner, was her incorrigible taste for camps, her camp-following bent, when there was so much uninhabited open space all about in which you could just take the air and see the sights unconnectedly.

They talked about a program of disaffiliation, these fugitives from the organized centers, all the while they spread hugging tentacles around each other and organized, organized. They enveloped each other in desperate bear hugs and talked about disaffiliation.

Lewellyn did not lean on anybody. He fundamentally did not like to touch anybody. Fugitives, he had found, were funnily enough great leaners and touchers.

Without particularly wanting to bait Penelope, just eager to take advantage of this rare occasion to have some words with her, Lewellyn said, "This Genet is a big queer, isn't he? He's always describing the size and shape of men's organs, like a big queer."

Penelope said, "I don't like that word."

Good. Fine. She was the big understanding liberal about queers. To her queers were Negroes of another sort, an abused minority. Anybody who made a face at queers she took to be a racist and the Ku Klux Klan in disguise.

To Lewellyn, who lent himself to all the queerest doings with queers, this liberalism was one of the true jokes. For one thing, the queers *loved* to be beat up. The mayhem rate among queers was much too high to be explained on the basis of uninvited hostility from the outside world, outsiders were definitely provoked, over and over, to do the beating by the beatees. To administer these beatings to queers was part of Lewellyn's main business in life, he made money out of it and also he rather enjoyed it. He considered the soft liberals' opposition to such roughness toward queers an invasion of *his* right, too, a restraint of rough trade. This wasn't live-and-let-live. The queers only insisted on their right under the Constitution to be beaten up and the rough-trades only insisted on *their* right under the same dispensation to give them these ardently sought-after beatings. Yet these very liberal and very democratic defenders of minorities were forever quoting the Constitution as their source and their validation.

Lewellyn saw that he was going to have a lot of fun with Penelope, this beat who did not understand the true values of beatings.

"Well," he said, smiling in a friendly way, "if you don't like to call them queers let's call them something else, call them ordinaries."

"They're like everybody," Penelope said with her eyes on the move and her voice unstirred, "they need room to breathe. So many of them make wonderful artists."

To Lewellyn, who was no more interested in art and its variegated products than in canasta or petit-point, this was another cliché.

"This Genet spent a lot of time in jail, didn't he?"

"They make it hard for unusual and gifted people, that's the kind of world we live in."

"Come on, Penelope. Let's keep the record straight. This man wasn't locked up because he's an ordinary, they put him

139

behind bars because he broke some laws, he stole things and caused a lot of illegal trouble for people and was stupid enough to get caught. He'd still be in the cooler if some other ordinaries like André Gide, and similar softheaded people like the Paris existentialists, hadn't gotten together and formed a committee and circulated petitions and generally stirred up a lot of pressure to get this particular ordinary out."

"Thank God," Penelope breathed, eyes looking very far away and traveling, "thank God there are still people left to defend the artists and larger souls."

"You're overlooking something." Lewellyn was beginning to enjoy himself hugely. "You're against people being unkind to ordinaries because that's discrimination, right? But you're in favor of getting an ordinary like this Genet out of the jug because he's a sensitive ordinary and a gifted artist. Well, that's a terrible, terrible new kind of discrimination, Penelope, my friend. That's discrimination against all the other thieves and troublemakers who are in jail and who can't get fancy committees set up to spring them because they're *not* ordinaries and *don't* write books and plays. Is there anything in the Constitution or the Rights of Man that says a man should get special treatment over non-ordinaries because he's an ordinary and writes books? If you ask me, *all* the jailbirds, all of them, should be discriminated against, the ordinaries and the non-ordinaries too, for one simple reason, because they were stupid enough to let the cops catch them. That brings us to another question. Caryl Chessman."

The others at the table, History Jones, Prosper Merrymake, Worthington Rivers, Marga Countryman, were not listening, exactly. They were more or less aware that sounds were being made and their eyes were, with varying degrees of retardation, trying to track them to their sources.

"What, what about Caryl Chessman?" Penelope more or less said.

"Some people are developing very soft heads about Caryl Chessman too. He belongs to another minority, the rapists and knife-wielders. They're discriminated against all the time."

"I signed a petition for Caryl Chessman."

"Sure you did. Of course you did. That's what I'm saying. You didn't sign any petitions to save *all* the jailbirds who are in the deathhouses waiting to be executed, which might make some sense, though to my mind not much, because I think anybody who's stupid enough to get nabbed on a capital offense deserves the cyanide pellets. People like you don't spend much time opposing capital punishment as such, though you say those are your grounds for being against the execution of Chessman. No, you agitate and campaign for *Chessman,* one man, and forget about the others in the deathhouses. Why is that? Isn't it because you're not really concerned about capital punishment as such but have a soft spot for this particular rapist and knife-wielder because he's good at reading law books and messing around with the law and has written a couple books of his own, which qualifies him as an artist and therefore a sensitive soul more worthwhile in your eyes than the others who've been convicted for capital offenses, even though you're supposed to be against *all* executions and not just that of Chessman? So aren't you discriminating against all the other jailbirds, and picking out one rapist and knife-wielder to be kind and gentle to, one who needs your coddling a lot *less* than the others, simply because he puts words on paper and looks like some kind of special artist type to you, same as the ordinaries you're soft on?"

Penelope tried to gather her eyes sufficiently to glare.

"I think you're some kind of fascist," she said.

"Sticks and stones, Penelope," Lewellyn, chronic queer, trade, thief, troublemaker, rapist, knife-wielder, said, grinning broadly.

Then he was looking toward the door and his face was sober, almost studious.

The nine young punks from Mott Street, in their sweaters and blue-and-gold basketball jackets, were standing just inside the entrance, surveying the room.

At their van was the punk Lewellyn had roughed up, with a handkerchief tied around his temples. There were stains of blood on it. Farther down, his left cheek looked bruised and discolored.

As soon as they saw Lewellyn they began to thread their way over to his table, the one with the bandage leading the way. This one stopped three feet from Lewellyn and looked at him measuringly.

"You want more?" Lewellyn said in a flat, fact-finding tone.

"This time you're getting it," the punk said. "You're getting plenty, guy."

"I'll have to turn that offer down," Lewellyn said, almost sorry. "Just now I've got no use for anything you're in a position to give, which I don't think is much."

"We didn't come to ask any permission, guy," the punk

141

said. The people at the other tables were quiet and staring, sensing there was bad trouble here. "We're going to give it and you're going to take it. You'll be having a whole lot before we're through with you."

"You're through with me now," Lewellyn said. "You were through before you started. All nine of you handsome brave shits." Without taking his attention from the ringleader of the punks, his eyes remaining in close consultation with this punk's eyes, he addressed the others at his table: "History. Prosp. Back way. I'll hold these punks off. Got to get away because if there's a riot here the cops'll be on us in no time. Get to the studio fast. I'll catch up with you at the studio. Back way, fast." Then his voice came around to the hovering punks: "Well? You've got a present for me? Don't be stingy, friends, bring it out."

The punk with the bandage suddenly had a heavy steel chain in his hand but he never got a chance to use it, it never even got raised for a swing. As Lewellyn finished his last words of taunting invitation to these punks he was heaving to his feet and the table was heaving with him, propelled by his hand flat under the circle of marble and moving fast.

The table top caught the first punk in the chest and flipped him over backwards with such force that when he went down he took several of his friends with him.

Somehow Lewellyn's words had gotten through to History Jones, who alone of the stoned persons in his assemblage was still capable of registering and interpreting an occasional sound from the outside. History was on his feet too, herding the others toward the rear door. While Lewellyn stood and studied the scene his friends trooped toward the door and out, History serving as guide and usher.

"I do believe he's some kind of subversive fascist," Penelope was heard to say, and then the whole party was gone.

By this time the dispersed punks were all on their feet again and trying to reform their ranks, converging inchingly on Lewellyn. Some of the other people in the room had been scattering to get out of their way. Others resented being crowded and shoved and began to shove back. Several fights broke out on the perimeter of the punks' formation, taking a few of them out of the concerted action against Lewellyn.

But the punk with the bandage was still disengaged and edging his way toward Lewellyn, chain raised on the ready in his hand. Two of his friends were flanking him, only a step behind him.

Lewellyn retreated slowly, calculatingly, to the rear wall, close to the door.

His hand went unhurriedly to the pocket of his corduroy pants and when it came out it had a very long, very thin switchblade in it.

There was a clicking sound and the blade of this knife had flicked out to cutting position, a long, thin blade, nine inches from base to tip, and shining.

Lewellyn held the blade some distance away from his stomach, in the best cutting position. He was slightly crouched and his eyes were very alert.

"Any time you're ready," he said easily. "Just understand this, I'm not playing games, when I reach you I go for the deep parts of you. You'll have holes in you where you never dreamed of having holes. Well, gentlemen? Who's first?"

The three punks stood very still. Behind them their friends were busy trading blows and wrestling with some of the disgruntled esthetes in the room.

"You with the chain," Lewellyn said. "Wouldn't you like to step forward and get some air let into your soft parts? Please. You have my special invitation. No? I'll carve your initials on the *inside* of your stomach."

Nobody moved.

"That's too bad," Lewellyn said. "I thought we'd have a nice party and I'd do the carving. Well, if you change your mind, follow me out into the alley. I'd just as soon carve you up there as here. I promise you, I'll carve you like a Thanksgiving turkey. I'll cut you apart so they won't be able to figure out how to put you back together again."

He turned and stepped through the door into the alley.

His friends had taken off from this alley at top speed. He walked, with something of a saunter. The nine-inch blade was close by his side, hanging loose from his ready fingers.

23

THE FIVE Negro musicians were now neither infectious nor jolly. They were gathered in a corner of Prosper Merrymake's loft, making little concentrated flutters and spasms of sound on their instruments, their faces clamped in an Arctic calm. In the passage from the Waldorf railroad siding to this West

Broadway mambo studio they had somehow managed to discard their manic levee grins and now their eyes and mouths were fixed in the schizoid glaze that to them was authenticity and home.

They had discarded their clothes, too. All of them were nude, since it was Prosper Merrymake's one house rule that guests at his at-home's divest themselves of all falsifications, including garments. The musicians were always the first to oblige, on the theory that when music became stripped this clean the people making it ought to be similarly stripped.

They were standing with their heads close together as they blew toward nowhere their scampering, pellmell, rabbity sounds. As they played they passed a lighted reefer from hand to hand and each in his turn took an audible quick sip from it.

Alongside them were three young white men whom they had somehow picked up on their spring down West Third Street, hammering at bongos with various polyrhythms.

Prosper and Penelope, mute, were circling about the middle of the room in a laggard shuffle, their hands resting on each other's shoulders, their bodies slouched and lazing after the music's erratic beat. Prosper took a drag on his reefer and handed it to Penelope. Penelope took a hurried sequence of drags and handed it back, pressing her lips tight together and making choking sounds in her throat.

Alone, and quite mute, Marga was soloing at the far end of the room doing a dance that was part lindy, part mambo, part bop, part the contractile snaking which modern dancers have developed into a high art and which seems to have taken as its model sometimes the labor pains of a Peruvian five-year-old bride and sometimes the peristaltic action of the upper colon. Her eyes were closed. From time to time as she passed the black bed on which Worthington was sitting she would stop before him, hold out her reefer for him to puff, then continue on her jolting, weaving way, her eyes never once coming fully open.

Each time Worthington's slack lips accepted the offered reefer as a baby's might a pacifier. His lungs no longer knew what they were inhaling and his eyes no longer knew what they were seeing. He felt, sensed, rather than saw, that the object of all his battering affections, Marga of the beckoning honey hues, was jogging about spectacularly somewhere in the vicinity, stripped to her sensational honey hues, but his eyes

144

could not quite fix on her and his hands did not have the initiative to reach for her.

He, too, was quiet. History and Prosper had undressed him when they first arrived and he had offered little resistance outside of asking somewhat petulantly what kind of a damn old dance this was anyway, he being under the impression that they were all at a fraternity dance or commencement ball or similar social function.

Worthington sat with his legs pressed together, trying to hide his privates. He was fearfully aroused by the vauge sense of Marga moving about with no clothes on, and arousal was invariably to him a state that had to be hidden from all eyes. This modesty was not a decision deliberately arrived at but rather a mechanical shame reflex that began and ended in his central nervous system. He was there with his legs glued to each other and his eyes went forraging through the room after the sensational Marga. When she stopped to offer him a sip of reefer his lips went through their sucking movements by reflex too, as he pressed his legs closer together.

The musicians made their dry, squeezed sounds, sharp, jagged, rather like the breaking of thin glass, the sputter of tubed neon, the whine of wind tunnels, the pale complaint of oscillographs.

Prosper looked straight up. In the large mirror on the ceiling he saw his own head and Penelope's bobbing slowly as they danced, each with restless matchsticks that were diminished arms and legs somewhere behind it.

"The best dance is upside down," he said.

"I like capuccino coffee the most," Penelope said.

Worthington crossed his ankles in an effort to fuse his legs together and said, tried to say, thought he was saying, "She is a devil, a devil in her honeys, I tell you, and."

History put away his saxophone and crossed the room to where Prosper and Penelope were going in lagged circles. He put his hand on Prosper's shoulder and eased him to one side.

"Bongs," he said. He meant that Prosper was to go away and play the bongos in the corner. He put both hands on Penelope's upper arms. "Us," he said. He meant that he and this girl, this end of a female lady girl with her mattresses of thighs and pillows of boobers, were now going to dance.

She raised her hands to his shoulders that were matted with hair, as was his slab of a body all over, and they began to move, lingeringly, with an after-beat drag.

145

"All right, then," History said.

"If the capuccino is in a mug," Penelope said. "Got to be in a mug with the whipped cream floating."

"She, she, I'll give it to every honey inch of her," Worthington said, tried to say, doing his best to make his knees osmose each other.

The musicians made their jerky sounds of electronic tubes tocking and encephalographs in revolt.

Lewellyn Period was busy in the bathroom. He had dumped out on the flat porcelain top of the toilet's water chamber the small supply of cocaine which he generally carried in the secret compartment he'd had built into the handle of his switchblade for just this purpose. With a razor blade he had divided the white powder into half a dozen tiny piles, lined up in a meticulous row. Now he had a very thin and short glass tube inserted in one nostril and through it he was sniffing up the white piles, one after the other, carefully moving the end of the tube around to pick up every last granule of the friendly and all-therapeutic stuff. His lovingly attended abs and pecs vibrated potently as he inhaled.

He blew delicately over the porcelain work area to disperse whatever traces of powder might be left. He straightened up and put the glass tube away in the medicine cabinet. He took a deep breath and flexed his shoulder muscles. He felt warm and good, prepared for any and all delights. He unlocked the door and went out to join the others.

He was halfway across the room when the sound came at the door. It was a sharp, aggressive knock.

He stopped. Nobody else in the room seemed to be paying any attention to this. In a second the knock came again, more insistent.

A voice from the hallway said, "Come on, I can hear you in there, open up."

Lewellyn went to the door.

"Who is it?" he said. The knife was in his hand and his index finger was poised on the switch button.

"Penelope Gissings' friend Hoyt," the voice said. "I was with her at the Waldorf, we were supposed to meet here."

"Wait a minute," Lewellyn said.

He looked around at the others, thinking. Nobody was paying any mind to the disturbance. His fingers played on the knife handle. He reached for the door, unlocked it and opened it.

Hoyt Fairliss and Shoshana Gasharid stepped inside.

Hoyt's eyes bulged.

"What'd *you* come as?" he said with torrential disgust. "Lady Godiva?"

"I've been to parties as Lady Godiva," Lewellyn said, casually informative. "Certain parties. Other times I've been her escort. Even at parties where there weren't any women I've been sometimes Lady Godiva and sometimes her escort. That answer your question?"

By this time Hoyt and Shoshana had had an opportunity to take in the whole unlikely scene and when they looked toward each other he was sheer nasty and she was frightened, truly frightened.

"There are bad things here," Shoshana said.

"Bad?" Lewellyn said. The creepy hotness was all through him now and he was ready for all things, full of a reaching-ness. "Bad when the lost American dream is given some life? This is where we all become equals again by taking off the medals and decorations and that means everybody can have everybody else, the old lost American grabbag."

"I do not like what is building here," Shoshana said to Hoyt. "I think we should get your friends and go quickly."

"Nobody wants to leave," Lewellyn said. "Just when they've all become the Least Common Denominator, namely, flesh."

Hoyt looked at Lewellyn queerly for a moment, as though wanting to ask a question but unable to quite formulate it, as though there were a curiosity in him that had no pinpointed subject or frame of reference. Then he turned and went over to Worthington, Shoshana close behind him. He took hold of Worthington's shoulder and shook him.

"Put your clothes on, Worth," he said. "We're getting out of here."

"But your glortch on on," Worthington said to his joined ankles.

Hoyt's face was getting red. He looked with exasperation at Worthington, went off toward History and Penelope.

"Penelope," he said loudly, "get your clothes on. Do you hear? Get your clothes, I'm taking you home."

"Without a spoon," Penelope said into History's shoulder. "Because if you stir with a spoon the whipped cream gets mixed up and will not float on the top then."

"Us," History said. He meant that the two of them, himself and Penelope, were going to go on dancing, he and this

147

wild bustigerous everything of a goony redhaired girl, and Hoyt was to go away as quickly as possible.

Marga drifted by with her distinct calves, saying, "I do remember though that his name was Tuna Fish."

Prosper was somewhere behind her, playing the bongos.

Lewellyn had come up behind Hoyt.

"You're not going to get anywhere that way," he said pleasantly. "Come on over to the corner, we'll discuss it." He led the way to the exercise bars, Hoyt and Shoshana following. He turned and regarded Hoyt with growing interest. "What did you say your name was? Hoyt? Hoyt what, or what Hoyt?"

"Hoyt Fairliss. Now look, those two are out of their minds on reefers or something, you've got to help me get them moving before—"

"Ah," Lewellyn said. "Hoyt *Fairliss*. Well, now. How about that."

Now the look of unpinned and unfocused curiosity was back in Hoyt's face. He was examining Lewellyn with care.

"I know you from somewhere," he said, puzzled.

"You certainly do. I *thought* there was something familiar about you when you came in, there's more meat on your face now, of course, but all the same."

"If you would tell me your name."

"Lewellyn. Does that help? Lewellyn."

"Lewellyn. I see. Wait a minute. You don't mean you're, you're not the Lewellyn who—" Hoyt's mouth was stretched wide over the impossibility.

"You've got it, Hoyt." Lewellyn looked pleased. "*That* Lewellyn. That one, exactly."

"I went to Groton with this pig, that's a preparatory school," Hoyt said wonderingly to Shoshana. "He was thrown out in our second year for corrupting six of his classmates."

"Seven," Lewellyn said. "And you're the one who squealed on me, you, Hoyt Fairliss."

"Yes, I squealed on you," Hoyt said. "It was one of the few acts in my life that I can boast I carried out with no ambiguity or second thoughts. One of the few things I'm genuinely proud of is that I turned you in and with no hesitation."

"You may be proud of the incident but I'm heartily ashamed of it," Lewellyn said. "It's one of the few things I'm truly sorry about."

"I'll bet," Hoyt said. "You vermin."

"Please don't misunderstand," Lewellyn said. "This was the

148

first and only time I've ever been caught at anything and *that's* what I'm ashamed of. If I hadn't been caught and thrown out I might have corrupted another, well, let's see, according to the Kinsey figures, maybe another twenty or thirty of my classmates. Maybe, who knows, even including you, you confirmed and programmatic heterosexual, Hoyt Fairliss who loves only the ladies."

"You tried with me, you vermin," Hoyt said with his lips curled. "That was when I decided to turn you in with infinite delight."

"Well, who can tell?" Lewellyn said, close to a smile. "If I'd had more time I would have tried again with you and one time I might not have failed. It's my theory, and it's confirmed every day of my life by what I see and hear, that there's a little bit of everything in everybody. I consider it my mission in life to bring out hidden potentialities and get all kinds of people together in all kinds of ways. I don't know why you should be different from the rest by not having any hidden potentialities."

"You always had potentialities to be a total bedbug," Hoyt said, "and I can't say they were ever hidden."

"Mr. Fairliss," Shoshana said urgently, "I think we should go. I think that very strongly."

"Oh, no, miss," Lewellyn said. "I think you should stay. In fact, I insist that you stay. I would like you both to remove your concealing clothes and join the party and let all your hidden potentialities out. This is a special occasion for me. I haven't had a chance to meet with my friend Hoyt since that day he squealed on me and caused me all that trouble."

"We're going," Hoyt said tightly, "and we're coming back with the police. Since that's the only way to get Penelope and Worthington away from you."

"I'm afraid I can't allow that, Hoyt," Lewellyn said. "I can't have you bringing me and my friends to the attention of the police, really I can't. You turned me in once, true. We can't have any more of that."

Hoyt took a step toward him. Instantly the knife in Lewellyn's hand came up and the blade ticked out.

"Better not, Hoyt," Lewellyn said. "You're bigger but I'm better equipped."

The musicians were blowing all unconcerned, making their eerie, intergalaxial sounds.

"History," Lewellyn called out. "Get the boys over here.

149

Get them right away. This man came to take Penelope away from you just when the party is getting started. You've never been at a real party with Penelope before, have you, History? You don't want this man to take her away just when everything's getting started, do you? Listen to me, History. Get the boys over here."

He was speaking very slowly, distinctly, intently. Somehow his essential meaning got through to History. He stopped dancing with Penelope and went over to the band. In a moment the musicians stopped playing and put their instruments down. In another moment they were all approaching Lewellyn, forming a loose semi-circle behind him.

Hoyt was doing his best to keep Lewellyn and the others within range of his eyes. But History kept edging away, moving to one side.

Hoyt made as though to go for him, to stop him. Before he had completed his first step Lewellyn was close to him, making swiping movements in the air with his long blade.

"Right there, Hoyt," he said. "No more moves, please."

Somewhere on the far side of the room Prosper was still fingering the bongos and Worthington was slouched on the bed studying his bunched-up toes.

"I was a good host," Lewellyn said to his friends, watching Hoyt. "I invited these people to take their clothes off and join the party, but no. All they want to do is take Penelope away and spoil the party. You know we can't have any party without Penelope. Penelope *is* the party. It's the first time she's joined us in our little evenings at home and we can't let such a special occasion be broken up, now can we. We're just going to have to stop these people from trying to bust up our party by taking away the whole juicy party, namely, Penelope."

Now it was Shoshana who stepped forward. Her eyes were on fire.

"No more, miss," Lewellyn said, bending more at the knees, "not if you want to keep your good looks, miss."

"I have seen your kind," Shoshana said, her voice vibrant. "Oh, yes, many times. You pretend to be something but you are nothing, you do not exist on your own. The proof is that you have to crawl all the time into other people's lives with your knives and guns and create commotions there and it is all because when you stay in your own backyard you feel nothing alive. You have a little bit of everything in you, yes, everything that is dead and stagnant. When you look in the mirror you see fog with no shape. You are a great hero with your knives and your dead insides. I spit on dead ones like you."

And she was actually taking another step forward, her lips poised to spit into Lewellyn's face, when Hoyt got a grip on her arm.

"No use," he said. "He—"

That was as far as he got. History Jones had by this time slipped away to the other side of the room and picked up there a small iron dumbbell of the sort used for bicep building, he was now standing directly behind Hoyt, aiming one end of this weight carefully at Hoyt's head.

"Look!" Shoshana screamed. "There—"

A thud as the bell connected with Hoyt's skull. Another, softer thud as his heavy body landed on the floor.

24

SAMUEL. Help me. Help me I beg you. I can't move. Hurt, too. My head hurts. They, History, hit me with something. Hit me hard. When I came to I was tied up to these exercise bars. Standing here with hands over head tied to bars and ankles tied too. Handkerchief or something in mouth, can't talk. Head hurts something terrible. Miss Shoshana there inches away on Hardoy chair. Tied hand and foot to chair. Gag in mouth too. Her eyes keep going to mine and mine to hers. Horror in hers and I suppose in mine too. Samuel you've got to do something. There is a horror in this place and I can't move. They are committing horrors on Penelope and I can't move. Just help me get my hands loose Samuel. I ask no more of you. Help me with my hands. They are holding Penelope down on the bed and taking turns. Four of them holding her hands and feet while they take turns. She's not struggling any more. She fought when History went at her but that was the first time and now it's the fourth or fifth and she's not fighting any more. It is a total horror and the worst horror is that she is lying there very quiet now and no more fight in her. She has even stopped making those low sounds in her throat. I thought I was going to go out of my mind when she was still fighting and making those sounds because it sounded to me like she was saying, Hoyt, help, Hoyt, help, those words over and over without her lips moving. Now

151

there are no sounds and that is worse still. It began when Lewellyn told the musicians to hold Penelope down on the bed and came over to put his face next to mine and deliver the prologue for the horror. He likes best the role of master of ceremonies at all obscenities he can organize I think. Help me with my hands Samuel. Please. He put his face close and said, "She lives in a universe of Negroes, you know. Her heart bleeds for all kinds of Negroes, Genets, Chessmans, Negroes of all types, abused good souls and bold spirits. She comes from all the whiteness and she's drawn to all the blackness, which she equates with goodness and the free life. Well, she ought to do more than dance with the scorned ones and sign petitions for the trapped ones. She's got to show more solidarity than that. If she's for better treatment of all the way-out people I think she ought to desegregate more on her own and really treat them a little. Actually I think she likes them only because they're cut off from everything with all doors closed to them. That way *she* can come to *them* and only when *she* wants it. If they were free to come and go and mixing with her kind so they could look *her* up from time to time on *her* home grounds she wouldn't like it half as much. I think we'll arrange a little desegregation and solidarity for her now. History will give her her full membership in the delicious pariah class." He turned away and called, "History, you've been wanting some of that fine white meat, haven't you, friend? All right, then. There's the whole spread, it's a banquet, help yourself, my friend. Good appetite. Go. I'm giving you my little sister on a silver platter. I want to share everything with you because I'm the truest desegregationist and communal man around here, History. That's right, friend. Yes. All yours." That was when History began to understand and went over to Penelope. Lewellyn must have read my thoughts in my eyes because as he watched History going to Penelope and then at Penelope, she making those deep sounds in her throat and trying to get her hands and feet free, he said to me, "You should learn something from this, Hoyt. There are the ones who give the orders and there are the ones who carry out the orders. The dynamos and the sleepwalkers, you might say. I'm the pushbutton in the lives of these unflexed people. Our friends here aren't capable of setting anything in motion. That's what beat means, really. Disaffiliation means to cut loose from all the initiating causes in the world and to join up with the willy-nilly effects. They're drifters and floaters and gliders, these people. They'll go along with whatever currents come their way. It needs somebody like me to provide the currents, an initiator. I'm glad to be of service because I like to see things happen and I enjoy making them happen. I'm for as many things happening as fast as possible, all the time. I blow the whistle and they begin to dance. Something, eh? The way they need a push to get started and keep going just out of inertia." History was taking her, taking her. She was fighting hard and making noises. Lewellyn said to me, watching, "You shouldn't have turned me in in the good name of heterosexuality, Hoyt, really, you shouldn't have. There. Take a good look at your lovely heterosexuality. It's a ridiculous thing to make a program of, isn't it, now? All programs are a little ridiculous. I'm for a more open and improvisational style." His eyes were very bright. They're brighter still now. The other musicians are finishing with her and he's with them, watching. There's nothing much to watch for though because she's very still now and corpselike almost. If only you'd help me get my hands back, Samuel. I could take care of everything if I had my hands. The hi-fi is on loud. It's playing a record of "How High the Moon." History Jones is singing, I think. Prosper and Marga are dancing delicately and with high style to the music, round and round. My hands, God, damn, it, my hands. Miss Shoshana is trying not to look at me and I'm trying not to look at her. There is nothing to do with our eyes, nothing. There are tears in her eyes now but I think they're tears of rage. Mine are getting wet too. I think I will close my eyes while I keep working my wrists around in the ropes and try not to see and not to think of this supreme dirt. I will think of something else. Lids closed fast. Samuel, do you remember the day we went to visit your old college friend at the Brookhaven labs? Remember what he looked like in his anti-radiation monkey suit, cut off from the beakers and reagents by several feet of lead and watching everything through feet of glass? Manipulating from his safe hiding place the mechanical arms and fingers inside the compartment, putting reagents together and separating them without ever touching anything himself? I took away two words from that meeting. Insulate and manipulate. That was when I began to understand what you were up to with State, at Yalta, with Alger Hiss at San Francisco setting up the U.N., what you're up to now with your international law. You don't have contact with far-off people. You never learned their languages. Out there it's all contamination. You put walls of lead and glass between you and them and then *pretend* you're talking to them, all the while you cleverly, agilely, from your safe hiding place, move the mechanical fingers around, regrouping those others, shifting them, turning them this way and that, making them dance to your tune. Now I'm not sure I want to become a professional diplomat-manipulator. It would be nice to cultivate a different side of myself, if any trace of it is there, whatever talent I may have for making contact with the strange natives of those contaminated places on the other side of all the glass and lead, for talking to them in their own languages, for offering them something more substantial than beads and trinkets, sometiing that might even help to clean the bilharziasis trematodes out of their intestines. Wear as little insulation as possible and cut down the manipulation to the minimum. I have been spending this night with a group of people who are totally insulated one against the other and in lieu of truly talking to each other can only reach out with long mechanical arms to manipulate one another. This is the horror of tonight because these men are taking Penelope through several feet of glass and lead, *their* insulation and *her* insulation too, and the only way they can touch is with mechanical arms. Exactly as it was between her and me these two years past. A breakthrough is needed, Samuel. A genuine breakthrough. The carapaces have for once to be cracked off and a simpler atmosphere created in which direct, living touch is again possible, something to negate the Lewellyn overseeing. The worse horror here tonight is not that they are taking Penelope but that they are taking her across vacuums, across light years, with an engrossed Lewellyn M.C.ing from his ice-capped mountain top. No use, Samuel. I simply can't get my hands loose even by an inch. Oh, my head hurts. I am all ache and there is a nausea in me too big to contain. My eyes are flooded now. I appear to be really crying. Tears of rage, probably. Commotion out there. Have to look again. Lids up. Oh, Jesus. Oh, my, Jesus. They are lifting Worthington out of the chair they dumped him in. Carrying him across the room. Lewellyn saying to him, "She's dark and she's lovely and she's yours, she's a lovely dark dancing lady," he coming back from his sprawl and coma, "Gentlemen, my name is, gentlemen, you will be good enough to," Lewellyn looking my way and saying with a smile, "Beacon Hill and Grosse Point, inspired coupling, marriage made in the Dow-Jones heaven, wouldn't you say, Hoyt?" If I could get my hands on that one's neck. I can't get free, I can't. Jesus, Samuel. Dear Jesus. She is. She—

Gentlemen I must insist that you set me down immediately. Ah. Gentlemen my full name is Worthington Rivers the Third and if you would do me the courtesy to release me without delay I am fully capable I assure you of handling this matter on my own. Ah. Yes gentlemen I am from Grosse Point we have quite a few acres there and the house though not ostentatious does have thirty-three rooms and I assure you that this is a matter I can and will take care of single-handed. Ah. Gentlemen it is for the most part electrical and hydraulic equipment that my father produces in quantity and that I will be producing with him once I finish my graduate studies and I wish you to rest assured that I am fully equipped to carry through projects on my own and without several pairs of hands holding to various portions of my anatomy and conducting me here and there. Ah. I don't believe that we have been formally introduced and I consider that you are taking undue liberties with my person and ah gentlemen you must you really must put me down this ah instant. Ah but she is honey all through and all her honey is mine ah is mine. Ah I wish that I could see her face but there seems to be cheesecloth over both my eyes but in any case she is a thing of rare honey. Ah gentlemen. Wait. Gentlemen. Something is decidedly wrong. Oh, gentlemen, ah, gentlemen, I urge you, put me down immediately, something is infernally wrong. Gentlemen this is not supposed to be happening. I must state my objections in the strongest terms gentlemen. I know that I am screaming but she is not supposed to be screaming blackly and rising up this way and blackly blackly erupting gentlemen please gentlemen I insist gentlemen do something this is impossible I will die from her black sounds—

It was just then that Shoshana managed to get her left hand disengaged. Her eyes darted to Hoyt's to blink an arresting semaphore while she wiggled the hand violently behind her back in hope that he would see it.

He did. His own eyes widened.

"Guh," he said through the gag in his mouth. "Ocket. Ocket. Guh, ocket."

Nobody paid any attention to them. Worthington was on his knees at the foot of the bed, head buried in arms, making keening dips and saying in the accents of prayer, "But your glortch on." Penelope was flat on her back, rolling from side

155

to side, saying something that might have been, "Want self back, self back." Lewellyn and History and the musicians were standing around the bed in studious poses. At the other end of the room Prosper and Marga were still doing their slow angular dance to the tune of "How High the Moon."

Hoyt began to indicate wildly with his head and eyes, trying to direct Shoshana's attention to a spot down a ways and very slightly to his left. He said, "Ocket, ocket, guh."

It finally dawned on her that he was saying something about his pocket, presumably about his left jacket pocket. Maybe that there was something in his pocket.

Checking to make sure that nobody noticed, she brought her free hand forward and slipped it into his jacket pocket.

Her fingers closed on something hard.

She brought it out.

It was a gun, a peculiar-looking kind of gun.

He had been telling her about the gun in his pocket.

Hoyt was nodding furiously at her and blinking.

She knew what to do now. Nobody had to tell her. She laid the gun away on the chair under her thigh and with her free hand began to work at the ropes still holding her. In a moment she had her other hand free, in another moment, her feet. Nobody saw.

Lewellyn was saying to the others around him, "You see how blood is thicker than water? When two representatives of the ruling classes meet and join forces, join together all their forces, there's quite an explosion. Of course, they don't always recognize each other. He thought he was having a nice roll with honey-colored Marga and she probably thought she was getting a fast one, a very fast one, from the hairy saxophone player. Still, blood will tell. You outside people can't reach her that deep way from across the tracks and social barricades—"

Shoshana was on her feet and shouting, "You there! The short one! Yes, you, you come over here!"

All the faces turned to her and set with urgent scholarship.

Lewellyn looked attentively at the gun in her hand.

"Now, now," he said placatingly. "What's all this? Just take it easy, miss."

His hand began to go lazily, almost absentmindedly, as though making a carefree gesture, toward the nearby side table. His switchblade was lying there.

The gun in Shoshana's hand rose higher, aimed at him.

"Oh, no, no such thing," she said. "Absolutely not. You

156

move for that knife and it will be the last move you make on this earth." She meant it. "You come over here," she said. "Without delay. The others stand still."

Lewellyn began to walk her way. She backed off to a safe distance.

"That will do," she said. "Turn to the wall, please." Lewellyn turned to the wall. "Untie Mr. Fairliss." Lewellyn reached up and began to untie Mr. Fairliss.

As soon as Hoyt was liberated from the ropes and the gag he said to Shoshana, "Keep the gun on him. And watch the others. I'm going to settle some scores with this one. If anybody makes a move in any direction you know what to do."

"I will," Shoshana said. "I will be most happy to."

"Now," Hoyt said. "You, comrade from the ruling classes, friend Lewellyn." He was talking so slowly that there was a comma after every word. "Blood will tell? Really? Let's get some of your blood out in the open and look at it close up and see just what it tells."

Lewellyn was backed against the wall, standing rigid. Hoyt took a step toward him.

"You like to make everything happen?" Hoyt said into his face. "Make something happen. I invite you. Make something happen that will prevent you from doing all the bleeding I've got planned for you."

Hoyt thought, I've been on this senseless rampage this past day and night, I've been snarling and clawing and taking potshots at all kinds of people and what a bore, what a bore, flexing the muscles really isn't for me, the hitting doesn't do any good, and thinking that, bored, far past emotion, he raised his fist and let it go like a battering ram down on Lewellyn's skull. Thinking, I'm tired of hitting people, hitting is something entirely remote from me and my true projects in this life, what I'd really like right now is to be sitting somewhere in the sun reading a good book on bilharziasis or the Dead Sea scrolls or looking at Miss Shoshana's handsome Beirut legs, with his head full of that thought, he let his fist go like a sledgehammer in Lewellyn's face. Thinking, I've gone through an important transition this night, I was always addicted to big breasts but now I'm suddenly thinking of legs, I'm thinking of Miss Shoshana's great legs, his head bursting with this important thought, he slapped Lewellyn's left cheek with all his might, then the right cheek.

Lewellyn slumped against the wall. He was not out entirely but neither was he alert.

Shoshana came forward and Hoyt reached to take the gun from her. She got a grip on Lewellyn's neck with both hands and shook him until his eyes flipped open.

"The worst thing about you," she said, "is that you are impotent. The others at least participated, at your urging, and you only watched. You are the kind who will never know what it feels like to have a commotion of your own, you can only live through other people's commotions. You are impotent and that is why you make a big philosophy out of being free to do everything and you will never be able to do or feel anything because you are impotent and the vilest thing of all, a watcher, and all your glorious freedom is to watch. On any and all borders, naturally, the filthier the better. Where scum such as you can take up membership in all the filthy commotions not your own."

She spat into his face with all vigor.

The telephone was lying on the floor a short distance away. Hoyt went to get it. He picked it up and dialed one digit.

"I'm turning you in again, Lewellyn," he said. "I'm turning all of you in. All the lively things you like to make happen you'll have to make happen for the next few years in a jail cell."

He listened. Then he said into the receiver, "Operator, this is an emergency. Give me the police. . . ."

It took only minutes for the first squad car to arrive. When the police came in Hoyt still had the gun trained on Lewellyn, who was still leaning groggily against the wall.

For the first time this night History Jones was shocked into impeccable English. He began to say very rapidly: "You must not misread the situation here, gentlemen. There is nothing in the least or slightest amiss here because although the signs might superficially seem to indicate that there have been certain excesses and indulgences here this evening, certain somewhat wayward practices, that is far from being the case, actually what we have here is a calisthenics class for all-around bodybuilding and we meet here every Saturday, a few of us who are interested in improving the stance and body tone, merely for purposes of—"

Hoyt said to Shoshana, "Watch this, it's the best kind of joke that happens on the worst borders," and he aimed the gun at Lewellyn's face and squeezed the trigger.

A long stream of vodka squirted into Lewellyn's astonished, battered eye.

Shoshana looked at Hoyt in absolute amazement.

Hoyt went to the bed and leaned down to put his hands on Penelope's shoulders.

He said, "It's all right, Penny, it's all over."

She said far down in her throat, her lips not moving, "Want self back, want myself back, I want myself back."

"It's done, Penny," he said. "It's over, no more."

When the explanations had been made and the police were beginning to round these people up, Worthington was still going on about the necessity to put the glortch on, Prosper and Marga were still dancing dreamily, the hi-fi was still playing,

How hee the moo.

They, just the two of them, began to circle Washington Square, round and round, he limping a little.

It had rained during the night. The pavements were still wet, the air was freshened. They drew in long gulps of the clean and cleansing air, and they talked.

This night's featured lovers, Penelope and Worthington, who had become one without knowing it, were in good hands: she safe in a private room at St. Vincent's, her raving demands for the return of herself momentarily stilled by heavy sedation; he tucked away and fast asleep in a high suite at the Lower Fifth Avenue Hotel, no doubt dreaming of women like bombs, exploding women, women like shrapnel, all in a swirl of menacing blackness; and History Jones and Prosper Merrymake and Lew-Ellen Earth-Mover with their associates and followers were gathered at the Charles Street precinct house, Marga most likely making Martha Graham movements in her continuing attempt to say what was too heavy on her mind with her body, the others doing their best to convey to the night-tour detectives their philosophy of the gangshag as the Twentieth Century All-American communal supper; though maybe Lew-Ellen Nameless was saying nothing, since his one idea was to be everything and not get caught and this philosophy was in both halves at the moment beside the point, there was no earth of any type to be moved by such as he.

Once as they passed a newsstand on Sixth Avenue Hoyt thought to buy a morning paper. He turned to the sports page and when he read there the news that yesterday afternoon, nineteen eons and a blink ago, the Yale crew had scored a dramatic upset and won the Goldthwaite Cup at Derby, he nodded as though he had learned something unutterably profound, then dropped the paper in a trash basket. On top of it he laid the water pistol he had bought in Derby when he was momentarily Worthington Rivers, saying to himself more than to Shoshana, "And now, real projects."

When the sun came lumbering up with its pimp shoulders over the N.Y.U. administration building, in the shadow of which Prosper Merrymake had once been touched by Hieronymus Bosch on the left groin, these two were still walking and talking.

25

"AM I A MAN of my word? I said I'd take you to some interesting borders."

"You overkept your promise. We passed all the borders and kept going."

"Passed the jokes too?"

"Not all. The most ghastly we kept in sight."

"Namely?"

"Those wretched shrunken excuses for men did not mean to hit Penelope. She was only a gangway."

"For her own gang."

"Who hits so hard as the gang turning on its own? But they were only striking at themselves *via* Penelope."

"She took quite a beating."

"Because of what she is? No, that only explains how she happened to be within reach. Because of what those people are *not*, not fully, what they'd like to be, have to be, insist on being because they don't know what else to be, despair of being."

"I see your meaning. You're saying these hipsters want to be like us allegedly inside people and can't quite make it? So when they hit at us it's because we're more them than they are?"

"You are in their eyes a mirror image that outdoes them."

"We add the finishing touches to them? That's what you're getting at?"

"Precisely that. Exactly that. One of the really interesting borders, of course, is that between the blurred man before the mirror and the sharp-outlined man he thinks he sees *in* the mirror. Knowing he himself is so much fuzz."

"Don't these wretches notice that a lot of us mirror dwellers keep losing our outlines too? *Changing* them, anyway? Slipping in and out of Roman pimp suits?"

"These people are not trained to distinguish between degrees of Worthington. All they see in the mirror is a horde of Worthingtons with skins equally tight and contoured. This makes them gnash their teeth. They want tight and admired skins too."

"You know, we used to have revolutionaries around here, rebels, true bohemians, people who were so busy scrambling for the exits in their hurry to get the hell out of the establishment that they *never* looked back, never saw *any* visions in *any* mirrors. *These* apprentice bums aren't *trying* to get out."

"Far from it. They took momentary cover on the outside and now are standing around there hoping some kind soul will let them *in.*"

"How do *you* know so much about them?"

"The European and Middle Eastern press is full of their doings. I have read some of their poems and novels."

"Isn't the beat world a little remote from your main interests?"

"Oh, no. Certainly not. My field of study is D. P.'s. It makes no difference whether they were pushed out or went of their own accord, people on the edges of things all act pretty much alike. I am a student of the way in which D. P.'s simultaneously walk away and look back. Or stand in one spot and stare at their feet."

"Well, you've got a point about *tonight's* D. P.'s. To them society is one big walled fortress, a stockade. They're hoping to storm it without firing a shot or taking up a battering ram."

"I know these border people and their tribal ways. They circle the big stockade in a slow shuffle and dream of the nice inside. Not as a target for bombs, only as a place to take up residence."

"Their complaint is that the fortress will not collapse merely through the magic of their presence."

"Once in a while a particularly bold one will shake his fist and make a pouty face. Beyond this, they have no weapons."

"They circle, and they recite angry free verse and play limp saxophones, waiting for the walls to melt away."

"Never suspecting that for this is needed a *Communist Manifesto* or at the very least a Zola's *J'accuse,* plus some very strong Jericho trumpets. The true stormers of walls, being responsible people, must also have in their hip pockets careful blueprints for electrification and low-cost housing and an exact program for measures against all the bilharziasis worms. This is a test of their seriousness, to show they are looking for more than a place to sleep and keep dry and strike poses before a large audience. Those who are given to recitations and musicales seldom can meet this test. They know more about sprung rhythms and flatted fifths than about stringing electric lines and killing bad trematodes. The suspicion arises that they do not truly wish to overhaul the establishment so much as to find themselves a nice address there."

"Listen, maybe you ought to organize a Development Corporation for these hipster tribes. Bring some sanitation and light into *their* dark camp lives while they're hanging around."

"It would not work. They have no fondness for their present camping grounds and dream only of moving. Not on. In."

"You know, you're right. Sure. Once in a while, when they've inhaled enough marijuana bravery or shot in enough cocaine audacity, these outsiders, just because they are dying to be insiders, will take a poke at some true insider who wanders their way. For his two-way mobility, the insideness he can't lose, the keys to all desired kingdoms which are built into his fingers."

"We agree, then? These are Arabs who desire not only to move into the Jews' homes but also to *become* Jews? This is sufficient motive to kill and maim all Jews within reach, and to steal the chickens of those *not* within reach."

"Revolutionaries complain about the chains put on them by orthodox life and only want to slip out of them and get away. These miniature people who pose as angry are really only hungry, they have a hunger for all the chains of orthodoxy."

"But the doors to the inside, to the lovely chains, do not open. So they turn their attention to a Penelope simply because she is handy. She is one elite door they can force open when all the others remain shut tight against them. It gives them the illusion that they are up to something and moving ahead, that is, inward. Of course, why the Penelopes should offer themselves for such breaking and entering rituals is another matter. Also, why the Lewellyns should bother to organize and supervise them."

"Take this a step further. Cut off from the main group, not so much by official edict as by their own doing, by their original panicky gravitation to the camps of the bearded and sandaled and dungareed and unbothered on the outskirts, they don't wander off into the open spaces one by one as true rebels would, rather, they form their own *out* groups. They are so orthodox that they have to do everything, even their rejection of groups, *in* groups, no doubt rehearsing for the group life they'll have on the inside once they get in. All projects are group projects. Love becomes a gangshag."

"Sometimes when I went skiing in the mountains in Sweden I used to see the gangster wolves. Do you know why wolves travel and hunt in teams? Not because they are so ferocious. Because under the snarls and showey teeth they are cowards, afraid of everything."

"It's lonely there on the outside of everything, where the self-made rejects roam. They huddle together for warmth and reassurance. They never engage the true enemy."

"How could they? If they saw him they would not even recognize him, he looks exactly like them, like what they are secretly trying to look like only more so."

"But sometimes, sometimes they're able to draw a blind stray away from the central pack. A Penelope."

"Then they pounce on her all together, to show how brave they are. But it must be a joint venture, because they are afraid in their impotence to move as individuals."

"These poets and musicians of the sacred individual life, who write bumpy odes to the proud me and make up jazz homages to the unfettered condition. Walt Whitman, all you proud openers of roads, what have you wrought?"

"This gangshag style shows, does it not, that they are only trying to outdo the orthodox in their orthodoxies? This is only another togetherness. Of the terrified."

"That's the big joke, all right. Penelope, running at top speed from the orthodox world, was the victim of the most orthodox people around, people exquisitely trained for the pack life of the large herd, whose one beef is that the pack won't invite them in despite all their qualifications."

"And they are so blind, they see Penelope not for the stray she really is but as the one in charge of handing out the engraved invitations, the mistress of all inside ceremonies. This was not sex they were after. It was retribution for being left off all the insiders' guest lists when they are ideal candidates for all central doings."

"This has implications, Miss Shoshana. You might say that on this, as on all borders, there are many dramatic cases of mistaken identity."

"My father, for one. You, for another."

"What border am I on?"

"The very interesting one between Mr. J. Press and Signore

163

Giacomo D'Amici, if I remember the names you mentioned. It is only an extension of the border we have been talking about. You have your own private Jews. Whom you spy on from a distance."

"Granted. Penelope's another case in point. The worst thing is that nobody recognized her. She was outwardbound, feverishly looking for all the doors that would lead her irrevocably out. She had a terrible thirst for the outskirts. Lewellyn too. He invents outskirts. And Prosper and his gang are *inward*-bound, traveling toward the center or wanting to, dreaming of rejoining the larger pack because their small and excluded one doesn't give them enough warmth."

"Somewhere on the far social margins the outward-bound and the inward-bound are fated to meet."

"That's the whole point, right? Because they happen to find themselves in the same peripheral place at the same moment, they both assume they're facing and heading in the same way. It's not so. They're moving in opposite directions, their paths just momentarily cross. If one sees a mirror image of himself, his imagined, finished self, in the other, a perfect, undiluted, 100-percent pure image, it's only because each is wearing the costume of the other and also talking the other's language."

"What do the centrifugal and centripetal have in common except compulsiveness?"

"Sharing momentary quarters on the outskirts of town doesn't make for identity between inners and outers, no."

"You know, there is a very big lesson in this."

"About the geography of disenchantment?"

"Also about work. The first reason for working hard during the day is to tire yourself out so that you will fall into bed at an early hour and so avoid nights like this one. The night becomes a tarantula to those who do no useful work during the day, who simply move compulsively to and fro."

"I can vouch for that. Since I've been writing my dissertation I've begun to look for the tarantulas each time the sun goes down. I go to one minute and fro the next. That's the story of my life, lately."

"May I ask you something? Why do you always refer to the Middle East and foreign policy as though you had lockjaw and your tongue were missing?"

"It is a cornerstone of my political philosophy, Miss Shoshana. Let me put it this way. When the powers, those on the American side as well as those on the Russian side, lay plans for this or that Aswan dam without taking this or that bilharziasis fluke into account, they are not thinking of a real

164

place called the Middle East and they are certainly not formulating a true foreign policy for anybody. They are children playing children's games, and what they're up to has to be discussed in the accents and with the vocabularies of childhood. The powers, all the powers, are playing in a nursery yard that has to be called the Miwwel Eatht, and what they're playing is a game of skin-the-cat that properly should be referred to as Fowwin Powithy. This is a technical question of nomenclature, but important."

"Your political philosophy is that developments should be talked about with the names and the accents suited to their maturity levels?"

"My meaning, essentially, is that in politics as in all fields certain matters should be discussed in adolescent lisps, others should be described in the thin sopranos of the seven-year-old, and still others, a surprising number of them, have to be referred to exclusively in gurgles and coos. I wanted to write my dissertation around this theme but my professors in the department of political science did not consider it a fruitful line of inquiry. This is why, since I started work on the dissertation, I've been looking around for the tarantulas every sundown. Too much of me is chronically unemployed."

"I begin truly to see. Yes, the secret is to work hard and with results. To see dams taking shape and mud huts lighting up. The more illumination there is, the easier it is to close the eyes and sleep peacefully. Tarantulas and all crawlers avoid the light."

"Tonight, Miss Shoshana, we had an object lesson in what happens to those without gainful employment to truly mobilize the self."

"Yes. Those who make big noises and discuss capital-letter subjects without once considering the many small bilharziasis worms in life."

"I want to go back to your earlier remarks on the gangshag, if I may. I feel it is a theme worth exploring. May I ask what are your views on love?"

"I suspect it is a thing you can recognize when you have it, feel it, but I know no words to hold it. I suppose, whatever it is, it must when it has some mature quality have something in common with the feeling which led my father to organize his energies against the bilharziasis worm."

"I propose we approach it in this light: what is the relationship between the gangshag and genuine love-making?"

"Ask first: what is the relationship between the hangout and the true community?"

165

"Consider that I have asked."

"It is, I would say, a matter of glue. In the hangout, where people drift together simply to have a roof over their heads and some momentary warmth, no matter in which direction they are compulsively traveling, all they can have in common is a geographic thing, location. There is no subtle glue to bind them together and make them feel as one. In the true community, on the other hand, people feel themselves facing the same way and held in a common matrix, up to their hips, at least."

"Your point is that the presence or absence of this matrix affects their methods of lovemaking?"

"You cannot make true love unless you feel something in common with the other person, some glue binding the two together, at least to the hips. In the hangout, where your partner is a perfect stranger, you make not love but war, real war or mock war, which is wuv, not love."

"These overgrown piglets we saw tonight were making war?"

"On themselves, as I have said. On all reminders of their unsprouted selves. Penelope, who is just such a reminder in spite of herself, happened to wander onto the firing range."

"Aggression can then take the form of sex?"

"Often it has no other form to take, particularly among the unemployed and unconnected and uncalled-upon. The bed is where much war is made in the guise of love, or wuv. When strangers are deposited there who do not even recognize each other as traveling companions."

"What exactly are your views on the proper making of love? What distinguishes true love from war or wuv? Would you care to say a few words on that?"

"I will try. I believe that true love and not a variety of wuvwy military assault is being made when there is a true sharing of the experience and the one is reasonably joined in with the other. At least to the hips, but ideally higher than that."

"This sounds like the togetherness you were referring to a moment ago."

"It has nothing in common with this togetherness which is only a facial pretense, designed for the billboards and the magazine covers, that the happy glue is there. I am talking not about those who put arms around each other for the benefit of the cameraman but about a true sharing of a thing in which one cannot be completed without the other, where

166

there is a true and felt joining, and pleasure is taken in this joining, and gratitude is therefore felt. This is where the mirrors are most important. In bed it is vital, I would say, that the one should be able to look at the other and automatically feel that he is looking into a mirror and seeing a great part of his innermost best self reflected there. This can happen, of course, only when there is enough glue present to make the two people feel they have something in common and are somewhat like each other, not stray pieces of flotsam accidentally heaved up together in a storm. Love, if you insist on a definition, is the highest concentration of glue, which generates the most convincing mirrors."

"By this criterion there was no sharing of any type this night."

"Ah, but you forget, this was a gang operation. The members of the gang were sharing the smell of battle among themselves. To provide a moment's semblance of the psychic glue and so give the hangout the momentary feel of a true community."

"Penelope was only an excuse for them to get together in something concerted and lively?"

"Most certainly that, I would say. An excuse for them to be close in something, bound by wuv, and to have the illusion that they are not stalled but are up to something, something with the shape of an enterprise. The chronically unemployed and disconnected invent surprising forms of ersatz labor."

"You must have seen this many times in the Arab refugee camps?"

"Over and over. I would even suggest that there is about any such ganging up among men, such locking together of men, whether against a woman or anything else, something homosexual. Among Arab nomad tribes, as you surely know, there is traditionally a very great deal of homosexuality. Ask any T. S. Lawrence."

"The gangshag is a homosexual project? Interesting."

"It brings men together in a schoolyard or poolroom intimacy, does it not? *Against* woman? For other types of men sex is the fullest opportunity they have to get *away* from the world of men, to pull back from the usual male fraternity, which finally is the most cut-off and falsely glued gang of all."

"Miss Shoshana, to come back for a moment to your observations about sharing. You think that between men and women there should be a general sharing?"

"It makes no difference what I think. Those who are most

contented in life do it without any theories from me, aim for something like it, at least."

"And does this concept of yours embrace, if you will forgive my wording, orgasm?"

"Well, Mr. Hoyt, there is some relation between sex and orgasm, would not you say? I think it would be troublesome and self-defeating, a negation of the entire enterprise, to share the one without the other, though many try, many have no choice but to try. Perhaps some of the fringe people are doing further research on this matter, I have not kept up with their experiments. I have my own bias in such things, you know. I am a businesswoman, when I begin an enterprise I wish to bring it to a successful termination for all concerned, I do not like wasted effort, jobs half done, I am interested in results. Those of the fringe, having no true concept of work, unable to form a perspective about the end of a job because they never begin any jobs, do not care about results, they are only interested in processes."

"This is proving to be a very encouraging discussion, Miss Shoshana. I am finding many favorable overlappings in our thoughts. Let me just point out one thing. During the Orphic rites tonight, Penelope had a full, rich, unmistakable climax. Under *those* circumstances. This I find not in accord with the criterion of true sharing and extremely distressing."

"I do not understand the question you are asking."

"Before I ask it I must go into a few personal considerations. Forgive me, there is no other way. You see, Penelope and I have conducted some experiments in the matter of sex without sharing. Let me sum it up this way: she was capable of climax, fully, deeply internal climax, but only long after my own, only on the condition that I remained and was perfectly still, still as a corpse. It gave me the uncomfortable feeling that I was accidentally present at some weird necrophiliac rite."

"You find that strange?"

"You don't?"

"Not in the least. There are women who find sex monstrous, an outlandish happening that must take place on the outskirts where all forbidden rites are practised. They therefore can manage to bring it off only with thorough monsters, outlanders, the hairy and steamy ones from across the border, that is, the Jews."

"You suggest that that was my role with Penelope?"

"Just the opposite. I am suggesting that she needed a wilder fur-bearer than you or any man could possibly be. Such women need the long time after the man is finished to close their eyes and summon up in their minds the most fantastic violating monsters, only because the real partner is *not* monstrous enough. They see jumping on them giant toads, crusty crawling things with darting forked tongues, dinosaurs, unicorns, snakes, all the misshapen creatures that lurk on the borders, in short, Jews. Sex is to them the supreme violation, carried out on the outermost rim of things, as far beyond the pale as possible, by the most fiendishly snarling wolf packs. In their minds sex cannot work at all between those who have something in common, if both partners belong to the human race it smacks of incest, for their tastes it must be the human torn and mauled by the wolfishly animal. The excitement that comes from such violent images involving two creatures with no possible glues between them, a helpless victim and a slobbering violator, *this* must be what leads such a woman to climax. It is the mind that does the main work, the mind creeping over the border in search of strange and very Jewish outrages."

"Yes. Sex from the viewpoint of Clausewitz. But in that case, why keep the man near? Why not dispense with him entirely?"

"To keep it from being outright masturbation, Mr. Hoyt, that is, a loner's game, which all enterprises in the hangout ultimately are. To keep up the formalities of communal sharing while the mind is free to yield to its own pictures of monstrosity by turning the Mr. John Smith now close by into a flame-snorting beast, without his knowledge or consent, of course. To set up the physical conditions within which the most violent fantasies can be given their head."

"Why is it so important that the man be perfectly still?"

"Perhaps if you become active you only intrude on her fantasy violations, you force yourself into the picture as engineer rather than mere impresario, no, stagehand waiting in the wings. If the woman allows you a dominatingly active role in her pleasure as well as your own it is an admission that, how is it said in the song, it takes two to tango, which negates the whole creed of the hangout, where all performances are essentially solos even when carried out in a mob action. Do not forget, the monsters who so stir such a woman are not really there, they exist only in the woman's heated head. At such a time who would want a forceful reminder that there are things outside the head?"

"How do you know so goddamned much about it?"

"For the best of reasons. I am a woman, and all women

169

have monsters of one dimension or other in their heads. Just as men no doubt have their monsters too, perhaps of other categories. Perhaps *their* fantasy is that they are the toads and unicorns so many ladies have such a fantasy need for. That I can only guess, but about the woman's side I *know*. There is a fringe of darkness around the woman's thoughts of sex as certainly as around the man's. This darkness is the hardest to dispel, we do not as yet have the proper electrification for such borders. Such Jewishness."

"You say you have these monsters in your head too. Do you follow Penelope's procedures in letting them prowl loose?"

"No. My darknesses are not so profound, I would like to think, and I am not happy with them as she must be with hers."

"Would you say that you are more interested in pushing them away to make more space for the man?"

"Definitely. May I add this, that I would hope that on his side the man would be fighting off *his* darknesses to make room for *me*. I do not wish to be crowded at important moments."

"One more point I'd like your views on. The fact remains that tonight Penelope was not allowed the luxury of letting her fantasies go. Her unicorns would not play dead. Yet she came to climax with one of these real-life unicorns, fully, convincingly. How would you explain that?"

"Well, Mr. Hoyt, tonight for the first time she did not have to *invent* attacking monsters. Tonight when she opened her eyes she saw that the demons that ordinarily dance only in her head would not go away, they were there in person, lurching up and down the room. It must be most upsetting, the worst nightmare of all, to open the eyes and feel your nightmare swarming over you, crushing and rending you, not to be turned off by turning the light on. Upsetting, and also very exciting, to those whose tastes trend that way."

"Ah, but, Miss Shoshana. A big but. The violator who roused her finally to the full was not exactly one of the breathers of flame and smoke, it was Worthington. *Worthington*, being the passenger, as usual. *Worthington* propped up and steered. Some unicorn."

"Which only shows, Mr. Hoyt, does it not, that on the more remote borders there are many, many cases of mistaken identity?"

"It makes sense. It does. If she did not have such a burning need for the big toads and lizards, if she had not been withering away with a thirst for the ultimate violation, she would not have gone prowling on the outskirts among the hipsters. She was hunting for outrages. As Lewellyn was thirsty to inflict them."

"This brings us to a further point. What leads a member of the elite central group to move toward the outlanders? Perhaps each person fashions her own monsters out of the peripheral shapes and colors that most violently negate herself and her past. This is why Jews have been so useful to the world, they are a rich source of negations, the most enduring Negroes. There were no poetry-reading mambo instructors and schizoid saxophone players in Penelope's background, I would gather. There a poet was a man who needed a haircut and a Negro was an ambulatory something that brought in the roast beef."

"Ah, now you've hit on a thing, Miss Shoshana. The trouble with me in Penelope's eyes, yes, yes, you must be right, was that I was not *enough* of a monster. Simply because, no matter how I try to disguise it, no matter how I hunch my overgrown shoulders and cover myself with Italian clothes, I look too much like her and my color remains her color. Even though my physique is defiantly broad, I'm still part and parcel of her past and therefore can't convincingly imitate any of the snorting animals in her head. The truly qualified monster can't be a member of your own family, for God's sake. The conclusion is not to be avoided, I couldn't under any circumstances, no matter how hard I tried, bring this girl to the full and fully shared culmination. It was a doomed enterprise from the start. I wasn't black and monstrous, that is, Jewish, enough."

"If that was the case, why did you persist in the project?"

"Why, indeed? I'm coming to see it now. I was making war with this girl, and therefore wuv, not love. It was not what you call the true sharing I was after, since all the circumstances of our lovemaking excluded that. I was only unleashing my big guns against her because *I* needed some target practice too, against those who are too much like me. She *is* too much like me, you know. In her orthodoxies and in the way she stands her orthodoxies on their heads, both. Except that I finally can't stand either side of myself, the ruled or the unruly, and she dotes on *both* of her sides, while claiming she's the world's foremost hipstress. I spent all my erotic energies in military strategies, and each time I marched into battle against her, through her, made her *my* gangway, I kept on complaining about how she denied me and my rights and needs. My one true need there was for the target practice.

171

Otherwise, of course, of course, I would have picked a partner who was a less spectacular target. There are such. Miss Shoshana, I'd like your opinion on something. Would you consider it a fair statement of the facts that you are very much, very dramatically, unlike me?"

"In some ways, Mr. Hoyt. Not, I hope, in all. Not so much that the mirrors would get clouded too badly. I cannot be the total Jew in your vision. Still, among other things, I have an occupation. There are enterprises in my life. These help to keep the worst monsters tied up."

"Yes, it's a good thing to be busy. The tarantulas of idleness and unsocketedness don't like to come out when there are bright bulbs of enterprise all over the place. Tell me, Miss Shoshana. This is really important. In this matter of sex and orgasm, in the very interesting comments you were making about the sharing up and down the line, were you advancing a theory or were you, if you will allow me to put it this way, speaking from, well, experience?"

"Mr. Hoyt, my dear young man, there are some questions that are not to be put into words or answered in words. Another level of discourse is called for."

"Ah, Miss Shoshana, ah. What eloquent answers you can and do give. I have the very strong feeling that you have answered my question fully, with an excruciating thoroughness. I like your answers enormously, I want you to know that. You give such answers as can bring down all the walls of all the fortresses. Your answers are of the type to erase all the borders and light up all the darknesses with memorable fireworks. Now, if you don't mind my getting rather technical, one further point. Regarding the geography of the joyful occasion on the lady's side, the exact location of the good phenomenon, do you consider that it should occur on the periphery of things or at some more central marshalling point?"

"Mr. Hoyt, this question too calls for another type of communication at another time. I will only say this, as to my feeling about peripheral happenings in general. Events that originate and unfold on the edges of things rather than going to the very heart of the matter tend to generate more flashiness than true substance. What we saw tonight would tend to prove that, I think. I believe that the more inner the orientation, the better. Outward-bound people interest me least of all in the intimate aspects. Border phenomena are not after all at the core of things."

"Miss Shoshana, do you mind if I babble for a moment? I

172

feel an enromous babble in me, I must let some of it out. You have some refreshingly *central* business in life, busyness, projects, programs. You don't seem the sort of person who needs to attack all her jobs in concert with others, you don't have the gang mentality, though you apparently work well with people you enter into association with, there's room in your life for colleagues. That's very exciting to me. I would appreciate the opportunity to work with you on some of your more central projects. Not because I need company at all costs but because I would welcome *your* company, also, I have a fearful urge to find something that will keep me busy and I suspect that with your projects, your many projects, I might keep very, very busy. Also, it occurs to me that just possibly I might show up fairly presentably in your mirror, and you, for sure, in mine. Tell me this, Miss Shoshana, dear Miss Shoshana, do you think you might find a place for me in your work? Is it possible I might fit in somewhere in a reasonably central spot?"

"Hm. This takes some thinking about, Mr. Hoyt. It is an exacting work we are doing over there."

"No test is too severe. I only ask to be tried, in any area where there's a place for me, a reasonably central one, that is."

"All the same, you seem to have qualifications. You speak several of the languages of the Middle East—"

"So that if I met an Arab farmer disguised as a kibbutz worker on this or that smudged border I would not have to shoot him, I could talk to him in his own language."

"Yes. Assuming that you would be prowling up hills that are none of your concern."

"If I could keep busy enough, centrally enough, I certainly would not feel the need to go crawling up dangerous hills, Miss Shoshana. It might very well turn out from an exploration of the immediate landscape that there were equally good hills close by, hills that gave as much as anybody could reasonably ask from hills, ones I could climb standing up, in broad daylight. But let me tell you what my goals are, the ones I think recommend me for this work. First, there is my very strong interest, which exactly parallels yours, in seeing a job of work brought to a successful and mutually satisfactory conclusion. Aside from this, my basic aim is to tire myself out sufficiently during the working day so that I will be in the mood to fall into bed at an early hour, with no thoughts of tarantulas or other monsters. If I had some help in that direction, more specifically, a good collaborative arrangement, especially if that were the case, I would have no thoughts of prowling, none at all."

"You do have certain qualifications. You know the importance of the bilharziasis worm as few do."

"And do not overlook this, Miss Shoshana, I am one who takes a very strong position on sharing up and down the line. I stress that because while I am not given to gang activities I *am* oriented toward the more important joinings and sharings."

"That is to be considered, Mr. Hoyt, Hoyt. In the Middle East, as elsewhere, there are too few people who are genuinely dedicated to the important sharings, which no doubt means that there is a bit of Miwwel Eatht there and everywhere. Yes, I think we might find a place for you. A central place. Hoyt. Hoyt."

"I look forward to this joint enterprise, Miss Shoshana, Shoshana, you fine girl. I like the smell of mutuality about it. I sincerely hope and trust, more, I positively anticipate, that we will find this a mutually profitable partnership, one which generates an impressive amount of binding glue and lights up the best border jokes. Forgive me if I babble, dear Shoshana, employed Shoshana, Shoshana of the trickier sharings and the more lasting mucilages, there are runaway joys and ferments in me, I'm in the mood to make up songs and dances about our corporation papers. Ah, there is a way around the tarantulas. There are roads to a fine and heavy-lidded exhaustion. There are lovely development corporations, ones that can make a hash of all borders and install some very bright mirrors. I mean to do a lot of basic research into these matters, if you can find the time to work centrally with me. Let's cross the street, shall we? To that Whelan's over there by Sixth. I want to make a long-distance call. There's somebody I have to tell about my new career, my Middle East that can be described without baby talk, the fine fingers of occupation that are starting to crook at me, my beckoning career in sweet glue—"

26

HELLO, SAM? How are you, Sam? Sorry to get you out of bed but I've something to tell you. Well, yes, Sam, I know I owe you a letter. That's the reason I'm calling, in a way, I just figured out what to say to you and I thought I'd do it over the phone rather than by letter Yes, I've made up my mind. Let me put it this way. Tonight, Sam, I identified the soup spots on your old school tie. I *know* that's not an answer, Sam, it's just a way *into* the answer. What I mean about the soup stains on your old school tie is, you remember how you backed up Acheson in defending Alger, Alger Hiss? You just didn't think a Harvard man could steal government documents, that was about it. Well, I found out tonight that you were wrong, Sam. Hiss did what they said he did, and tonight I learned why. He was bored. He got plain damn bored in State and he wanted to get into the exciting way-out world of the Whittaker Chamberses with their conspiratorial pumpkins and all. Hiss got bored up to his ears in State, Sam, and that's the reason I'm not going into State, I'm afraid of getting bored and landing in all kinds of trouble looking for something lively to occupy my time. It all has to do with the search for commotions, Sam, which commotions you've got the best talent for and which are most readily available and central. Now just hold on, Sam, I've got to explain this point by point, it doesn't help to shout. You see, tonight I got a postgraduate education in boredom and its off-shoots. I took an advanced seminar in boredom and where it can lead. It scared the bejesus out of me because I suddenly realized that I've been bored out of my mind ever since I started working on my dissertation and thinking about a future in State. Now just a minute, Sam, let me state my case. The fact is that this past night I got an offer of a very interesting job. It's hard to explain, it has to do with installing pumps and generators in Arab refugee camps and starting campaigns against certain worms known as Bilharzia. It seems to be right up my alley, I feel a great enthusiasm for this job and I mean to take it. The big challenge in this is to push past all the borders to the true centralities. No, I can't go back to New Haven, this thing won't wait. I'm off to Detroit with one of my associates this afternoon to scare up certain low-cost pumps, from Worthington's father as a matter of fact, and then we've got to rush over to Beirut and get to work. Now here's the thing, Sam. Please don't interrupt, there are all sorts of practical matters to discuss, and no, I'm not drunk. The main thing is, I can't get back to New Haven so would you send somebody up there to close out the apartment, my end of it anyhow, and ship my belongings home?

You don't have to pack up my clothes, though. I wish, I make a special point of this, I definitely want you to have my entire wardrobe burned. It's all Italian pimp clothes, you see, and I have a suspicion I'm outgrowing them. What? How do I know what kind of clothes I'll be wearing in Beirut? Loincloths, burnooses, something, I'll shop around and see what fits. I assure you, I'm *not* drunk. Sam, I'm really sorry about this State thing, I don't like to let you down but you wouldn't want me to wind up with a lot of soup stains on my old school tie. Listen, while you're at it, burn all my ties too, will you? Sam? Are you there? Sam? Sam'l?"

AFTERTHOUGHT

VERY HIP people will object that their brothers have here been presented as speaking a broader, richer, more nuanced tongue than they in fact do. That is so. A more phonographic rendition of their somnambulistically flattened and laconic rhetoric would make it quite impossible to write books or, indeed, anything more sustained than a postcard: a novel developed around a vocabulary of twenty or thirty words must be repetitive to the point of schizophrenia.

But there are signs that here, too, life is beginning to imitate art. Lately, in various odd corners, a few *post*-hipsters have started to show up, groping their way back from the Arctic Circle of Cool in an attempt to rejoin the human race and the English language. They should be helped in every way to get home and begin communicating again. Heresies of all kinds are to be encouraged.

The idea of Community (where Etiquette governs easily) vs. Hangout (where peace is just barely maintained with a minimal set of House Rules) was first formulated by Harold Rosenberg well over a decade ago. This has always struck me as a wonderfully witty and suggestive thought, but Mr. Rosenberg is not in any way to be held responsible for the rather facetious use made of it in these pages.

B. W.